The Flight of The Griffin

The Flight of The Griffin

C.M. Gray

Copyright (C) 2015 C.M. Gray
Layout Copyright (C) 2015 Creativia

Published 2015 by Creativia
Paperback design by Creativia (www.creativia.org)
ISBN: 978-1517057886
Cover art by http://www.adipixdesign.com
This book is a work of fiction. Names, characters, places, and incidents are the product of the author's imagination or are used fictitiously. Any resemblance to actual events, locales, or persons, living or dead, is purely coincidental.
All rights reserved. No part of this book may be reproduced or transmitted in any form or by any means, electronic or mechanical, including photocopying, recording, or by any information storage and retrieval system, without the author's permission.

To my children,
...Dylan and Yasmin...
... that my light may one day shine through their eyes...

Contents

1	An Uncommon Evening	1
2	A New Day Dawns	15
3	The Book of Challenges	27
4	A Hunter's Moon	39
5	Set Course for 'The Isle of Skulls'	53
6	Something's Down There	66
7	Bleak Fortress	75
8	The Towers	84
9	A Walk in the Dark	93
10	To Battle a Demon	103
11	Gathering Skulls	112
12	A Rude Reception	121
13	A Minsten Tale	131

14	Finding the Hidden	141
15	The Tree of Truth	156
16	Different Paths	170
17	The Flight Of The Griffin	181
18	Seas of Sand	190
19	Walking the Knife's Edge	202
20	What's a Mudlark?	211
21	The Guardian and the Flail	221
22	Tipping the Balance	237
23	Fishing	257

Chapter 1

An Uncommon Evening

The floorboard creaked under the sole of his felt boot - a calculated risk whenever entering a sleeping man's room uninvited.

A breeze fluttered the loose linen curtain, and the sleeper stirred at the welcome respite from the hot sticky night. The prowler slowly exhaled the breath that was starting to burn in his lungs, every sense tingling, receptive to any change in the room or a sound from the street below.

The sleeper, thankfully, continued to sleep.

The street under the second-storey window was silent, the night given up to the occasional rounds of the city watch and those set on a darker business, the never-ending cat and mouse game that went mostly unappreciated by the law-abiding citizens of the sleeping city.

The summer had been one of the hottest people could ever remember, taxing the energy of the city's inhabitants to the limit. Several of the more elderly citizens down at the port could be heard explaining that, 'in their day', the summers were often this hot, and indeed often hotter. Of course, these were the same group who would entertain the regulars at the portside taverns with tales of goblin hordes, ferocious sea serpents or the time the winters were so cold that the seas had frozen solid.

'A man could have walked from here to Minster Island without ever seeing a boat or even getting his feet wet,' was a much-repeated reminiscence. Whatever history really concealed, it was a hot summer, and this, a particularly humid night.

Pardigan watched the now softly snoring form and, moving his foot from the traitorous board, crept towards the cabinet that he knew held his prize. It was an elegant cabinet - its construction given over to more than mere function. Gracefully curved legs supported drawers and shelves that were fronted by a scrollwork of intricate designs. He inserted the blade of his knife between the edges of the middle left-hand drawer and felt for the hidden catch. If the information Quint had given him was correct, the false front should spring open. A prickle of sweat tickled his brow and he wiped it absently away. Glancing over to the still-sleeping form, he applied a little more pressure on what he hoped was the catch.

Nothing.

The merchant stirred, smacked his chops, exhaled wetly and then returned to snoring. Pardigan tried again.

Most people hated the fat merchant, known for his cheating ways and vile temper, so he and Quint had set about the business of planning to rob him with great enthusiasm. The break had come quite by chance when Quint had met the apprentice of a cabinetmaker who'd been happy to talk about the merchant, and the cabinet he'd helped his master build for him.

'The shame of it is that the true beauty of the cabinet will never be appreciated,' the apprentice had moaned. 'Such a cunning mechanism my master contrived to conceal the hidden safe-box, nothing of the like have I seen before, nor I fear will I ever see again.' He had been all too happy to describe and even sketch the piece for Quint who, of course, had shown great interest, marvelling at the skill of the cabinetmaker and, naturally, his gifted apprentice. Several glasses of elder ale had kept his new friend's throat well lubricated, an investment in tonight's escapade that they had both placed huge hopes in.

Up until this point, the information seemed to be good; the cabinet did indeed look like the sketch that he and Quint had spent so much time studying. Pardigan's hopes had soared when he'd first set eyes on it as he was slipping over the windowsill. Right up until now that is, as his frustration grew. Because the Source damned catch simply wouldn't shift - if catch it was. Pardigan was beginning to wonder if the real catch hadn't been poor old Quint, whom the apprentice had conned into buying several glasses of elder ale on another blisteringly hot day.

Without warning, the warm still of the night was disturbed as the door to the bedroom opened with a creak, causing the hairs on Pardigan's neck to stand up. He slowly turned, half-expecting to be staring at the tip of a crossbow bolt. Instead, a large grey cat slunk around the door, ran across and rubbed against his legs, purring as it sought attention. He ruffled its ears, before gently pushing the animal away. Without a backward glance the cat walked over and leapt up onto the bed. Settling comfortably against the sleeping merchant, it lay watching as Pardigan renewed his efforts.

He applied his knife once again. Nothing was happening with the left-hand side so he moved his attention to the right. An audible click echoed around the room, rewarding his efforts as the false door opened, wobbling the washbasin that sat precariously upon the cabinet's top. The merchant turned over, groaning loudly and ejected the cat from the bed. It meowed, padded over to the open window and leapt to the sill. Ignoring Pardigan, it sat regarding the street below with a critical eye.

The merchant continued to sleep. He was back to breathing heavily, his fat sweaty chins bobbing with the effort of sucking in the warm moist air.

Pardigan returned his attention to the cabinet. Behind the false front was a small opening. Several moneybags had been carelessly tossed on top of some papers, a few old books and some rolled documents that had been stacked neatly above on two shelves.

Pardigan hadn't had any real idea what he might find, but when he and Quint had been working out the finer details of the plan, they'd had plenty of time for speculation. Jewels, money and magical items had been on the hoped-for and expected list, but Pardigan now noted, with a certain touch of dismay, that there was a distinct lack of necklaces, rings and brooches in the safe. He turned over a few of the papers to see what they hid and wondered at the markings on them. He could read after a fashion, but only the local low-speak, enough to tell the difference between a bag of beans and a bag of rice. High-speak was for merchants and nobles.

He slipped several of the more promising-looking papers into his coat along with the moneybags, and then a small knife without a scabbard caught his eye. He picked it up. It had a blade about a hand's span long and a plain blue jewel set in the pommel. He put it into his pocket and cast a last glance over the remainder of the contents. With a sigh, he gently reset the false front, watching the merchant's face to make sure he wasn't disturbed as the catch clicked softly back into place. Satisfied that he hadn't been heard, he straightened and tested the new weight in his pockets. With a smile, he crossed to the window. The cat watched him approach then meowed in irritation as he brushed it from the sill. Taking care to mind the loot in his pockets, he straddled the windowsill and, with one eye to the street for the city watch and the other on the still sleeping merchant, made his way carefully to the ground.

Dropping the last few spans, he landed safely and offered up a silent prayer of thanks to the Source. Then, after casting up and down the street, he drew in his first real breath for what seemed an eternity and moved off towards the sanctuary of the poor quarter. Keeping to the shadows, he kept an eye open for both the watch and for any opportunist thieves that may be lying in wait for a rich victim like himself.

* * *

The grey cat continued to watch as he scuttled away, noting his haste now he was in the open. The way he looked back and forth for danger, seeing everything, but understanding so little.

She'd been waiting for something like this to happen for several weeks and now she felt both excitement and regret that the game was to move on. *Maybe I was beginning to enjoy the lazy life of a house cat too much*, she wondered. The easy life did have certain merits, especially for a cat. Licking a paw she cleaned herself one last time, enjoying a few final moments in this form, and then leapt from the window, shimmering before spreading wide, snowy white wings and gliding silently in search of the departing figure.

* * *

Pardigan hurried down the darkened alleyways, the houses crowding closer together the further he got into the poor quarter. At several points, the buildings actually touched above him and the alley became a pitch-black tunnel, blocking out even the faint ambient light that had lit his progress so far. Earlier in the evening, the oil-lamps would have been lit, but it was late now and the oil had long burned away. He came to The Stag, an inn on Barrow Street that was favoured by traders from the market square. The murmur of a few late drinkers came from behind the heavy closed door, then the sound of a glass smashing and a woman's shrill and angry cry prompted Pardigan to move on before the drinker was tossed onto the street, illuminating him in the light from within.

At the end of Barrow Street he slowed to a cautious walk. Market Square was in front of him, a regular hangout for drunks and beggars who tended to group together. Even at this time of night there would probably be a few milling around. These people didn't seem to keep normal hours. You could be walking around at midday and most would be sleeping like it was midnight, and then times like now, they would be up and about sucking on a bottle and probably wondering idly where the sun had gone to.

Keeping to the shadows as best he could, he moved into the square being careful to skirt the darker parts at the edge. Picking up his pace he had to clamp his hand over his nose and hold his breath as he sidestepped several piles of rotting vegetables; the warmth of the night rich in their pungent odours.

Several of the square's occupants were dotted about but none seemed interested in him. Three drinkers grouped around a spluttering fire were singing and laughing as they passed a small barrel. Pardigan slowed and watched for a moment, fascinated as they took turns, upending it and laughing at each other's efforts as more of the liquid splashed down their chests than into their mouths. Pardigan shuddered, and wondered at the mystery that was adulthood and at what age you lost your mind and did crazy things like that.

At 12 years old, Pardigan dreaded the thought of waking up one morning as an adult. To have had all the fun sucked out of his life, replaced by the need to scowl at people and tell everyone off for not seeing the world his way. Growing old was inevitable, growing up was not. He and the others had made several vows that they would never grow up and would sail the coast in their boat *The Griffin*, for a lifetime of fun, adventure and good times. Whatever happens, I'll not be sitting in this square drunk, dribbling and howling at the moon like some crazy dog, he vowed. Casting another look at the small group, he moved on.

The square was crossed without incident and he started down The Cannery, a street so named because of all the fish canning shops that lined its sides as it went down the hill towards the city's little port. During daylight hours, it was one of the busiest areas of town, with fishermen hauling their catch up from the port and the canneries bustling with wagons shipping out their product all over the realm. At this hour, all was deserted and Pardigan passed down the pungent street without incident, a few squabbling rats its only nocturnal residents.

Coming down into the port, there remained one final obstacle in his path - Blake's. The largest of the inns around the harbour, it never closed. On a warm night like tonight, even at this late hour, there could be people sitting outside hoping for the comfort of a small breeze to come in across the sea.

The sound of music drifted up to him accompanied by the sound of voices laughing and talking – there was no way he could escape being noticed. He would have to cross right in front of the entrance to get to where *The Griffin* was moored. Drawing his coat about him, he walked on, a shiver running the length of his spine - his nerves once again on edge.

A lone figure sat on a barrel under the main window, bathed in a pool of light from a lantern that hung above the door. Keeping his eyes averted and with his heart beating in his ears, Pardigan tried not to stumble on the uneven cobbles in his haste to get past. Nearly there, only Blake's to pass, almost there... Talking to himself often helped in times of stress, it was almost as if some of the burden of the moment was shared...Only a little way more...Nearly...

A sudden movement from behind and he spun round in time to see a dark figure loom up with arms outstretched. With a cry, Pardigan stepped back, tripped over something and then hit the ground hard, pain instantly screaming from his back and left ankle.

He lay writhing on the cobblestones gasping, fear and despair filling him as he realised he'd been caught so close to *The Griffin*. It was almost in sight, only a little further around the port, but this obviously wasn't to be his night after all. That's how my luck's been running lately, thought Pardigan, offering a silent curse to the Source. Shadows gathered about him and he tried to struggle up but someone flipped him face down and sat on his back. Powerless to move or even breathe properly - flutterings of panic threatened to overcome him. Footfalls surrounded him and he waited for the touch of a knife.

'You should have told us you were going to do it tonight.' The speaker tapped Pardigan's head with something hard. 'We could have helped you know.' He sounded cross.

'Quint?' Pardigan felt a wave of relief and then anger at being tricked like this. 'Get off me, you lump.' He felt the weight move and several pairs of hands rolled him over. A lantern was lit and he gazed up into the shadowy faces of his friends.

'Well, how did it go?' asked the tall scruffy boy holding the lamp. Tarent, for that was his name, reached down and pulled Pardigan to his feet. Waves of relief filled Pardigan and he smiled, his anger slipping away.

'You rotten...' he took a half-hearted swing at Tarent who moved aside easily. 'Why did you jump me? I thought you were...'

'Serves you right, now tell us...' hissed Loras, the fourth and final member of *The Griffin's* crew. Smaller than the others with a tangled mop of red hair, Loras was peering up at Pardigan with a frown etching shadows on his face. 'We found your bunk empty, and then Quint told us about your plan.'

'Which he wasn't meant to carry out yet,' added Quint.

'So we came and waited for you here. You've been ages.' Loras was moving from one foot to the other, clearly agitated. 'Quint seemed to think you'd have plenty of coins and would be in a better position to settle our bill than we are,' he glanced back into the inn, a worried look on his face. 'Like I said, you've been ages and we were hungry.'

'And thirsty,' added Tarent. 'So we appear to be a little in arrears with the good landlord here.'

Loras reached out and dusted Pardigan's cloak. 'Sorry about the surprise, but you should have included us, so... how did it go?' All three waited patiently for some sort of response.

Pardigan finally shook his head in wonder at his friends, then checked up and down the path for observers. Reaching inside his coat, he pulled out a moneybag, recently the property of a certain local merchant, and fished out a silver coin that he tossed to Tarent. 'Settle up here and let's get back to the boat. I'll tell you all just how well it went when we get there.' Tarent disappeared inside the inn as the others moved off towards the gently bobbing boats of the port eager to hear more.

Now, back in the company of his three friends, Pardigan finally felt safe. They were a strange group, all with a different story of hard luck and the tough times they'd had before finding each other. They'd since formed the closest thing to a family that any of them had ever known -

even the boat that they called home had a sorry tale. Quint had found it in a terrible state, rotting in a small river, off the main estuary to the city. Having nowhere better to go and all alone, he'd started to live on it. The boat had conveyed the feeling of abandonment and the only other inhabitants had been a few mice and lots of spiders. Quint had spent the first few weeks alone and in fear, expecting a gang of cutthroats to reclaim their vessel at any moment. Then, as the weeks had turned to months, he had realised *The Griffin*, for that was the name he had found under layers of grime, really was abandoned and he began to relax. The hull was sound, had no leaks and it had several cabins plus a good-sized cargo area. The problem with the boat had simply been neglect. Whoever had abandoned her hadn't left any clue to their identity, but abandoned she most certainly was.

About ten spans long, *The Griffin* made a wonderful home, blending in wherever the boys moored her. They spent most of their time in the rivers hidden from the world, but made several trips into the port cities for supplies and a change of scene. Pardigan, of course, was the practised thief, bringing gold, food and supplies to the boat whenever they were needed. He felt no remorse from his exploits, saying it was a harsh world and if he didn't take stuff then someone else would. Quint often found the rich targets for Pardigan and was the only one who had known how to sail, making him the logical choice as Captain. As the oldest, Quint was the unofficial leader of the group.

Loras had once been apprenticed to a magician, but the old boy had died before passing on much of his craft. When he had left, Loras took what he could of the books and spells; the boys had found him appearing dazed and confused, with soot all over his face, blowing up tree stumps in the forest.

'That's great!' Quint had said, obviously impressed at Loras's efforts, 'How do you do it?'

'I haven't the foggiest idea,' Loras had replied. 'I was actually trying to make the stumps grow new leaves; they aren't supposed to blow up like this.' He'd looked questioningly at a tatty old book held together with string. 'I think I must be doing something wrong - maybe there's another page missing?' He was waving his wand again, hopping about and trying to read, all at the same time. Quint had brought him back to the boat and Loras had settled in well.

The fourth crewmember was Tarent who was the laziest person that any of them had ever met, or so they often told him. Fortunately, he hid this flaw in his character by being one of the nicest people you could ever want to meet. He slept more than anyone had a need or right to, and could spend the most amazing amount of time merely gazing out to sea, or up at a star-filled night while the others were working. To many this would have grated and annoyed, but he would also talk and talk and talk, which was a good thing. He would tell about the night skies or monsters from the deep and he knew the reason why a compass always pointed north or how to make the ticker fish bite on a hot afternoon. After supper Tarent could always be relied upon for a good story to lead their minds around the world or bring enchanted sea creatures up from the deep. His body could be lazy, but his mind was as nimble as an acrobat. He was one of the crew, and shared many of the responsibilities of leadership with Quint.

The Griffin was waiting for them at the end of the quay, dwarfed in the shadow of a large black barge. The fragrant aromas of spices and herbs rich on the warm night air attesting to the cargo the barge was carrying. They clambered up the gangplank and Quint waited at the top until the last of them came aboard, then he pulled it in, sealing the boat from the land. He glanced over to the barge where a sailor was smoking a clay pipe, watching them. Giving a wave that was returned; he slipped down the hatchway pulling it closed behind him.

Down below, two lamps were already lit, the slight breeze from the open portholes enough to make the flames flicker, sending shadows dancing around the cabin. Everyone had settled; waiting for the news as Pardigan stood at the table and, without any ceremony, started to empty out his pockets.

He carefully placed the bags on the table, side by side, eight in all. The boys watched without saying a word as each bag made a soft chink, the cord drawstring falling softly to the side. Eight bags. Four were blue, one red, one yellow and two were of common canvas. The papers and books were passed across to Tarent, while the small knife was placed upon the table alongside the bags.

They hadn't believed Quint when he'd told them of the plan; hadn't actually thought that Pardigan would come back with anything except a tall tale of a daring escape and some would-have-beens and should-have-beens. They hadn't thought they'd really be seeing moneybags this evening. They all sat and stared.

Loras eventually broke the silence. 'So what's in 'em?'

'I haven't had a chance to look,' said an exhausted Pardigan. He waved them an invitation to the table.

Loras jumped up and tipped out the contents from one of the canvas bags. Copper coins fell out and rolled around. 'About thirteen shillings in coppers,' he muttered, pushing the coins with his fingers. He picked up a red bag, untied the cord, and upended it. More coins hit the table making an altogether different sound, the buttery colour of gold glinting in the lamplight. 'Seven sovereigns and one royal crown,' said Loras after a moment, his interest growing. The other bags were duly opened and all but the yellow bag held coins of gold, silver and copper. The yellow bag held a necklace that sparkled with precious stones as Loras held it up in awe for the boys to see.

'It's beautiful, Pardigan. Who, in the name of the Source did you rob? Was it the King?' They all stared at Pardigan.

'What sort of trouble are we in?' asked Loras, as the peril of their situation suddenly dawned upon him. 'What are we going to do?'

'Come on, let's not panic,' said Quint. 'Did anybody see you, stop you or question you at any point, Pardigan?'

'No, nobody saw me and I'm sure I didn't leave any clues,' stated Pardigan confidently. 'I'm *very* good at what I do.'

'Course you are, but come morning the city will be in uproar about this - we have to play this with cunning and no mistake.'

Quint looked at each of them in turn; lastly he turned to Tarent. 'What do you think?'

Tarent sighed. 'If we up and sail on the first tide come daybreak, the watch will be after us like a shot. We can't be appearing guilty.' He pondered a moment. '...Even if we did want to give it all back, which I don't think we do'? He glanced around the group seeing shaking heads, 'Well we couldn't, could we?' Everyone shook their heads again. 'We keep the coins, some on the boat and some we take up river and stash back at the moorings.'

Quint nodded.

'The papers I'll look over tonight to see what we have, then we either burn them or plan on their use. What we don't do is leave them here to be found if we do get searched. Source willing, we can up and leave in a few days' time and be back on our usual moorings for further plans.' He turned once more to Quint.

'Agreed,' said Quint. 'Check the papers as quick as you can. The coppers we can add to our own cash box with a few of the silver as well, so we can get our normal provisions.'

'And the knife?' asked Pardigan.

They all stared at the knife, still lying next to the sacks. The blue jewel sparkled in the lamplight.

'It's a very unusual knife,' said Tarent in a soft voice almost as if talking to himself. 'The best thing would be to lose it over the side, or drop it in some back alley well away from here.' He glanced across at Quint, but he was saying nothing, simply staring with the others at the knife on the table.

It seemed almost to be calling out to each one of them, and they all knew they wouldn't be throwing it into the sea, or losing it anywhere else for that matter.

'Stash it in the stove for now until we can think on it,' said Quint. Sounds of ready agreement came from all around.

Pardigan placed the knife in the cold stove then piled old ash and wood over it. The cash was split between that which was staying, and that which was going, and then Tarent moved off to his cabin to check the papers. The boat settled down; Pardigan and Quint went on deck in search of fresh air before sleeping.

'I can't believe it was really there, false front and all,' whispered Quint as he lay back looking up at the stars.

'Oh, it really was there, just as he said it was and twice as lovely as the picture.'

'I wish I could have seen it. What were you thinking when you were creeping round the room?' Quint sat up and stared at Pardigan. 'Weren't you scared to the very marrow of your bones?'

'Being scared is what keeps a thief alive and not caught and hanged,' replied Pardigan. He pulled the knife from his pocket, and rubbed the blue gem with his thumb.

'I thought you put that into the stove,' said Quint watching him.

Pardigan stared at the knife, a frown creasing his face. 'I did, I'm sure I did but ...'

'Well you can't have, can you?' Quint nodded at the knife in Pardigan's hand. '*Don't* get caught with it, put it in the stove, eh?'

'I will.' Pardigan ran his finger across the long thin blade. It wasn't sharp but it didn't feel dull either, he could just make out signs or writing on the side in the dim light, but unfortunately it wasn't bright enough to see properly. 'I'm sure I put it in the stove, I remember covering it with ash,' he murmured as he slipped it back in his cloak.

The boys chatted about the night's events for a while longer. Pardigan telling of scaling the wall and creeping around the sleeping chamber as the fat merchant snored, puffed and farted, and Quint telling a lengthy story of how Tarent and Loras and he had managed to dine at Blake's on the slim hope of him turning up with a few coins to pay for it all.

'Blake would have skinned you all alive if he'd known you were eating and drinking all evening with no money in your pockets,' laughed Pardigan.

'Ahhh, but we had faith in you, my friend,' countered Quint, punching Pardigan softly in the arm. 'And besides, we were hungry and the iced lemon water at Blake's is the best in all of Freya; we needed it.'

'I know,' murmured Pardigan softly, 'let's hope this is a sign that our fortunes have changed.'

An Uncommon Evening

As the stars maintained their journey across the night sky, the city continued to sleep and the boys finally went below to their bunks, ready for a busy day.

* * *

The owl watched from the top of the boat's mast as the two boys disappeared and with a beat of her wings flew off, back into the city. It had been an interesting evening and she felt pleased that events were finally moving along. She knew the boys would need a nudge or two to put them in the right direction, but she had a good feeling about them, a far better feeling than she had when the merchant had got his greedy, pudgy hands on the knife.

She soared over the shops and buildings of the city enjoying the freedom of flight, the air flowing over her feathers as she rode the warm currents rising from the buildings below. She watched as the moon rose above the water, its reflection rippling upon the calm ocean, its pale light making long dark shadows of the boats in the harbour, giving a new texture to the cityscape beneath her.

She flew until she saw the world start to awake and with it, dawn break on a brand new day. Turning back towards the harbour, she glided down to alight upon the deck of *The Griffin* and, returning to the form of the grey cat curled up on a badly stored sail and there she slept, waiting for the start of the day's events to unfold.

Chapter 2

A New Day Dawns

Bartholomew Bask awoke in a groggy haze; his head thumping from drinking too much good berry wine the evening before and yet another awful night's sleep.

'This confounded heat is getting the better of me,' he mumbled. 'Thirteen weeks of blistering weather that torments me night and day - will there be no end to it?' He pulled his great bulk to the edge of the bed and sat with his head resting in his hands. Mornings were seldom good for Bartholomew Bask.

He eventually managed to heave himself up and stood, swaying slightly, squinting at the light streaming in through his open window. Padding across the room, he leant on the sill and gazed down, watching for a few moments, entranced, as always, by the clutter of shops and the human tide coming and going below him. A donkey and cart was causing a commotion a little way further down the busy street as the driver tried to pass several tables set up outside the little brewshop. The early morning customers, unwilling to move from their breakfasts, were goading the driver, who was arguing vocally while failing in his attempts to reverse his stubborn animal. Tempers were rising early these days in Freya.

Bartholomew drew in a deep breath, catching the aromas of morning brew, newly-baked bread and cinnamon buns. His stomach rumbled and his thoughts moved towards his own needs. Leaving the window, he crossed to the cabinet and filled the washbasin with water. After splashing his face he rubbed at his bleary eyes and stared into the mirror that hung on the wall, shuddering at the reflection that gazed back at him.

Dipping his head, he sucked up a mouthful of water from the basin and threw his head back. 'Aaauurrgghhh,' he gargled with relish, spat, and then returned to the mirror. Rolling his cheeks around a little, he frowned into the little piggy eyes that stared back and gazed down his throat past rows of browning teeth. He rubbed at them a little with his finger, flashed a toothy grimace, then satisfied with his efforts, rinsed his hands and dragged wet fingers through his hair a few times, to control the unruly grey mop. He picked up a shirt, hastily thrown over the arm of a chair the evening before, and sniffed experimentally. His nose wrinkled, but seeing no fresh one, he dragged it over his head and waddled out in search of his maid.

'*Hildy...Hildy.*' Bartholomew, cheeks wobbling with the effort, shouted down the stairs. 'Where are yer, blast yer gal, *Hildy?*' A crash came from somewhere below and a short while later a thin wisp of a woman appeared, scurrying up the stairs all skirts and fluster.

'*Trousers*, gal, where are me damn *trousers*...and a shirt, yer lazy gal, get me a clean shirt and be quick about it. This one's fit to crawl out on its own an no mistake.' He stomped back into the room feeling better for the exertion, then stopped short as a thought struck him. Turning back to the door, he bellowed once again.

'And bring me something to break me fast on as quick as yer like, and you'll hurry, gal, if yer know what's good for yer.'

Hildy had been in his employ for years and he would have never found anyone else that would dote on him and put up with his foul tempers like she did, but that didn't stop him from threatening to dismiss her several times each day.

A meek little woman of about fifty summers, Hildy wasn't really the 'young gal' he always called her. Her friends had tried for ages to get her to leave that 'nasty' merchant Bask but so far, she hadn't. This morning was no different from any other morning and that was fine by her. She would see to him and her cleaning and be out of the house by lunchtime. She ran to fetch him some food.

A glass of freshly squeezed orange juice, a pot of brew, six slices of toast, a large slab of smoked ham, half a dozen fried eggs, mushrooms and six rashers of crispy bacon. She added another plate to the tray, heaped with pancakes dripping in syrup, and then a basket of hot scones that she'd laboured over since arriving earlier that morning, then smothered them in butter and jam, exactly the way merchant Bask liked them.

Once ready, she carried it all up the stairs, struggling under the weight and resting for a moment at the top before kicking open the door to his bedroom with her foot. She didn't need to knock; he would be sitting on the edge of his bed the same as every morning *counting his sins*, she would always think to herself.

Bartholomew watched the tray arrive with a critical eye as Hildy placed it on the table close at hand.

'I'll be getting your shirt now, sir, all freshly pressed and clean for you.' Hildy laid out a napkin and started to back away towards the door.

Bartholomew, as was usual at this point, was lost in the smells and sights of his breakfast and hardly heard a word that Hildy said. He picked up a scone with his fingers and crammed it whole into his mouth, the butter dribbling unnoticed down his chin. Hildy stared at him in disgust, wrinkled her nose and left the room.

Some time later, after eating, Bartholomew began the task of dressing; squeezing himself into trousers that strained at the effort of holding him, and a clean shirt that already showed signs of its wearer with sweat patches forming under each armpit and a jammy mark on the chest from hastily wiped fingers. Once attired, after glancing to the door for any sign of Hildy, Bartholomew approached his cabinet and sprung the catch to the secret safe.

Bartholomew Bask, leading merchant of Freya, was known for his temper, but on this occasion he didn't explode, he didn't scream, he didn't do anything. For once in his life he was actually lost for words, lost for reason as his mind tried to convince his eyes that they must be wrong.

'Gone, everything has gone,' he finally mumbled, shuffling the few remaining papers. How much money had been there? He thought about it for a moment, his mind doing a dance as it added and subtracted and went over the business he had conducted for the last few days. He slumped to the floor. A fortune, there had been a ruddy fortune in there, and that's without a shred of doubt. He buried his face in his hands and tears started to slide down his quivering cheeks. With a jerk, he stopped sobbing and sat up - it must have been Hildy! His face turned red and he started to tremble. Hildy, whom he had cared for and employed for so long. How could it be? But there really was no other explanation. He stood up, fists clenched at his sides.

'*Hildy, Hildy* get yourself here this instant!' he bellowed. Her hurried footsteps immediately sounded on the stairs and moments later she came rushing into the room.

'Yes, Merchant Bask sir.' She bobbed a quick curtsey, catching her breath as she dried wet hands on her apron - her face was flushed from the heat of the kitchen.

Bartholomew stood up, hitching his trousers over his vast stomach. 'Have you been in here moving things? ... Taking things?' His voice was low and menacing.

'Taking things, sir? What would I be taking? I'm an honest woman and I don't take kindly to being thought otherwise.' She stared at him, trying not to become agitated. 'What is it that you've lost? Maybe I can help you look. It can't be far, whatever it is.' She started to move towards the cabinet and he watched her eager approach. What was he thinking? The girl was without a whit of intelligence and wouldn't have been able to open the damn cabinet even if she *had* known there was something in there.

'Get out, gal! Get out while I think.' He waved a hand in her shocked confused face. 'Out!'

Hildy stopped, then slowly retreated backwards out of the room, wondering at the questionable sanity of her employer.

Bartholomew sat back down to think the situation through. What to do? The watch - he must call the city watch to be sure ... but then there'd be questions he'd prefer not to answer, and if the thief was caught and found with so much money on him, there would be questions of unpaid taxes...no, not the watch. Bartholomew returned to his sobbing. What papers had been in there? Again his mind raced: several property deeds, but they could be re-issued. Also contracts for several business transactions that would have to be resigned and probably renegotiated at this point. He was going to have a very busy time of it, trying to salvage something out of this. Bartholomew wanted vengeance, he wanted to find the thief and he wanted to make him suffer, but how to catch him?

He stopped crying and jerked back from the cabinet, trying not to move. The more he was near it and the more he searched, the less a Mage would have to go on. Yes, he needed a Mage and he needed a good one. Bartholomew stood up, now under control. Snatching up his cane, he crammed a hat upon his head and left the house.

Hildy watched him waddle quickly from the house and went back to scrubbing the kitchen floor. Gone for another day and no more shouting to endure, she started to feel happy for the first time that morning and even started to hum a tune.

Unfortunately, she was wrong. Merchant Bask was back in less than a turn of the glass with a nasty looking man in tow. The stranger was scruffy and wearing a long gown, or some such thing that wasn't any fashion that Hildy knew about. Although they were back down again and gone in no time, without a 'Hello' or 'Get out of the damn way, gal,' most odd.

She went upstairs to find the bedroom in a state worse than usual. It appeared to have powder over half the room and there was a horrible smell as if something had been burning. Hildy wrinkled her nose, something she did many times a day in the employ of Merchant Bask, in fact, she did it so much that she now had permanent wrinkles on her nose from this very action. With a sigh of resignation she set about cleaning it all up.

A New Day Dawns

By lunchtime, she was ready to leave and was just putting her hat straight when Merchant Bask came home with his new friend. She had just stepped out and closed the door behind her, when the hot afternoon air was split by the sound of Merchant Bask screaming her name.

'*Hildy, Hildy*, by the light of the Source, where are you, gal? Come here this instant!'

'Aaahh,' muttered Hildy to herself, 'now what's his problem?' She thought for a moment of simply heading off down the street. After all, she'd finished for the day and a good job she had done as usual. He had no call to... The thought was left unfinished as Merchant Bask's head appeared out of the bedroom window, bright red and bug-eyed in fury. She saw him scan the street and then he noticed her standing below and pointed, screaming once more.

'Hildy, you stupid, stupid girl, you've cleaned it all, cleaned every last blessed bit!'

Staring up at merchant Bask, Hildy finally decided that he had gone completely mad. Now he's screaming at me because I've cleaned. The man's a raving lunatic to be sure. She decided there and then to take the advice of her friends, so with a flick of her skirts and one last wrinkle of her nose, she left the service of Merchant Bask once and for all.

Several of the people on the street watched her leave with the merchant screaming from his window. An elderly couple told him to mind his tongue. When he started to scream and shout at them, others joined in, until a small crowd had gathered and a number of objects were hurled up at him.

Forced to retreat back into the room, Bartholomew turned once more to his guest who was studying him closely, quite unaffected by the merchant's outbursts.

'Well, is there anything left?' panted Bartholomew, angrily wiping bits of tomato from his face. He sat down heavily on the corner of the bed and regarded the scruffy Mage, with a look of desperate appeal.

'As I first advised you Merchant Bask, there is a general confusion surrounding the room.' The Mage stood up from where he'd been examining the bottom of the cabinet. 'This makes it much harder to read whatever has transpired. What first appears to us cannot be readily applied to what one would normally associate with an act of theft.'

'What?' wheezed Bartholomew, his mouth hanging open.

The Mage went on. 'There are strong echoes of yourself, of course, and your cleaner. The makers of the cabinet are also evident, but these are easily set aside. What *is* confusing, are the strong echoes of a cat and a child.'

After a short silence, the Mage decided to venture the question that he felt almost unnecessary. 'Do you...have any children in the house, Merchant Bask?' The look that he received from Bartholomew was enough of an answer. 'Well I thought not, this is why I asked for more time and indeed stressed the need for a different approach. Alas the cleaning of the room has undone any chance of getting any closer to the truth. Why an animal's echo should be so strong I cannot fathom, however, we can be sure this was no ordinary animal, but one that carried an echo of magic about it. As to that of the child...' He shrugged and left the sentence unfinished.

Bartholomew frowned; it grated on him to pay for so little results, but to refuse payment to a Mage was...well, frankly...stupid. He pulled a silver coin from his pocket and handed it over; the Mage took it without question or apology for any lack of results and quietly left.

Bartholomew sat back and tried to think. My home has been invaded, my monies stolen and all I'm left with is an image of a magical cat and a child running around in my bedroom as I've slept. What unlucky star was burning over me last night?

He knew the cat to which the Mage was referring. He'd had it for about a month and had been getting quite used to it. Bartholomew glanced nervously around the room but as he suspected, detected no sign of the animal anywhere. He'd keep an eye out for it anyhow and if he saw it ... he felt the rage build within him again and drew in a breath in an attempt to calm down. Whoever has committed this filthy act will pay dearly, he vowed. What I need is a tracker, and with that thought, Bartholomew started to smile for the first time that day. I know of *just* the tracker that I need.

A New Day Dawns

* * *

Despite the late night, the crew of *The Griffin* were up shortly after sunrise. Loras went into the city to buy provisions while Pardigan and Quint stayed talking in hushed tones over a hot brew and stale buns.

The boys were anxious, half expecting the city watch to come storming down to the port and turn the boat over at any moment. The moneybags were all stowed safely away and the knife, so Pardigan assured Quint, was buried in soot at the bottom of the stove. It made sense to move part of the haul off the boat, but if the watch were indeed investigating at this point then they'd be searching any boat that was trying to leave. This was what Pardigan and Quint were discussing when Tarent emerged from his bunk.

His eyes were red and he'd obviously had little or no sleep. Sitting down next to Pardigan, he poured himself a cup of brew and placed two stacks of papers onto the table.

'This big pile is stuff that I either don't understand or is just nothing we can sell or work with. My vote is we burn it all as soon as possible.' He glanced over at the other two who nodded saying nothing, not questioning any of the papers in the pile, both were staring at the smaller bundle of papers.

'There's some interesting things here that we may be able to use.' Tarent slurped some of his brew and grabbed one of the stale buns, pulling it into small pieces that he fed into his mouth as he spoke.

'I've found one contract here worth keeping - it's a license allowing any vessel holding it to conduct legal business operations out of Minster Island. We could either sell it in a few weeks when the noise has calmed down, or even use it ourselves to do some legitimate trade.' He stared at Pardigan. 'This one paper could mean we are never hungry again. Thank the Source you never left this one behind.'

'I'm not stupid,' said Pardigan indignantly. 'I took all the good stuff.'

'Oh, and this one's interesting, but I can't say why.' Tarent ignored Pardigan and flipped a thin, tatty book from the pile on to the table in front of Quint. It was obviously very old and worn, as if handled many times over the years, and had some strange text in small letters crammed into every conceivable space. The only recognisable thing about it was a rough sketch of a knife on the cover. The boys inspected the book then Pardigan went over to the stove and brought back the knife, secretly glad that it was still there and hadn't found its way back into his pocket. He laid it next to the book. There was no mistaking it. The picture and the knife were one and the same, the stone on top, the shape of the blade; it was no coincidence.

'Well what's it about?' asked Pardigan, his interest sparked.

'I can't read it, can't even tell you what language it is I'm afraid,' Tarent yawned and got to his feet. 'That's it, the sum of my night's efforts. I'm going to sleep - you can deal with that lot.' He staggered back to his cabin and slammed the door. Quint rose and put the big pile of papers into the stove, he lit a match and they watched the papers flare. Just as the smoke became too much and he closed the stove door, they heard a shout on deck and he and Pardigan jumped up with cries of glee and scrabbled for the ladder - Loras was back with fresh buns.

In their efforts to be first to the ladder, the papers were pushed aside and the knife briefly touched the book. The cover transformed and the blue gem in the pommel glowed brightly, unfortunately, no one was there to see it.

The three boys came down the ladder into the cabin, helping Loras with several bags. Quint was crossly telling Loras that it looked like he'd gone on a crazy buying spree and that he could have brought them unwanted attention.

'All I got was the usual buns, milk and some blue fish for our supper,' whined Loras. 'Then some dried beans and other stuff for the stores - was that too much?'

'You seem to have forgotten the other two sacks Loras, the one with all the books in, and what's in the other bag?' asked Quint, calming down now that he was munching on a fresh cinnamon bun still warm from the baker's oven.

'Well the books I've needed for a long time and the bookseller has been holding them for me. They're the books I used when I was apprentice to Magician Pyper. They'll help me to continue my studies.' His face began to turn red. 'The other bag,' he started sheepishly. 'Well the other bag has a few luxuries that we can afford and it's not like I've bought anything too much, just dried fruits, sweet lemon drops, a game of Old Jack Bones, things like that. It's not like I've gone out and bought everyone a new pocket watch, is it?'

With a shrug Quint relented and they indulged themselves in cinnamon buns as Pardigan made up a fresh pot of brew. The day was starting to warm up now and sounds of the port awakening could be heard.

'Sounds like the barge next door is getting underway,' said Pardigan absently, as he glanced over the remaining buns deciding if he could fit one more in.

'They're bound up the coast to Sterling Port,' said Loras. 'I walked back this morning with their cabin boy. Says the barge's captain is right unhappy with the merchants in Freya. Says they can't turn a profit here and won't be coming back 'cos they're going broke.'

Quint stopped chewing, swallowed his mouthful of bun and stared at Pardigan and then Loras in turn. 'That's it!' he exclaimed excitedly. 'That's how we get the money out of Freya and back to the Moorings,' he put the remainder of his bun down. 'Loras, go wake Tarent, you and he can ship aboard the barge as paying passengers. When he's awake, go aboard and book passage. He turned to Pardigan. 'We split the money, we've split the risk. You and I can sail *The Griffin* away in a few days and meet up with them back at the moorings.' Quint grinned. 'We can swing by and pick them up. Sterling Port is only half a day from the moorings.'

Loras finished his bun, took a slurp of his brew and jumped up to bang on Tarent's door, before scuttling up the ladder to book berths on the barge.

Tarent poked his head out of the cabin as Pardigan and Quint were tidying away the remains of the papers and the food. As they did so the knife once again came into contact with the book. The blue stone in the pommel glowed brightly, and the book was once more transformed - this time, it was seen.

'What by the Source was that!' squealed Pardigan, jumping back.

After a moment, he and Quint hesitantly approached the table. The knife was now resting with the blade on top of the book, and the book had changed. No longer a thin pile of papers, barely held together with a threadbare cover, now it was a small leather-bound book, its title displayed in flowing script.

The Book of Challenges

A Masterwork by Magician Ignacius Pew, year 1024

Pardigan moved the knife away. The book returned to its previous state. He moved the knife back and once again the knife's blue stone glowed brightly and the book was again transformed.

Tarent approached the table. 'Did that just...?'

'A magic book!' cried Pardigan. 'I knew there must be magic stuff in that cabinet, but nothing like this.' He reached out and touched the book, making sure not to move the knife. As he did so, something leapt from the hatchway above them and landed hissing on the table. The boys jumped back, Tarent banging his head on the lamp, Quint fell back onto a chest and Pardigan tripped over his own feet - all three gazed up at the table from the floor. There, standing over the book was a large grey cat - it stared intently at the three friends and paced slowly round the table.

'What by the Source is...' started Pardigan, but was stopped as both the blue stone on the knife, and the cat's eyes glowed a bright flashing blue. 'Whooww,' cried Pardigan, falling back to the floor again.

'Where did that come from?' asked Quint, and the cat swivelled to regard him. It let out a loud '*Meow*,' and sat beside the book, turning its attention from one to the other of the startled boys. As they stared at the cat, Loras stumbled back down the ladder.

'We're booked!' he cried excitedly. 'We leave in an hour.' He walked over to the table and held out his hand. 'Where did you get the cat?'

he asked happily. It stood up to let him stroke it and pushed its head into his outstretched hand.

The boys all got to their feet, glancing from Loras to the cat, which Loras had now picked up.

'Can we keep it?' he asked expectantly.

'I think it may have already decided to keep us,' said Quint, '...or you anyway. Just try your best to keep it under control and find out if it's connected to the magic book, will you?'

'Magic?' exclaimed Loras. Tarent filled him in on what had just been happening and Loras was obviously impressed. 'My own magic cat,' he mused. He sat down and started talking quietly to the cat as Quint, Tarent and Pardigan took another look at the book. A slot in the book's spine held the knife while it was read. As they hunched over trying their best to decipher the script, Pardigan glanced over at Loras.

'I'm sure I've seen that cat before,' he muttered.

'Well it's not likely that you'd forget something like that in a hurry,' whispered Tarent, peering nervously over as it purred contentedly on Loras's lap.

They returned to the book, now held by Tarent. Running his hand over the cover, he passed his finger over the title then opened it. The other two waited expectantly.

'Come on Tarent,' urged Pardigan, 'what does it say? Can you read it?'

'Oh my' said Tarent, 'oh my, oh my, oh my.'

Chapter 3

The Book of Challenges

Bartholomew Bask was never one to frequent the bars and coffee shops of the city; he'd always associated them all with riff raff and the general flotsam of humanity. It was therefore an uncomfortable Bartholomew Bask who found himself on the waterfront, at one of the least probable establishments that he might ever wish to visit.

'Blake's,' Bartholomew muttered, scowling up at the sign that hung crookedly over the street. He shuddered and held a scented handkerchief over his nose. Casting a look about, more in case someone he knew saw him than from any worry of robbers or cutthroats, he entered and quickly scanned the room.

It was past early evening and the place was filling up. Several groups were sitting at tables, while others stood close to the serving counter, almost everyone seemed to be talking or shouting noisily. Several barmaids were working the tables, carrying tankards, bottles and trays of food. He stopped one long enough to whisper in her ear; she shook her head and nodded towards the bar.

'Talk to Blake,' she muttered - then she was gone, disappearing back into the crowd.

Bartholomew made his way to the bar, excusing himself politely as he navigated his bulk through the crowd, which only made several people laugh and caused one toothless old woman to slap his backside.

'Oh yer lordship, I'm so sorry,' she shrieked as he spun around with a squeal, bringing howls of laughter from her fellow drinkers.

Bartholomew hurried on.

Blake was sitting on a stool at the corner of the serving counter, a position where he could keep an eye on the drinkers, the barmaids *and* the cashbox, all at the same time. He was a large man but not a fat man; Blake was the kind you wouldn't want trouble with. The years had added a comfort layer and a big belly, but it was stretched across a large muscular frame. Bartholomew made his way over and tried to introduce himself.

'Mr Blake, good evening to you, my name is...' he faltered, as Blake cast him a quick look before returning to his task of watching the room.

'What do yer want and wot's it werf?' growled the innkeeper in a low voice.

'I merely seek...' started Bartholomew.

'Speak up, man,' growled Blake peering down at Bartholomew with disgust. 'If yer got something to say then out with it and let me be, I've a business to run or can't yer tell?' he gawped at Bartholomew. 'Well...?'

Bartholomew was sweating more than ever by this time and simply wanted to be done and gone from this awful place. He stared into Blake's dark eyes then summoned a little courage and a lot of voice. 'I seek the Hawk!'

Conversation stopped at several tables around them, and Blake quickly pulled Bartholomew to the side. 'Shhh, not so loud with yer 'awk business.' He glanced around Bartholomew's shoulder at the room and, satisfied that his girls were all working and a fight hadn't broken out in the last few heartbeats, he turned back to Bartholomew.

'You better 'ave a real good reason for asking for the 'awk' in ere, my fat friend, a real good reason.' He leaned closer and belched softly. Rank, stale breath wafted over Bartholomew, who blinked and held his handkerchief to his nose. 'Well? ...And not so loud, all right? What do yer want with the 'awk?'

Bartholomew started to feel a little ill. 'Oh dear...well...' he started. A short while later Bartholomew found himself being seated into what Blake described as a 'private nook.' A tankard of Elder ale was set down messily in front of him and Blake walked away. Bartholomew started to wipe down his shirt where the ale had splashed, and then noticed that he wasn't alone. The nook was quite dark and the other occupant had been sitting well back in the corner saying nothing. Bartholomew couldn't tell if the fellow was staring at him or even if he was awake. Was this the Hawk? He dabbed at the sweat on his upper lip and cleared his throat. 'My name is Bartholomew Bask, Merchant by trade,' he glanced around nervously, then peered into the corner, trying to make out more of the dark shape. Whoever it was, he was wearing a cloak with the hood up and Bartholomew couldn't see whom he was addressing, which disturbed him. 'I seek The Hawk,' he managed to hiss, then sat back and drank thirstily from the tankard.

The stranger slowly leaned forward, his face briefly caught in the dim light. Bartholomew could just about make out the features of a man - he blinked. A large nose was the first thing to emerge from the hood, closely followed by two gleaming eyes. The Hawk folded his hands upon the table and stared at Bartholomew.

'For what...and for why...' rumbled the Hawk, in a deep gravely voice '...do you seek Matheus Hawk...Mr. Bask?'

It took a moment but once recovered; Bartholomew presented a lengthy heartfelt description of his problem, how little he had to go on and what a travesty of justice it was that strange criminals could be allowed to wander the streets at night taking advantage of...

Matheus Hawk stopped Bartholomew with a slap of his hand on the table. '*Enough* of your prattle...I'm expensive,' he growled, 'but I can find your goods, if found they can be, and I can skin the hides from the thieves and hang them out for the crows if that is your wish?'

Bartholomew smiled; now this was much more like it. Those thieves, whoever they were, would indeed wish they had never heard the name Bartholomew Bask. He gazed across at the Hawk and shivered. He detected something exceedingly strange about this Hawk person and Bartholomew was grateful that it was to *his* side that he was now recruited.

Matheus Hawk had been a sergeant in the King's Guard - an army known for its brutish, violent behaviour, yet he had been discharged for having too heavy a hand. A big man, Matheus had loved to fight and inflict pain from an early age and had taken to war readily. He was cruel, and took a sadistic pleasure in the pain and suffering of his victims. The army wanted none of this. After receiving a number of complaints from the rest of his company, Matheus was court-martialled and imprisoned; but no prison could hold him and he escaped. He'd spent several years as a highwayman, robbing coaches and travellers, until one day he chanced upon a coach carrying two wizards.

The wizards had defended themselves well. Matheus had been badly beaten, and in risk of his life, but a lucky crossbow shot from Matheus had killed the driver and the frightened horses had run off, taking the coach with them. With nobody driving, the coach had careened off the road and into a ravine. Both horses and one of the wizards had died straight away, yet the other had survived for several weeks while Matheus tortured him until he gave up the secrets to his spells. The wizard had eventually died and Matheus had used his new-found skills to act as a bounty hunter and tracker. He'd made a name for himself, not only with the people, but also with the King's Guard. They now saw him as someone to arrest upon sight for continued acts of terrible violence. Matheus Hawk was not a pleasant man, but he was the best tracker in the entire kingdom, and Bartholomew always wanted the best.

Bartholomew handed the few pieces of evidence over to the Hawk and wished him well with his endeavours. 'How shall I contact you?' he enquired.

'You shan't,' growled the Hawk, sliding back into the shadows once more. 'If I want you or have news, then I shall contact you. Now leave me to my work.'

Bartholomew wiped his face and stood up. He wasn't used to taking orders, especially from someone in his employ, but thought better of mentioning anything to Mr Hawk on this first meeting; maybe next time, when they knew each other a little better.

He hurried back through the crowded bar and out into the night, confident that he had done what he could and that the matter was now in capable hands.

Outside on the slightly cooler street, Bartholomew thought again of the hands that the Hawk had crossed in front of him on the table. Long and thin with sharp nails like… like talons… like a Hawk for goodness sake! Bartholomew shivered in the warm evening air, then waved as he saw a carriage that was empty. I almost pity the thieves; he chuckled to himself as he clambered in and settled back into the carriage seat, but then again… maybe I don't. He was giggling as the carriage set off, back up to the 'better part' of town.

* * *

The barge left on time with Loras on deck waving back to Pardigan. Much to his dismay, the cat hadn't wanted to go with Loras, preferring to stay on *The Griffin* with the knife and book. Pardigan returned the wave as the barge left the harbour, slowly creeping out into the open sea.

Quint had gone off to purchase a few more supplies and to try and find out what the word on the street was about the robbery. If the watch were tracking the thief, they had to find out where they were searching and what they had to go on. Pardigan took a last look around at the other boats and the few people walking on the jetty, then made his way down below. At the bottom of the ladder, he peered around the gloom of the hold waiting for his eyes to adjust to the dim light. The book was on the table and the cat was curled up not far from it on a pile of sacking. It lifted its head and watched him as he came down into the room, making him feel awkward. Trying his best to ignore it, he crossed to the table and sat down so that he could read in the small square of sunlight that came in from the hatch. Touching the papers with the knife made the stone flare bright blue and the book once more transformed into the slim leather-bound volume they'd seen before. He studied the cover once more, his finger slowly following the words, his brow creasing in concentration as he read.

The title had appeared written in gold script and below this, was now a picture of a wizard, not the knife, and more tiny words that Pardigan could only just make out, but at least it was written in low speak.

> *The Book of Challenges*
> *A Masterwork by Magician Ignacius pew,*
> *In the year 1024*
>
> *The journey of challenge - written to be read by ones who are worthy, when times are correct.*

Hmm, interesting, thought Pardigan. I wonder if that's Magician Ignacius Pew? He doesn't look particularly happy. He opened the book to the first page, which was an introduction of sorts, from Magician Pew.

> This book was written way back when,
> A need was seen for cunning men.
> A journey's choice, you all must make,
> A challenge for all mankind, you take.
>
> I knew the day when I first took
> This magic pen to magic book.
> When need would rise, a call from man
> And so I wove a magic plan.
>
> The start is finished, the finish not
> I'll need some help to end this plot.
> So you who read these words of mine,
> Must be the heroes at the end of time.
>
> Although so young, you must be,
> I know you better than you know me.
> So if the four shall make this swift,
> This book will give you each a gift.
>
> So turn the page, but do take care,
> Peril and danger await you there.
> You will be right, you will be brave,
> I take these hopes down to my grave.
>
> Ignacius Pew, Magician 1024

Pardigan slowly read the rhyme through again, but still couldn't make much sense of it. It seemed to describe the crew of *The Griffin*, and that they all had to decide to make some journey together. What the guide - if that's what it was - didn't reveal, was *why* they should make the journey; a journey that promised to be both dangerous and perilous - as if they weren't in enough trouble as it was. He turned the page and found a clean white sheet staring back at him, as was the next

The Book of Challenges

one, then the next one. All the pages were blank except for the page of introduction. Maybe the knife has to touch each page? He touched the blank pages with first the blade and then the gem in the pommel, but nothing happened. He tried several other pages with the same result.

'Well that sorts that,' said Pardigan aloud. 'No more book. I guess he didn't finish it.' It had all been exciting until the book turned out to be a collection of pages never finished. 'What a waste of a magic book,' he murmured in disgust, and was about to throw it into a corner.

The cat leapt up screeching, forcing him to step back.

'Wohhhh, cat, I'm sorry. I won't harm your book, honest, here, you take it.' Pardigan held it out to the cat and the cat jumped up onto the table and placed its paw on top of it. Its eyes flashed bright blue, unsettling him further.

'Foolish boy,' purred the cat. 'Did you read the first page or were you just looking at the pretty squiggles hoping one day to understand?' Pardigan had never been insulted by a cat before but thought that this was indeed an insult.

'Of course I read it, but it finishes there. It's blank after the first page and anyhow, it doesn't make much sense...Hey! How come you can talk?' he added as an afterthought.

'Magician Pew never made large amounts of sense when he was alive, so I think it's asking a bit much for him to make sense now, don't you?' The cat purred and lay down across the book. 'If you read the introduction, there's a line that reads, 'A journey's choice you all must make.' It licked a paw and started washing itself. 'You will note by this that you must all decide to make the journey together, only then will the book reveal more to you.' It glanced up from its washing to stare into his eyes. 'So no throwing the book around, I've taken care of it for too long and will not let you destroy it now.'

All Pardigan could think to reply to all this was to repeat again, 'So, how come you can talk?'

The cat turned its head to one side questioningly. 'I'm a cat. Cats can't talk. Maybe you're going mad?' It went back to its cleaning then curled up and fell asleep on the book without speaking again. Pardigan stared at it open-mouthed, unsure what he could say or do.

By the time Quint returned, Pardigan had recovered from his chat with the cat. He'd tried several times to engage it in conversation and was doing so again when Quint dropped down the hatchway.

'What are you doing?' asked Quint, grinning. 'Loras will chat to anything, especially a cat, but surely not you, Pardigan?'

'But it spoke to me,' objected Pardigan. 'I was reading the book, well the first page, and it started talking to me.' He sat down at the table. 'It was actually quite insulting,' he added dejectedly. 'Only now I can't get it to talk again.'

Quint laughed. 'Pardigan it's a cat! Cats can't talk.'

'I did tell him that,' said the cat lifting its head. 'But he just wouldn't listen.'

'There you are, I told you,' said Pardigan laughing in relief as Quint stared in shock at the cat.

'It talked!' spluttered Quint.

'Yes, I know,' said Pardigan. 'Just don't get on its bad side, it can be *very* rude.' He told Quint what it had said and after carefully retrieving the book, Quint read the page while still keeping a wary eye on the cat.

'Well, we'll have to wait until we're back at the moorings and discuss this with the others. It does sound like fun though, eh, Pardigan? Challenges, danger and gifts, I wonder what the gifts are?' He skipped up the ladder whistling and Pardigan hurried after him.

The cat slept, and if a cat could smile, which they can, then the cat was smiling, happily.

* * *

Up on deck Quint was coiling rope and putting the loose objects into lockers making preparations to go to sea.

'I walked round the town for the last three hours,' he said re-tying a sail. 'I'm telling you there's no talk about a big theft,' he glanced at Pardigan. 'Nothing... maybe he doesn't know he was robbed?'

'Well maybe. I just can't believe our luck would be that good, but if he does discover it in a few days, and we're not even here, then we won't be suspected at all!'

'My thoughts exactly, so we're leaving on the morning tide. I'm off to pay our dues to the Harbourmaster, then we can take another walk around town to get another feel for things.'

They locked the hatchway and after paying the harbourmaster for their stay, they walked through the port and into the bustling town of Freya. The only gossip they heard about the merchant was close to his house, where they'd heard that he'd fired his maid that very morning and had been seen screaming at her from his window.

'Maybe he thinks it was her,' said Pardigan.

'Maybe,' Quint replied. 'Let's just keep moving and see what else is happening.'

They walked and walked, and listened to all types of gossip. There was much about the merchants and about the King and his troubles in the northern realms, but nothing more about Merchant Bask or his maid. They ate fried fish and shared a drink of lemon fizz from a bottle, all bought from a stall in Market Square, then headed back down to the port.

As they approached *The Griffin*, they got the impression that something wasn't right, so sprinted the last short distance, coming to a stop in front of the boat. The hatchway was open.

'We're being robbed,' hissed Pardigan as they crept up the gangplank. Nothing unusual could be heard from below decks, only the normal creaking of the ropes and a few groans from the old timbers - the normal sounds of *The Griffin* sleeping. The lock was still set but strangely the hatch was open, pushed to the side. Quint dropped down inside, quickly followed by Pardigan.

It was a mess with things thrown everywhere - crates upturned, bottles smashed, the contents of lockers all over the floor - and the cabin doors were all open showing similar scenes within. Someone had been searching for something.

'I think our secret's out,' hissed Pardigan. 'They got the book and knife by the look of it,' he muttered unhappily as he set the table back the right way round. 'Let's just get out of here while we still can. Whoever was here could come back.'

They spent some time despondently clearing up the mess and set the hold back as it had been, then got food ready for an evening meal. They had decided to eat up on deck and Pardigan was still below cutting bread, when he noticed the table. There, sleeping as if nothing had happened was the cat - her head propped on the book.

'Where did you come from?' he gasped.

The cat lifted its head and regarded him sleepily. 'Oh, you're back. You've had a visitor,' it purred. 'Not a very nice man at all. I'm glad to see you had a tidy up.' It rose and stretched as if it had spent the afternoon sleeping in the same position. 'He was looking for... things, but didn't find anything, he got very upset. I think you'll find his calling card on the back of the mast there.'

Pardigan turned to look at the mast and at first couldn't see anything. Then at the top, near where it went through the roof, he saw a black mark. He clambered up onto a chair to get a better look.

'It's a spell,' purred the cat. Pardigan froze.

'It's a listening spell, really quite clever. It lets whoever set it know when you return, so he can listen to what you're saying.' Pardigan crouched on the chair, not daring to move, and stared at the cat. The cat stared back at him. 'Don't worry, I stopped it working. He'll think the boat is empty and you're still away.'

'You... stopped it working?' said Pardigan.

'I did,' purred the cat and went back to sleep.

A little uncertainly, Pardigan decided to look at the spell mark a little closer. It was the outline of a hawk burnt into the wood - he reached out to touch it.

'I wouldn't do that,' the cat purred, opening an eye. 'He may have left traces of something very nasty for you to touch... I would have.'

Pardigan slowly pulled his hand back and got down. 'I bet you would have,' he muttered under his breath.

'There's a good boy,' purred the cat.

'Where did you go during all this?' asked Pardigan.

'I went...away, you wouldn't understand, so don't even try.' She curled back down, returning to sleep.

'There you go insulting me again,' muttered Pardigan and he went off to tell Quint.

They cast off at daybreak and slipped out of port into open sea, both boys feeling that they were being watched, but both very glad to have some water between them and whoever their uninvited guest had been.

Chapter 4

A Hunter's Moon

The trip up the coast to Sterling Port took the boys three days, during which they were blessed with good weather and good winds all the way. Sailing gave immense pleasure to all of them, but it was Quint who truly revelled in it. As the wind became stronger he made his way to the very front of the boat and stood on the bowsprit, where he indulged himself in shouting and laughing into the face of the sea.

Spray covered him, bursting in a rainbow of colours time and time again as he held on, bracing himself against the pounding of the waves that tried to dislodge him. Several times he had to grab for the safety rope to stop being washed over by a particularly big wave but simply laughed, loving every moment. Eventually, he dripped his way back to Pardigan at the helm.

'Oh, Pardigan, you just have to try it, it makes you feel so...so...alive!'

Pardigan excused himself from the fun on the grounds that he didn't want to be speaking with the fish anytime soon.

On the second night of the journey they entered a protected anchorage to rest and get a good night's sleep. They caught some fish for their supper and slow roasted them above glowing coals. The mouth-watering smell made their stomachs rumble and they ended up eating them while they were still hot enough to burn their fingers, cramming bits of fish into their mouths as they laughed at each other's efforts.

After eating, they sat back contented, gazing up as the stars began to appear.

Quint was thrilled to spot 'sea fairies' in the water as every wave that formed a crest glowed an eerie greeny blue in the starlit night.

'Its small creatures caught in the tide,' he explained excitedly. 'For some reason, when they're moved they glow like that - sailors call them sea fairies, Tarent calls it phosphorescence. Watch this.' He stood up, pulled off his clothes, and dived over the side. As he entered the water, his trail was lit by thousands of bright lights as the creatures glowed. He came to the surface grinning and shouting. 'Come on Pardigan, come and play with the fairies.' He slapped his hands about in the water and laughed as it all glowed back at him, lighting his face a greeny blue.

'Do they hurt?' questioned Pardigan, standing on the edge of the boat, unsure if he wanted to be in the water with a million angry fairies.

'Course not,' said Quint, splashing water up at him. 'Come in and stop being a baby.'

Pardigan held his nose and jumped into the water, keeping his eyes closed until he surfaced. Opening them, he saw the bubbles around him hissing and glowing brightly. He splashed about, delighted as the water lit up around him.

'Well, it doesn't hurt me, but what about the fairies?' he shouted to Quint.

'I've not heard any of them complain yet,' replied Quint. They swam about for a while, playing with the unusual show of colours, then lay floating on their backs, gazing up at the night sky.

Climbing out, they lay on the deck to continue their star watching, each trying to see the next one that would shoot on its journey across the heavens.

Unseen by the boys, the cat leapt from the boat, and flew away across the moonlit water on soft, silent white wings.

* * *

The next morning they were away early. Pardigan made a brew before they left and they munched on the last of the cinnamon buns as they returned to open water.

'We've had a good run up until now, so we may make Sterling Port by early afternoon,' said Quint scanning the horizon. 'That's if nothing nasty happens with the weather,' he added. Pardigan was also watching the skies but not merely for the sight of black clouds gathering. The mysterious intruder back in Freya still had him unnerved, and he couldn't shake the feeling that they were not only being followed, but were being watched as well.

They sighted Sterling Port late in the afternoon after an exciting passage. *The Griffin* had sped along with its sails straining to drag the ungainly hull through the water. Porpoises had led the last part of the voyage, ducking and diving in front of the boat, their antics causing the boys great delight. However, by the time they could make out the Towers on Sterling's harbour walls, they were ready to feel solid ground under their feet and to catch up with their friends.

Clouds of gulls escorted them in - wheeling and crying with the hope that *The Griffin* was a fishing boat with scraps to eat. They passed into the little port, and were surprised to see Loras running along the harbour wall waving at them.

They watched him run past a three-masted ocean trader being unloaded with the help of a large wooden crane swinging bales and crates onto the quayside. A waiting army of carts and porters was busily moving the cargo up to the warehouses and trading halls of the town, causing a heady aroma of spices to fill the air. A group of urchins was urging the porters on, hurling insults and jokes, ready to run in and snatch something if the chance was presented to them.

'Ahoy *The Griffin*,' shouted Loras happily.

Tarent stood up from where he'd been propped against the wall reading and raised a hand in greeting and they both ran down to where *The Griffin* was coming in to dock.

'How did you know we'd be in today?' shouted Pardigan, as he threw a mooring rope to Tarent.

'We could still be days away but you look like you've been expecting us.'

Tarent glanced over at Loras who was helping tie the other end of the boat to the docks. 'You better ask our magician friend about that, he had a visitor,' he answered cryptically.

When *The Griffin* was safely moored, sails stored and they were signed in with the Harbourmaster, the boys all gathered down below. Tarent replaced the coins in the stove, visibly relieved not to be carrying them around with him, while Quint and Pardigan told of Pardigan's conversation with the cat. Loras was in awe of the book and its magical abilities. He was sitting with the cat on his lap, stroking her fur, but had to put her down to see and touch the book for himself.

'Well?' said Quint. 'What shall we do? We find ourselves in the middle of an adventure and being asked to take it to another level,' he glanced around the group. All eyes were on him, including those of the cat. He carried on, 'This seems too good to miss but it also sounds dangerous. We know someone's following us and that he's after something that we have,' he glanced across at Pardigan, 'or rather took. I can only think it's the knife and book. To stay here means sooner or later he'll find us. The book at least gives us a chance to move on and I for one vote that we take the challenge, whatever it is.' He sat back down.

Pardigan stood. 'Let's do it!' was all he said before resuming his seat.

Loras was nodding all the time, clearly excited. 'Oh yes, we must. A chance like this for magic and adventure is...is...is, oh absolutely, my vote is yes.'

Tarent stood and stared down at the book, then nodded to Loras. 'Did you tell them how we knew they were coming in today?'

'Oh, right,' said Loras excitedly. 'Of course.' He held the cat up, which hissed a warning for being handled too roughly. 'Oops sorry,' said Loras. 'Well...Mahra here came to see me and told me you were coming.'

'But the cat has been with us,' said Quint. 'You're telling us that the cat, who by the way, was on our boat out at sea. That this cat here; came to see you from on another boat a long way away. It had a chat with you, then came back to our boat?' Loras nodded happily. Without waiting for an answer Quint glared at the cat. 'Cat or Mahra or whatever your name is, I think you owe us an explanation before we go making any decisions on what we're doing. Right now we're being played with and I don't like it.'

The cat stood up, stretched, and walked around the centre of the room her eyes flashing bright blue as she glared back at Quint and leapt up onto the table, changing form as she landed. Sitting in front of them was a girl with short dark hair. She was small, about the same size as Loras, had a pretty face with big blue eyes and was dressed from head to foot in tight grey leather. She looked around at their shocked faces, eyes flashing an even brighter blue, and giggled.

'Hello, boys, I'm Mahra and I suppose you're right, maybe it is time we had a little chat.'

'Well, she didn't look like that when she came to see me,' said Loras, 'How do you do that? Where do you come from? What...'

'What are you playing at, Mahra?' interrupted Quint angrily.

She turned to regard him with feline eyes. 'Calm down Quint...I'm not playing games with you; I'm merely your...guide or advisor, if you decide to take the challenges. Your friend here stole the book and knife,' she nodded at Pardigan. 'I watched him do it. It doesn't matter how he got it. The question you now face is whether to continue with what *he* started.' She sighed and settled herself more comfortably. 'I have been the guardian of that book for centuries and there has never been a group that have managed to open it until now. I'm actually starting to believe after all this time that we may finally get to complete this. Maybe then I can do something else other than follow a book about for years and years.'

'So how do you change into a cat and how did you get to Loras?' asked Quint, calming slightly now that Mahra was talking with them.

'I can change when I want to. I'm not too sure what my true shape really is any more, I think it's this one, but I do so love being a cat, and an owl, so maybe I'm really one of those.' She thought for a moment.

'No, I think that this is my real shape, I just don't use it much.' She looked down at her arms. 'I mean, it's not much good for anything is it? It can't fly, it's not very agile, what's it for?' She seemed to drift off again, and her eyes started to close, then opened again.

'Oh yes, this is important, so listen. It doesn't matter what decision you make, but every one of you must decide for yourself and make a conscious decision. Don't just follow your friends; decide if this is the path for you, or not. The future is fraught with danger, the path will often be uncertain, but then, isn't that the case whichever way you choose to walk in life?'

She stood and walked around staring deeply into the eyes of each of them. '*The Book of Challenges*' was written a long time ago, by a magician who foresaw a time in the future when this planet would need to be set on another course. The reality you all take for granted is set in a fine balance between Chaos and Order. A great spell was cast to stop the world slipping into a time of Chaos by altering the consciousness of every living thing. The spell was sealed within three crystal skulls and each was carefully hidden until it was time for them to be united, this will allow the spell to complete and balance to be restored.

To do this, the Magician needed to enlist the aid of others who wouldn't be born for many generations. I was charged with guarding the book and the knife and to await those that would one day use them. It's been a very long time, but maybe now we're truly at the end of time, our heroes have finally been found, and we can try and find the skulls.' She yawned. 'I need to sleep; it's just one of the things about being a cat for so long. Make your decisions, and if all of you are in agreement, each place a hand upon the book and the next pages will be revealed.' These last words were softly spoken as she transformed back into the cat and lay upon the table already dozing off.

'But what about the person following us?' asked Pardigan, 'What are we going to do about him?'

Mahra lifted her head and said in a sleepy voice, 'He follows now but won't find you...yet.'

'Yet...? Yet...? What does she mean yet?' exclaimed Pardigan, jumping to his feet, but this time Mahra really was fast asleep.

They talked until way past dark and broke the discussion to eat beans and bread before continuing, reading Magician Pew's rhyme several times. They all liked the mention of gifts, especially Loras who was sure they would be magical gifts, but they were also concerned about the dangers, particularly, in Pardigan's case, the one following them, but in the end they had only one choice. The unknown dangers would have to remain unknown for now. There was little they could do about them so there was no point fretting. Finally, each stood and, making his decision, placed his hand upon the book.

The last was Pardigan, who hesitated, staring around at the others, aware of the importance of the moment. Laying his hand upon theirs, he said, as the others had before him, 'My decision is made; we should take the challenges and see this future for ourselves.'

The knife in the book's spine flared, causing Mahra to wake for a moment, and then it went back to its normal state. They stared round nervously at each other.

'Well,' said Pardigan, 'Let's open it.'

Tarent reached for the book and keeping it flat on the table so they could all see, he opened it. Moving past the introduction, he found that the next page was no longer blank. He read it aloud...

> *Welcome friends, welcome all,*
> *You swiftly answered my Ancient call.*
> *Four you are, that I can see,*
> *Please accept these gifts from me.*
>
> * * *
>
> *Magician, place your hand upon this book,*
> *Please tell your friends not to look.*

They all stared at Loras.

'I think that must be you, Loras,' said Tarent turning to face away with the others.

Loras glanced about the group. They had their backs to him, leaving him quite alone with the book - he grinned nervously.

'All right, here goes,' he said, closing his eyes. As he lowered his hand the stone glowed and small blue streaks of energy flickered up from the book. When the glow faded, the boys turned expectantly. Loras appeared almost unchanged; the difference was in his eyes.

'What is it, Loras?' whispered Pardigan. 'What happened? What's it done to you?'

Loras shook his head. 'I don't know. I don't feel much different, except... except it all seems so... so clear in my mind, like... like a cloud has been lifted.'

'I'm not sure I want to put my hand anywhere near that book,' muttered Quint. 'I think it's messed with his head, he's gone a bit weird, hasn't he?'

'Weird!' said Loras. 'No, I'm not weird, watch.' He pointed at the mast and everyone fell to the floor. It wasn't wise to be anywhere near Loras when he was pointing at anything, lest you lost an ear or something.

They glanced up when there was no explosion.

'Oh Source!' said Pardigan, peering over the table that he'd dived under. 'Loras, that's incredible!'

Loras was still pointing at the mast but tears were streaming down his face and he was smiling. 'Do you know how long I've dreamed of being able to do that?'

From out of the old wooden mast, a single small branch now grew with three leaves and a tiny acorn.

'The book has taught me to control and understand the magic I've practised, and the chance to learn more and become a real magician.'

It was the first time any of them had heard Loras say anything like this; he was always one to argue that he was already a real magician. They glanced around at one another and then down at the open book, another page had become visible.

> *Travelling with you - I can see,*
> *A thief of great ability.*
> *For you I shall attempt to free,*
> *Your many talents magically.*
>
> * * *
>
> *Place your hand upon the book.*
> *And tell your friends not to look.*

Seeing that Loras was all right, well a bit strange, but apparently unharmed; Pardigan moved his hand to the book. Again the gem flared a dazzling blue and Pardigan felt fingers of ice creeping up his arm and down his spine. Pressure built behind his eyes, then the gem, and his world, returned to normal. He noticed firstly that he was wearing different clothes, which startled him. Everything was a light grey - a cape with its hood folded down was draped over his shoulders, soft black boots came up almost to his knees and he instinctively knew he had a knife tucked in the left boot. He was also aware of another knife at his side and checked his belt to confirm this.

'Well?' said Quint, concerned for his friend.

'I'm not sure,' whispered Pardigan. 'I don't feel very...different...yet.' He glanced around the boat and then out of the porthole, 'I do feel something...calling me...it's...strange but...'

Outside, the moon was up, its reflection dancing upon the water. Pardigan felt something within him leap forwards and before he knew it, he was over the water and on the jetty opposite, looking back at *The Griffin* as it lay by the harbour wall some thirty spans away.

What by the Source was that? He swayed on his feet and the answer came to him as if whispered in his ear: 'place shifting.' He glanced across at *The Griffin* again and imagined himself in the hold with his friends, and then with a whoosh and a rushing of air, he was there. The worried looks on his friends' faces made him smile. 'Well that's going to take some getting used to!' and he explained what had happened.

Mahra raised her head. 'I'll help you all to understand your gifts, they were all explained to me such a very long time ago, but I do remember.' She yawned. 'Think, hide.' He did so and vanished from their sight.

'Oh Source, that's incredible,' came a voice from roughly where Pardigan had been standing. He reappeared, grinning at everybody.

'Those are your working gifts but you also have gifts of defence,' purred Mahra. 'If I remember correctly you should be able to find one if you point at that cup and think burn.' She indicated a cup near her then moved out of the way.

Pardigan pointed at the cup and mumbled 'Burn,' a needle of white energy leapt from his finger and struck the cup, which cracked in two, each piece flying in different directions.

'I'm starting to like this,' said Pardigan, staring intently at his finger.

'The lightning is only mild; you'll have to work on it. At the moment it would scare someone but you're a long way from inflicting any real harm on anything... unless you take a serious dislike to cups, I suppose.' Mahra resumed her place. She seemed to think for a moment. 'Just as well really, maybe Pew wasn't as crazy as I thought. Your weapon of choice is the knife - try throwing one.' Pardigan produced a knife from the collar of his cloak and with one fluid motion sent it spinning with a *thunk* into a cabin door. He smiled.

'Who's next?' said Mahra. 'Come on step up; let's get this over with so we can get on with the next bit.'

'Next bit?' questioned Quint.

'Yes, dear, the bit after this bit, now be a good boy and read the next page.'

They peered down at the book again; Tarent turned the page with trembling fingers. The next page was now visible.

> *Your leader is a fighter true,*
> *My gift is coming now to you.*
> *Awake now hero of the bow,*
> *For my magic now begins to flow.*
>
> ** * **
>
> *Place your hand upon the book.*
> *And tell your friends not to look.*

'That, my friend is you,' said Tarent, looking with some relief at Quint.

They all turned their backs on Quint and the book, and heard the hesitant movements of their friend. The flash came and they slowly turned to see what had happened. Quint was standing quite still. Like Pardigan his clothing had changed. He was dressed in steel grey cloth with a hooded cape that fell from his shoulders to below his knees. A long black bow glimmered at his side in the flickering light of the lanterns.

'Quint...you all right?' Pardigan made to place a hand on Quint's arm.

'I'm...yeah, I'm all right...really,' murmured Quint. The others waited silently, giving their friend and leader time to come to terms with whatever changes he'd experienced. A moth flitted around the room and in one swift movement Quint drew an arrow, spun around and let loose, pinning the moth to the side of the ship. The whole action a blur, taking less time to complete than his friends' eyes could follow. Quint seemed surprised then glanced down and opened his cape; a sword hung upon his belt with a dagger to balance it on the other side.

'I love magic,' whispered Loras. He walked to the far wall and eased the arrow from the wood. The moth dropped into his outstretched hand and fluttered feebly. He cupped both hands around it and a blue glow shone from between his fingers. Opening his hands, the moth fluttered free, unhurt from the experience and sensible enough to head straight for the porthole. The boys all faced Tarent.

He studied his friends; all changed but still the same. Friends he had known for such a short time, yet felt he had known forever. He turned to the new page and, sure enough, the text was there. He read aloud in a steady voice:

> *Although the last, he is not least,*
> *I call upon the fledgling priest.*
> *His knowledge is a weapon true,*
> *And with twin blades he's one of you.*
>
> * * *
>
> *Place your hand upon this book.*
> *And tell your friends not to look.*

With a hand that shook, Tarent reached out and felt a warm blue mist enfold him as energy coursed through his body. Understanding dawned upon him as if a veil had been drawn from his mind and a smile lit up his face.

He knew himself to be in the Source, the source of all light and love. He was part of the Source and as one with the Source. A feeling of completion and belonging enveloped him and he understood the direction he must travel. After what felt like an age later, he opened his eyes to see his friends staring at him. Glancing down he saw brown robes and a long cape and was holding a wooden staff gripped in both hands. He twisted it and the two halves separated, twin blades flashed into the room. He replaced them expertly and returned the smiles of his friends.

The cat stood and stretched, then changed into the girl they had seen before. She smiled around at them. 'I have been waiting nearly a thousand years to meet you all and it is a real pleasure to do so at last. Magician, Fighter, Thief and Priest of the Source; it is such a thrill to see you. Magician Pew described you so well. Let me try to give some small explanation of what is happening to you.'

'Long ago, in a time now known as the Great Age, a future was foreseen by several of the leading magicians. They saw a day when the world would be at the very tip of all that was good and on the first slippery slopes of decline. For this world as we know it to exist, there has to be a balance, think of it as good and evil, positive and negative, or Order and Chaos. All are similar and related, yet each is completely different. There is the necessity for a little Chaos in the world to complete a balance, but no room for evil in the hearts of man. What the magicians of old foresaw was a point of balance between Order and Chaos, the forces of nature. That point of balance, if allowed to pass, would mean Chaos becoming greater and greater, gradually leaving no room for Order. However, if the battle between the two could be halted at the right time, then a period of perfect balance, of peace and plenty, could continue indefinitely.'

'To accomplish this, a great spell was needed. This spell was conceived by my master, Magician Pew, one of the greatest magicians of all time.'

'And you were there to see all this, a thousand years ago?' asked Loras.

'Oh yes, I was there,' Mahra confirmed. 'Many years of work went into the spell's casting and placing into three crystal skulls, but to complete it, someone had to wait for the right time to unite the skulls. That time, it would seem...is now. *The Book of Challenges* was created and heroes plucked from the future to use it. You are those heroes. You are the soldiers for Order, you must complete the challenges to finish the spell and stop the world from slipping further and further into the control of Chaos and the dark days of true evil.'

'We already have a mystery soldier recruited to Chaos, although he may not even realise it. I believe he is the one who now tracks you, and Chaos will be aiding him in every way that it can. For now at least, it would seem the balance remains.'

The stars shone down brightly and an orange moon hung large and low on the horizon, its glow scattered on the water's surface. Tarent was leaning back against the mast; he shivered as he sought the omen in his head -*A Hunter's Moon*. He instinctively knew this omen prophesied trouble and, more to the point, that a demon would walk the earth. Well isn't that wonderful, he thought. Just what I needed to know; magic, danger, and now demons, what joy knowledge can sometimes bring.

* * *

Matheus Hawk was not a happy man. He'd tracked the thief easily enough to a boat anchored in the harbour. A simple 'find' spell had allowed him to trace the boy who had been in the merchant's room and a morning's vigil had singled out the old hulk, hiding in the corner with several youngsters living on board. Matheus had a horrible reputation, which he was always careful to nurture. It paid to have people fear him in his line of work; however, setting himself and his methods loose upon children was lower than even he had been prepared to go. He had decided to wait until the boat was empty, search it, retrieve whatever was the merchant's and leave. If the merchant didn't like it, then so be it; they were, after all, only youngsters.

It had started to go wrong when nothing of the merchant's could be found on the boat. Magic didn't seem to work and even the listening spell he'd placed had failed to perform, which was strange. The final thing to take the edge from his humour had been the sight of the boat slipping out to sea early the next morning. He'd learned a valuable lesson in underestimating the thieves simply because they were children. Had they been adults he would have confronted them from the moment he'd traced them and slaughtered them without a regret, thought or prayer. He vowed to chase them down and children or not, he would show the world once more that being tracked by Matheus Hawk meant you should live what little remained of your life in absolute terror.

Chapter 5

Set Course for 'The Isle of Skulls'

The book was now starting to fill, and each of the boys spent time reading through it. The fifth page after the introduction was now visible and causing much heated discussion.

> *Challenge of the Skulls*
>
> *A haven of the evil mind,*
> *The house of skulls first you must find.*
>
> *An Island fortress you will see,*
> *Then seek the skull that links to me.*
>
> *Sail away north-east from here,*
> *Mahra, my cat will make things clear.*
>
> *When you arrive, you will see,*
> *That things are not as they should be.*

Pardigan looked over at Mahra. 'Well, what does it mean?'

Set Course for 'The Isle of Skulls'

'You can't need my help already surely?' she purred. Lifting her hand to her mouth, she began to lick it, then remembered that she wasn't in cat but human form and frowned. 'It means my little group of heroes that the first challenge is to get yourselves to the Isle of Skulls and find the... skull that...' She waved her hands in the air absently. '...that it links to Magician Pew... somehow. Listen, I don't pretend to understand everything that you're supposed to do,' she added in an irritated tone. 'Magician Pew was never the clearest person with his language. And apparently, for some reason known only to himself, he decided that he had to write your instructions in rhyme. This, remember, was all conceived over a thousand years ago and was probably necessary for the spell... I don't know!'

The boys glanced at one another and Tarent shrugged. 'Mahra, we're not asking you to know everything, just to help us as much as you can. How far is this island? I don't think it's on the charts, and have you any idea what we can expect when we get there?'

'It's not on your charts for the same reason that the next page isn't in the book before it's meant to be read. Simply sail north-east and after a day or two I'm sure we'll find it.'

'Sure we'll find it?' echoed Quint. 'You don't know?'

'No,' said Mahra. 'I don't know. I also don't know what to expect when we get there, but I seem to be remembering things when the need arises. My mind has probably been affected in the same way as the book and the island. Which means the spell is still active and extremely powerful.' She paused for a moment. 'When we get to the island, either I'll know a little more, or we'll just have to follow our instincts. I'm sorry but that's all I can tell you for the moment.'

They realised that although thin, it was all they had. As for the agent of Chaos that followed; not much could be done except stay ahead of him and act with the best of their new abilities, if and when he did show up.

The next morning Quint and Pardigan went ashore to buy provisions and have a last look around the town of Sterling. Quint reluctantly left his bow and sword on the boat, but both boys carried knives.

'I've never carried a blade before,' said Pardigan. 'It's strange, I'd feel quite naked now if I didn't have one with me,' he felt the knife under his cloak and sighed. 'A wise man once told me never to carry a blade. He said there would always come a time when you'd cross paths with a person that has a greater ability, who'd take it away from you and...' He left the sentence unfinished, drawing a finger across his throat theatrically, and then shrugged his shoulders.

'Do you really feel different?' asked Quint. 'I mean me, personally, I feel... strange. I know I'm me, but I'm not the me that I recognise... do you know what I'm talking about or am I babbling?'

'Yeah, I feel the same as you. I guess we all do, but I think we'll get used to it; I hope so anyhow. I do like feeling a little special. My only worry is whoever's following us. Knife thrower or not, and I don't care if I *can* go invisible, he scares me. I'm not sure why exactly, but he does.' They continued to walk into town chatting in low voices, so as not to be overheard.

By mid morning, they were back on the boat and *The Griffin* got underway, heading once more for open sea.

* * *

Matheus Hawk sat huddled in concentration over a cast-iron brazier – the hot coals painting his face with an orange glow. He added another pinch of powder from a bag, and smoke billowed up, filling the room and stinging his eyes, but he was past the point of caring. The spell he was casting was a seeing spell and it wasn't working. He was searching for the boat that housed his quarry, yet time and time again it was proving to be unsuccessful. His patience was growing thin as he watched visions change in the coals through red-rimmed eyes. He'd been doing this for several turns of the glass and was becoming extremely fatigued, but still he pushed on. Constantly the visions moved from boat to boat, as scene after scene was shown to him, yet nothing appeared that was remotely like the boat he had entered in the port.

At last he could take it no more. Turning from the brazier he stood and stretched. Clenching and cracking his knuckles, he strode to the window and threw the shutters wide. Smoke billowed out allowing light and air to flood back into the room. Breathing deeply, Matheus stood staring down into the street. Knowing his tactics would have to change he contemplated his options. This was no ordinary matter of tracking down some common thief or fugitive. Magic was involved here, potent magic, and if Matheus had come to enjoy one thing beyond all else, it was his magical skills. The chance that he could acquire new knowledge was even more tempting than any reward the fat merchant could put in front of him.

There was a powerful spell that Matheus had used only twice before and was hesitant in using again, but he was considering it now. To request the aid of demon kind was fraught with peril. Matheus knew he was a powerful magician, but was also aware of his limitations and knew even he would have problems controlling a demon, but if an agreement of some sort could be made ...

After eating a sparse meal of raw vegetables and cold rice, he spent the afternoon in meditation. By nightfall he was decided, ready and prepared.

The brazier was re-lit and several clay bowls of carefully prepared herbs and powders set to the side. Placing the brazier in the centre of the floor, he then spent some time and care, drawing a series of complex patterns and designs around it. While he worked, his mind went back to the sessions with the one he had called 'the magic man'. The crippled magician, desperate for medical aid, food and water, had begged Matheus for help, but had received only the bare minimum necessary to keep him alive; alive enough for Matheus to extract the information he craved. He'd written these scraps of knowledge down on small blocks of parchment and he was now studying them while scratching his charcoal stick on the floor, sending whirls and spirals off to the four corners of the room.

Energy began crackling along the charcoal lines changing from intense blue, the colour of Order, to a dark crimson red, the colour of

Chaos. Matheus was sweating freely in the stuffy atmosphere, yet he pulled the hood of his cape over his head, to better concentrate on the complex rituals of the incantation ahead. He had read and re-read the passages necessary several times over, and felt confident in his ability to perform the task. Yet, he remained uncertain of what direction to take once the task was complete; that of calling the demon into this realm.

Much would depend upon careful negotiation to see if he could persuade the demon to do what he wanted. If all else failed, he had set call-back spells at various stages of the pattern and was confident he could return the demon should anything go wrong.

Still, it was with some measure of uncertainty that Matheus finally took his position, sitting cross-legged in front of the brazier. Drawing several deep breaths, he commenced a deep rhythmic chant. As the brazier smouldered, he dropped different herbs and mixtures onto the glowing coals, repeating this at odd intervals. Around him shadows and lights danced upon the walls, smoke moved in patterns through the thick air and the energy in the room grew until every hair on his body was standing on end. Even the dust on the floor was dancing, drawn along the patterns as the energy crackled and glowed. It was becoming less and less blue, and more and more the deep crimson red of Chaos, as the spell's energy sank through the layers of awareness and into the realms of darkness. Down and down, sinking lower and lower, Matheus moved through the darkening mists, seeing strange beings and spirits. Some noticed him but most did not, each caught up in their own private nightmares. The chant no longer resembled a collection of words, but had become a vibrating mixture of energy and sound that twisted together controlling the spell. Window shutters, that had been carefully closed and bolted before he'd begun, now rattled and banged with an urgent fury.

Drawn by the noises and the strange glow coming from the room, the landlady of the hostel was trying to force her way in, but the normally flimsy door wasn't budging. It now seemed fixed as if made from iron. A mixture of concern for her room and fear of the strange noises, smells and lights from within lent her a reckless courage as she tried with all her might to gain entry. After a particularly loud ripping noise and a further shaking of the building, which sent plaster and dust raining down over her head, she finally gave up and ran shrieking down the stairs. In her wake she passed several guests peeking round their doors with white scared faces and large fearful eyes. Violent crackling and rumbling sounded like thunder throughout the building, as if a violent storm were confined and dancing within the small upstairs room. Cracks began appearing in the walls and roof tiles were now raining down, smashing onto the street below.

Completely unaware of his surroundings or his slumped body, Matheus had become one with the spell as he continued down through the ever-spiralling levels of spirit, seeking the lowest realms of darkness - the place where the demons dwelt.

* * *

Water washed back over the deck, as another wave was met head on. *The Griffin* seemed to come alive at times like this, attacking each new wave with a crash and a slap that sent water spraying over the delighted crew as the deck bucked and fell beneath them.

Quint was standing at the wheel teasing every bit of speed from the old boat, while Loras, who had been sent forward to stand on the bowsprit, kept watch for any logs that could still be a hazard to them this near to the coast. Loras didn't like this duty much and was holding on in fear; his cold wet fingers locked around the safety rope as the bucking boat nearly tossed him overboard for the umpteenth time.

Pardigan and Tarent were perched along the topside of the boat adding their weight to allow her all the speed she could muster. They hung over the side, leaning back with outstretched fingers competing to touch the rushing waters that sped past beneath them. Free from the cares and worries that life had recently brought them, the crew of *The Griffin* sailed on in search of a magical island.

When Loras crawled back into the wheelhouse, Quint could see how green he was so sent him below to change into something dry. The rest of the crew were enjoying themselves, feeling free for the first time in days. Thoughts of people following them, new magical abilities and mysterious challenges were thankfully forgotten for a time as they busied themselves with the familiar tasks of helping to keep *The Griffin* sailing hard. The land was soon lost behind them and after several turns of the glass the last of the gulls that had been following also departed.

Open water was a terribly lonely place and Quint felt himself fighting down the worries that came bubbling up, doubting his ability to navigate and never finding land again. On this heading he had no idea when land may be reached and had the worry that if it was a small island, they might miss it altogether, especially if they arrived in darkness. He continually kept an eye to the compass and also to the wave tops to try and guess where the tide and currents were pushing them. Despite the burden of command he still managed to enjoy the sail and kept most of his fears at bay knowing that if they did go on and on, then in two or three days they could turn around and come right back the opposite way. For now, it was simply a great time to be alive and he smiled as the spray washed back over the boat. It was all too much for Quint and it wasn't long before he called for Tarent to take over at the wheel. With a last look at the compass and instructions to keep the boat on course he pulled off his shirt and made his way carefully to the bowsprit to take up his favourite position. Tying himself securely to the safety rope and bracing himself against the rise and fall of the boat, he lifted his arms high in the air and once again laughed and shouted his defiance at the sea.

* * *

Having waited for a rich victim all evening and now most of the night, the two thieves standing quietly on a dark street corner were becoming increasingly frustrated. They stepped back into the shadows and watched as three more people left Blake's and walked up the cannery towards Market Square. Driven by desperation, they quietly followed, keeping a safe distance behind. Halfway up the Cannery the three stopped, exchanged a few final words, and the tall skinny fellow broke from the other two and headed down Weaver Street, his companions continuing on up towards the Square. Seeing their opportunity at last, they hurried to the corner of Weaver Street and peered around. It was dark, the oil in the street lamps long burnt out, but they could hear the shuffling sounds of their victim as he ambled along towards his bed.

'Let's get this done and go home, I'm way past fed up with this.' The speaker slapped a billy-club into his hand and started into the shadows. The second thief drew his own favourite weapon, a long thin knife, and followed him, eager now that the waiting was at last coming to an end, and it would soon be time to play - this was the bit he liked best.

They slipped into the darkness, following the sounds of the retreating figure and broke into a quiet trot in an effort to catch up with him.

'Shhhh...' The first thief stopped, holding out his hand to halt his partner. 'I don't hear him.' They both listened - straining to make out a sound in the warm still night. Two cats sang close by and a dog was barking in the distance, but Weaver Street itself was silent.

'Come on, he's here someplace.' They followed each other further up the street with hands held outstretched in the still, inky black air.

'Look! What's that?' Standing unmoving, in the only ray of moonlight to reach between the buildings, was their victim. His arms spread to either side as if in welcome, a hood covered most of his face and his cloak hung low to the ground. The two thieves approached cautiously.

'Tell you what, old feller... you throw over yer purse and we'll just leave, then yer can go back to yer nice comfy bed. You can cry to the watch about all this in the morning, eh?' They slowly edged forward, but the stranger didn't move.

'Give us yer money or I'll cut yer,' hissed the second thief glancing up and down the street. 'Oh... for the sake of the Source!' Unable to wait it out, he moved in quickly, pretending to stab down and then at the last moment switching to a thrust to the stomach. It was his best move, but it was the last thing he ever did. There was a flap as the stranger's cloak moved, then a crunching sound and then the thief was simply a dark crumpled shadow on the ground. The stranger rose to stand over him once again, slowly spreading his arms in unholy welcome.

'Jeb? ...Jeb?' The surviving thief stared at the cloaked figure then back to his fallen friend. 'You scum! I'll do fer yer and no mistake.' He leapt in, jumping over the fallen body, and sent a thundering swing with his club towards where the cloaked stranger's head was... except his head was no longer there. He glanced around in the darkness then felt hands flutter gently against his face - a nerve was pinched below his ear and, unable to move, he let the club fall with a clatter to the cobblestones. The stranger was behind him now, fingers sinking painfully into his eyes as a deep gravelly voice whispered into his ear.

'I'm sorry to disappoint you, my friend, but I'm not the easy victim you thought I was, and unfortunately ... I'm not known to be terribly forgiving. You may have heard of me, my name is Matheus Hawk.'

The thief was unable to cry out, even though a scream threatened to burst inside him, he merely shook and a dark patch appeared on his leggings as he soiled himself.

'Aaahh splendid, I shall take that as confirmation that you have indeed heard of me, very satisfying, yes... very satisfying.'

Defenceless, the thief felt the bony fingers on his face continuing to move until his face was a torn and bloody mess. The pain flared to an intensity that should have left him unconscious, yet somehow the stranger was keeping him awake and aware of everything. He thought of his wife and his children that he knew he would never see again, and then despair joined him as he fell to the ground. The stranger placed a hand over him and a red glow lit the dying man's face.

'A last present before you go,' muttered Matheus. He pulled his hand away and the thief fell to the dusty street, dead - burnt into his skin was the dark image of a hawk.

'You should think it an honour to die at the hands of the Hawk, you pathetic amateur.' Matheus glanced either way along the street and seeing nothing, pulled the hood of his cloak further over his head and once more, continued on his way, melting back into the shadows.

The spell had gone well and soon he'd be ready to begin the chase and track down that boatload of brats. They wouldn't slip past him again, for now the odds were heavily against them. The darkness of Weaver Street echoed with his deep laughter, they wouldn't have a chance, poor pathetic children. Pathetic maybe, thought Matheus. Yet I shall make sure I get them this time, oh yes. This time there shall be no excuses and no mercy.

* * *

By sundown, the crew's spirits had calmed, and *The Griffin* found herself moving along in far more tranquil waters. Quint was back behind the wheel with Loras as company, while Pardigan and Tarent made a pot of brew and prepared food below decks. The stars were coming out and Quint was able to confirm that they were still on course for the Isle of Skulls. They'd taken one sail down and were now set for a steady and hopefully uneventful night.

Quint was showing Loras how to recognise the group of stars known as The Lady. He explained that several stars forming a picture was called a constellation and The Lady was one of the main constellations sailors looked for as she would always point to the north giving a ship an easy reference to steer by in the night sky. Loras had heard the tale many times before but loved to hear Quint or Tarent tell how the stars got their names and how each constellation was related to the others by ancient tales and legends.

'You see where The Lady points over to the left there? Well that's north. To her side you can see her faithful hound, Naxis. The tail of Naxis will guide us on our course of northeast.' He stared upwards and pointed to a bright point that shone above them. 'You see that bright light there? That's the planet Regis. It never stays still. Legend says it's travelling the sky forever searching for a place to rest. During the summer months it will search high in the sky but as the winter sets in, it will start to search lower and lower on the horizon. The ancient Nearans called it the 'lost boy' and believed it was forever seeking its mother.'

Loras always felt sorry for Regis and saw it as another member of *The Griffin's* crew with a story as similar as any of theirs. He gazed up at the star-filled sky as Quint unravelled more and more of its stories and was almost disappointed when Pardigan came up to relieve him. Going down into the main cabin he saw Tarent reading a book in a hammock, swinging lazily with the roll of the boat and Mahra, who was once again in her human form, eating a tin of fish with her fingers. She smiled at him.

'It's easier to get the can open with hands than it is with cat's paws,' she wiggled her fingers at him by way of explanation for her current form. 'Would you like some fish, it's very good.' She offered him the tin as he walked over to the table and sat down.

Taking some of the offered fish he put it on a plate with some bread and studied Mahra. She was back to munching on her fish in a delicate cat-like way, poking a finger into the can like a claw to hook the last bits of fish out.

'Tell me about yourself, Mahra, if you don't mind, of course?' he asked. She glanced up at him and smiled again.

'I don't really know what to tell you, Loras, I don't remember that much. For the last thousand years or so I've been following the book, making sure that the knife stays with it and waiting for all of you to find it. I've been thinking a lot over the last few days, about where I came from mostly. I haven't thought about it in a long time but you all changed that and got me to reflecting. I remember Magician Pew very well, he was a nice old man and I think...' She stopped and stared off for a moment. 'Yes, I'm almost certain I was an apprentice to him or something like that, I'm sure we were close anyway.'

'An apprentice, like me!' cried Loras. 'I was an apprentice, but it didn't last very long.' He pulled at some bread as he remembered. 'I was living with my grandmother after my parents died and I think I was too much for her to look after. One day she took me with her to visit an old magician and spent ages convincing him to take me in as an apprentice. He seemed happy enough and was very good to me, trying to teach me all kinds of things but I wasn't with him long enough to learn much. I came back one day from collecting plants and mosses... and he was dead.' The cabin abruptly went quiet. It was almost as if *The Griffin* herself was listening. Tarent put his book down and Mahra stopped exploring her tin.

'He was just sitting,' Loras continued. 'Outside in the sunshine on his favourite chair, smiling. I actually made him a cup of brew and had been chatting to him for a while before I realised that something was wrong.'

Mahra held out her hand and placed it on Loras's arm. 'He would be proud of you if he were here, Loras, you're a real magician now.'

Loras smiled at her. 'Thanks, yes I'm sure he would be, but I don't really feel like a magician yet, not really, even though I know inside that I am. So what about you, Mahra, do you remember your days as an apprentice?' He went back to munching on his bread, watching Mahra expectantly.

'Like I said, I don't remember much at all. I don't think I was any good as an apprentice. I don't think I can do much real magic, except to change into a cat and an owl.' She thought for a moment. 'I think there's another animal I can change into as well.' She took a last bite of fish, her head tilted to one side, then she fell forward to the ground. By the time her hands had touched *The Griffin's* deck they were paws again. Though not the small grey paws of the cat that had become so familiar to them, this time they were much larger, and black. A Black Panther was now staring up at Loras with deep yellow eyes. A deep, low growl sounded in her throat. Loras gawped at the large cat and dropped his bread. Tarent was still watching silently from the hammock. Time seemed to stop in the room as the panther stretched revealing large claws. She walked around behind Loras, past the silent Tarent, then back to where the tin of fish sat on the table. The panther made to stand on its hind legs and Mahra the girl was reaching for the tin before either Loras or Tarent could see the change take place.

'Yes, it's a panther,' said Mahra as she poked around the tin for any last bits of fish - she started licking her fingers. 'It's been a while since I chose that shape, but yes, I can do panther, cat and owl.' She seemed completely unaware of the effect that her change had on either of the two boys. Loras glanced over at Tarent who simply shook his head, speechless.

'Mahra that's astounding, I mean it's astonishing,' spluttered Loras. 'To be able to change into another animal like that must be so ... can I learn to do that?' As a small boy Loras had never felt powerful and had always felt the need to rely on others. The thought that he could possibly change into a panther, so big, proud and ferocious was...inspiring to him, it had struck a chord deep within him.

Mahra scrutinised him thoughtfully, still licking her fingers.

'Well you're the magician, Loras, you tell me. I haven't a clue how I do it and I couldn't begin to explain it to you, except that I picture the shape and sort of...feel my way into it.'

'I have to read my books,' said Loras, hurriedly stuffing the last of the fish and bread into his mouth.

He ran off to his cabin, slamming the door behind him.

Mahra glanced questioningly at Tarent. 'Was it something I said? He seemed a little...excited.'

Tarent shook his head. 'I think we may have more animals than people around here soon.' He laughed and went back to his book while Mahra started searching for another tin of fish.

Chapter 6

Something's Down There

Quint woke with a start and sat up. Listening intently, he tried to bring some sense to his sleep-befuddled mind. *The Griffin* was creaking and rolling normally and he couldn't detect anything immediately wrong. He drew a deep breath and lay back, concentrating with every sense tingling, seeking the information that would set his mind at rest or at least explain what had set off his inner alarms.

There... and again... a faint scratching sound on the bottom of the boat. Tumbling out of the hammock and crashing against the table in his haste, he raced up the ladder to get on deck. It was some time around dawn. Pardigan was at the wheel with Tarent beside him, both oblivious to anything unusual.

'Something's scraping the bottom of the boat.' He scanned the horizon, trying to gain a bearing on where they were. 'Have we come close to any land or rocks?'

'No, we've not sighted anything since we left the moorings yesterday. Should I come around or take in the sails?' asked Pardigan. Quint nodded and clambered out to gather in the main sail. The boat started to lose speed as soon as the sail dropped and he returned to the wheel.

'We have to stop and see what this is. There was definitely a scraping sound coming from under the boat, I don't like it; something's not right.' Pardigan let off the ropes to the foresail and it began flapping in the wind as the boat came to an eventual stop, dead in the water.

The Griffin bobbed and splashed with the rise and fall of each wave, it was strangely silent without the steady chop, chop, chop that normally accompanied the movement of the boat.

'Tarent, get a sounding; find out how deep we are.' Quint started hauling the foresail in, tying it down so it wouldn't snap free, his eyes still searching the water around the boat and a worried look on his face. Tarent began swinging a sounding lead on a long rope from the front of the boat; it landed with a plop and rope started to pull through his fingers as the lead went down through the deep blue water.

'We're deep, Quint, very deep by the feel of it. That's thirty spans and still no sign of the bottom.' He started to pull the rope back up, coiling it at his feet.

There it was again! Now they could all hear the scraping noise that had woken Quint. It was like they were going over the top of an underwater tree or branches of coral; the long twigs running along the timbers of the hull. By now they were all gazing over the side, but nothing could be seen, it was intensely blue and obviously very deep.

The noise came again, this time accompanied by a strange tapping sound.

'I don't like this, I don't like this at all,' said Quint. 'Something's down there.'

'Aaaauuugghhh!' Tarent cried out, as the rope was snatched savagely through his hands. He jumped out of the way before it could snag his foot and drag him over. He stood cradling his injured hand, peering over the side to where the last of the rope had disappeared leaving a trail of hissing bubbles.

Mahra came scrambling up the hatchway, the first time that she'd been on deck since they had set sail.

'What's that noise?' she asked, her head tilted to one side listening.

By way of an answer the water at the side of the boat erupted and something large and black came flying up at the group, spreading wide leathery wings and showering them with water. It swept up Loras, enveloping him in an embrace and, continuing in its motion, leapt back over the side into the depths, leaving a frothing trail behind as the only evidence that anything at all had happened. It was all over in a flash. The rest of the group reacted in a daze, then began shouting and rushing around at once.

'It's got Loras!' screamed Pardigan, 'Whatever that was, has dragged Loras off. We've got to get him, Quint, we've got to get him or he'll drown!' He was peering down into the water desperately hoping to see something of his friend in the inky depths.

The scraping sound returned, only this time it didn't sound like twigs or branches to them, it sounded far more like the sound of fingernails being drawn slowly down a writing slate.

Quint could feel the hairs on the back of his neck stand up and a shiver shuddered down his spine. He sighted along the length of the arrow notched in his bow ready for whatever would come. 'Something's coming, let's be ready this time.' The tension on the boat was immense as they gathered themselves. The water around the boat started to boil and several white shapes erupted up onto the deck. Tarent's first sword cut one neatly in two. Both halves of a vaguely human skeleton, neatly parted across the chest fell clattering to the deck. His second sword caught another across the back of its legs, sending it against the bottom of the wheelhouse, its bony fingers clawing at Mahra, who roared. Her hand flashed out, changing at once into a large black claw and the skeleton exploded in a shower of bones that scattered, rattling over the boat then back into the water leaving a trail of hissing bubbles.

Pardigan was also busy, whispering 'Burn, burn,' as lightning flashed from his extended fingers causing mayhem among the attackers. To the crew, the attackers seemed like a wall of bones as they attempted to push them back with more leaping from the water, fighting to get past or climb over the ones already on board. It appeared their only weapons, were the stiff bony fingers they held out attempting to rip and tear at anything that they could take hold of. They were extremely fast, but the crew of *The Griffin* were proving to be faster.

Pardigan was already bleeding from a vicious cut to his side and Tarent and Mahra both had gashes to their legs because parts of skeletons, which they had thought beaten, continued to move, clawing at them from the deck.

A flurry of blows from Tarent sent three skeletons tumbling over the side. Then almost as quickly as it had started, the attack was over, leaving the group breathless amid an eerie silence.

They stood motionless but on guard, *The Griffin* rolling and creaking beneath them, waiting for the next wave of an attack that didn't come. Quint glanced around and seeing that everyone was still on their feet breathed a sigh of relief. The skirmish was now over but Loras remained missing. He saw the concern on the faces of his friends and whispered a silent prayer to the Source that Loras would be all right.

Loras found himself in a world of confusion. One second he was standing on deck with his friends, peering into the water. The next moment, he was wrapped tightly in something warm, wet and leathery. He couldn't move and he couldn't breathe, and struggling didn't seem to be doing any good as he vainly attempted to free his arms and kick his feet. His ears were filled with a rushing gurgling sound and the world had gone alarmingly black. He wasn't sure if it was because his eyes were closed or if they were in fact open, he simply couldn't tell. Panic began to overwhelm him and he let out a whimper of dismay. It was a huge effort not to scream; attempting to control his emotions and think clearly wasn't easy. It didn't help when a voice started speaking, echoing into his head as if he were standing in a large empty room. His fear entered a new level and he froze as the voice rasped like dry sandpaper, drawn across stone.

'Swe-e-et meat... swe-e-et food... oh, so lo-o-ng... so very very lo-o-ng...' the voice droned into his head and Loras felt another rising wave of panic. Struggling vainly against the sides of his leathery prison he began to feel madness take hold of him.

'I wi-i-ll eat you, the-e-n... your friends... on-n-ne by one... swe-e-et so... swe-e-et.'

Close to blacking out from lack of air, the need for escape reached a climax and he felt an explosion of energy release from his body without any direction from him at all. The leathery wings that held him parted with a hiss of bubbles and the voice in his mind gave a shriek of pain before tearing away.

'Aaaahhhhhh!'

Loras found himself free but deep underwater and still unable to breathe. It was dim, he couldn't tell up from down and it was cold, bone numbingly cold. He began to gag from lack of air and in the last moments that he had before blacking out for good, he saw bubbles around him, created when he had parted from the creature. Holding out a hand weakly, he trickled the last of his magical energy into enlarging a bubble of air and sucked it greedily into his aching lungs. He kicked feebly in the direction the bubbles were going, frantically searching in the dim light for another bubble that was close enough to enlarge. It wasn't easy when all that he could see was blurred and confused, and his mind simply wanted to shut down. But then he saw one, enlarged it with a trickle of magic, filled his lungs and felt a renewed burst of hope, energy and the will to survive.

The water gradually began to get lighter, giving his hopes and his strength another boost; he desperately kicked again towards the light and his friends. Eventually, the dark shape of the boat showed against the sparkling light of the surface and, with a rush and a gasp, he broke surface amid a confusion of light, sound and relief.

Hands grabbed at him and dragged him onboard where he flopped like a freshly caught ticker fish, sucked in his first breath of real air and gave himself over to the friends he had almost given up hope of seeing again. Coughing and spluttering he squinted his eyes at the brightness and lay back exhausted, feeling the welcome heat of the deck seep into his back and the warmth of the sun on his face. All about him was a babble of sounds as his friends voiced their concerns through the water still rushing in his ears. Turning on his side he vomited. His throat felt raw and his lungs ached as he sucked in breath after welcome breath.

As his vision cleared he gazed up at his friends' worried faces. Coughing again, he tried to speak, to say he was all right and so incredibly relieved to see them. Then as he glanced past Pardigan's legs, a monstrous black shape emerged from the water. He still didn't have a voice, and the sound that came from his mouth was no more than a croak, but he lifted his hand and pointed. They all turned around at the same time. To Loras, everything seemed to be in slow motion. He only had enough energy left to send a weak spark of energy at the demon as it rose to its full height, opening huge wings ready to fall upon the group. It screamed as it pounced forward, mouth gaping in angry indignation at being bested by Loras and robbed of its prize.

In the same moment that Loras's spell found its mark, Pardigan's knife buried itself into one of the creature's huge red eyes, quickly followed by two arrows fired by Quint, which entered its heaving chest with two dull thuds. The demon's scream turned shrill as it pulled at the arrows and tried frantically to release the blade from its eye. Emitting a moan of agony and frustration, it toppled, only to meet the twin swords of Tarent that parted its head from its body. The demon's body hit the deck and thick black acidic gore flooded the boat, hissing and splashing over the feet of *The Griffin's* crew.

The whole episode, from stopping the boat to the present, couldn't have lasted longer than it took to drink a cup of brew, but *The Griffin's* crew had experienced their first skirmish with Chaos, and had won.

'That's disgusting,' said Mahra, looking down at the steaming mess of dead demon and then at Loras, who was covered in black hissing goo. He was far too exhausted to do or say anything and didn't care what he was lying in. Mahra rubbed at a splash that had got on her leathers, the only tiny drop to reach her, and went below to change into a cat and clean herself properly.

Pardigan helped Tarent push the huge carcass over the side, which was no easy task, then sluiced the deck while Quint rinsed Loras off with several buckets of seawater before helping him down below to wash off properly. They then scrambled about hoisting all the sails, eager to be off lest something else was lurking in the depths ready to attack.

The Griffin sailed for the rest of the day with no other incidents and by nightfall, the boat was once again rigged for ease of handling in dark seas. The going was good with only smaller waves and a stiff breeze pushing them on. Loras was asleep in his cabin but had woken earlier complaining of nothing more than a sore throat. His eyes however, were sunken and surrounded by dark rings. He looked awful and Mahra sent him back to his bunk with a warm brew sweetened with honey for his throat.

'I don't like the look of him,' she confided to Pardigan. 'That thing was a demon and they can be nasty in many different ways. Loras was under that one's control for far too long.'

Tarent had been in to see Loras several times attempting to heal him saying that he felt that the ability to heal was one of his gifts. However, as he was unpractised, it only aided Loras a little on each visit, and drained Tarent of his energy at the same time.

The Griffin made her way steadily on with the crew changing shifts every three hours during the night.

By morning the sky was decidedly dark and hostile and the sea had risen again, sending the little boat surging from crest to crest with water pouring over the decks and often down into the cabin through the hatchway. To add to their problems, the temperature was dropping and the crew were all beginning to feel quite miserable.

Quint came below around mid morning having been relieved by Tarent and sat with his hands wrapped around a cup of hot brew, dripping water onto the table in front of him.

'I don't like this, Mahra, the weather is worsening and we still haven't sighted this island. It's raining hard again, visibility is awful and the sea is churning so much it's almost impossible to keep a course. I'm seriously starting to think we should turn around.' He blew dejectedly into his steaming cup. 'We don't know what's out there, we nearly lost one of my best friends back there and, for all we know, demons or something may be about to attack us again.'

'We're getting close now, I'm sure of it,' said Mahra. She looked cold and seasick. 'Magician Pew said to sail on this heading and that was enough. I'm sure that if there had been anything more to it I'd know... but I don't. I'm sorry.' She searched Quint's desperate features.

'We have to go on.' Draining his mug, he turned for the hatchway without saying a word.

For the rest of the day they kept going, holding as close to a heading of north-east as the heavy seas would allow. Tarent continued to visit Loras, pouring healing energies into his friend and by evening, the magician showed definite signs of improvement. Pardigan and Quint were now exhausted being the only full-time crew sailing the boat. It was almost dark when the ship's bell rang and Pardigan's head appeared at the hatchway, accompanied by a cascade of water.

'*Land!* There's land ahead of us, I need anyone up here that can help right away.'

Everybody who could muster the energy scrambled up on deck to see what was happening. The sea was still pounding them with waves and the light of the day was almost gone. Lightning flashed overhead, illuminating a boiling angry ocean and the dark shape of the island. Jagged rocks protruded from the water, like a row of vicious teeth surrounded by hissing foam, daring the boat to approach.

Quint shouted instructions and Pardigan cautiously edged his way forward through sheets of spray to look for a way through while Tarent took the wheel.

'Bring us hard over and around those rocks,' bellowed Quint, over the ever-increasing howl of the wind and crashing of the waves; worry for the boat's safety creasing his face. 'We're losing light fast, we're going to have to move closer to find an anchorage. Keep looking for rocks but bring us in, Tarent. There has to be a way through.'

They shortened the sails and slid towards the darkness of the island. Several times Pardigan shouted that rocks were ahead, forcing them to change direction while Quint stood in the middle of the boat with an oar, fending them off from anything they came too close to. Thankfully, as they made their way further in and past the first rows of rocks, they were more out of the wind and the sea started to become a little calmer.

Something's Down There

They lit lanterns to help guide them through the last part and eventually dropped anchor about three boat lengths from a small sandy shore.

Once back below decks, the assembled group was a sorry sight as they stoked up the fire in the old stove. Everyone and everything was soaked and they were all completely exhausted. Much to everyone's relief, Mahra volunteered to keep watch for the night, so after cooking and eating their first hot meal in several days, they went to their damp beds and quickly fell into a deep sleep.

The Griffin lay at rest in the shadow of the Isle of Skulls, and while her crew slept, a white owl watched over her. Mahra flew over the sleeping ship and her cry sang out, echoing between the hostile rocks as she soared along the jagged rain lashed cliffs - and as she flew, she started to remember.

Chapter 7

Bleak Fortress

Morning found the crew chilled and miserable. Pardigan had woken first. When Mahra came down from the hatchway, she found him huddled over the stove trying to light a pile of damp kindling with numb fingers. She walked over and laying a hand upon his shoulder crouched down beside him.

'How was the night, Mahra?' asked Quint, shuffling in as Pardigan placed a kettle on the stove. 'Did we have any visitors?'

'No, but I did have a chance to look around a little.' She shivered and held a hand out to the still cold stove. 'I also remembered more about the island. I'm fairly sure I know why we're here and what we're here to do.' She glanced up as Loras and Tarent, blankets wrapped around them, shuffled in and sat down.

'With the storm blowing I couldn't do more than explore the sheltered side of the island, but as I was flying, all sorts of memories came flooding back to me; some good, some not so good. The real name of this island is The Isle of Skills, not the Isle of Skulls; this was the home of the Academy of Magicians.' She smiled at Loras. 'It was here that the apprentice magicians were brought to learn their skills and to study under the greatest magicians of the day. The Academy was ruled over by the four most senior magicians, they were known as the 'Council of Four.' My master, Magician Pew, was one of the four. Then there was Magician Clement, he was a nice old man, always doing magic with flowers and nature.' Mahra stopped talking as she remembered the old magician for the first time in centuries.

After a few moments Loras cleared his throat with a polite cough. 'Who else Mahra? That's only two so far.'

'I'm sorry,' she answered. 'Yes there was Pew and Clement, then Magician Barrick and then...' she drifted again but this time without the smile. 'And then there was Magician Credence Bleak. Credence Bleak was in fact the highest ranking of the four and he ruled the Academy with a will of iron.' She shivered. 'Not a nice man as I recall. I do remember that he and my master never saw eye-to-eye on very much; they were always arguing - naturally he championed Chaos. Anyway, eventually the magicians fought and death rained down upon the island. From what I can remember Magician Bleak survived for a time, plotting his dark spells, but the Academy was no more. Please remember that this was all a very long time ago.

Magician Bleak would have known that one day the heroes would be walking the halls again in a bid to complete the great spell on the eve of what Chaos is claiming as its time of triumph. He understood that in this distant future the heroes would have to be stopped for Chaos to reign alone. He would have known the skull we seek and will be trying to stop us, even from his grave.'

* * *

Thankfully Mahra's report only dampened their spirits a little and they were eager, after drying out their clothes, to explore the island and do their best. Loras placed some protective spells on *The Griffin* with a warning to the others that if they returned before he did, they could undo the spells by naming the boat three times.

'If you don't and you forget...well, you don't want to forget, all right?' Loras seemed pleased with the spells he'd placed and no one doubted that they'd be effective in keeping the boat safe.

They made their way to the little beach huddled down in the small rowboat against the ever-present drizzle and gazed through the mist and rain at the walls of dark grey granite that loomed up ahead.

'There's a narrow path cut into the cliff that runs to the top,' started Mahra, but her words were carried away on the wind. 'I remember one of the biggest worries of anyone coming back to the island,' she continued a little louder, 'was that they had to climb the path to get to the Academy.'

Loras peered up from under the hood of his cloak at the huge storm-lashed cliff, imagining himself as a newly arriving apprentice and despite the circumstances, felt a thrill at being here. The place where magic was born and taught to the gifted. He sighed and pulled his cloak a little tighter around him.

The boat crunched up onto the sandy beach and the crew jumped out with Mahra making a fuss that she'd got her feet wet.

As always, it felt strange to have solid ground under them rather than the steady motion of *The Griffin* and they trudged off after Mahra, crunching through the sand with their heads bowed against the rain. The climb was every bit as perilous as Mahra had warned. The slick rain-lashed path sometimes disappeared into the cliff's shallow caves, where they could thankfully catch their breath out of the wind and rain, but, for most of the climb they were exposed out on the narrow slippery path with a sheer drop to the beach only one wrong footfall away.

As they neared the top, they became even more exposed to the elements. The wind howled with an even greater fury, tugging and pulling them towards the edge, as if deliberately trying to pluck them from the cliff face as they held on; slowly shuffling forward. Thunder crashed overhead and lightning danced upon the cliff above them, showering them with pieces of stone and forcing them to constantly flatten against the rock face trying not to look down.

They were on hands and knees as they eventually crested the top and made their way to the relative shelter of a group of large rocks, to gain their breath and rub some life into numb, bruised hands.

'Was it always this miserable here, Mahra?' shouted Loras over the howl of the wind.

She looked down at the four cold unhappy faces peering up from under their hoods and crouched next to them.

'No, I remember the isle as a place of sunshine. It was always windy, but that was a good thing. We would sail around the island or fly kites, seeing who could make the best and what magic could be used in the construction. The storms came when Magician Bleak tried to bring the world to Chaos,' she glanced around. 'I think he finally did bring this little part of the world to Chaos, but I can't think that even *he* expected it would turn out like this.' The wind changed direction and icy rain drove down with renewed ferocity, chilling them even further.

'What you're seeing is the very heart of the Chaos storm that's been changing so many things on this planet,' shouted Mahra over the noise. 'It's been storming here for centuries but the imbalance has only been felt as far away as Freya, with its incredible heat, since this year.'

Quint stood up ready to move. 'Come on, my friends, let's get out of the rain and see if any magicians are still at home.'

The dark stone of the Academy glistened in the rain and lightning lit its sides sending bolts of energy crashing into the towers. They moved off along a path choked with thorn bushes and tall weeds that led up to the forbidding fortress. It was enormous. If it was an Academy, then it was certainly well fortified with towers at each of its four corners and a tall inner sanctum that rose higher than the surrounding battlements. Windows dotted the upper levels of the outer wall but none was in reach of even the tallest of ladders. A large hole, that at one time must have housed a massive door, now gaped like a hungry mouth as the crew approached. Its stonework had caved in at the sides as if something had ripped the huge doors from their hinges and tossed them away, leaving loose stones hanging down like ragged teeth dripping a constant flow of water.

The Academy waited patiently, glaring down upon its first visitors in over a thousand years.

* * *

Bartholomew Bask stared across the small wooden table into the stern unsmiling features of Matheus Hawk. It was distressing to be back in Blake's so soon. He was sweating freely, his piggy eyes darting around the room constantly expecting any one of the drinkers to attack at any moment; rabble.

Bartholomew lifted a hand away from the table, peeling the lace of his sleeve from one of the many sticky patches, with theatrical disgust. He took a deep breath and wiped his brow with a perfumed handkerchief. Lifting it to his nose, he inhaled deeply in an effort to keep away the heady aroma of the bar and its patrons. 'Oh dear, oh dear, oh dear,' he muttered, casting a glance at the hooded figure opposite him. For a moment, he was in danger of losing his self-control and running from the building, but then he gathered himself and managed to ask his first coherent question.

'Mr Hawk, I'm confused. If you know who the thieves are, why am I not sitting here with my belongings in front of me? I am, we agreed, paying you for results, not moonlit meetings in this Source-forsaken gutter hole.' He cast around quickly to be sure he had not been overheard.

He'd spoken briefly to Blake upon arriving and had decided that Blake was not a person he wanted to upset. A nasty common man with an obvious aversion to bathing was how he'd summed him up. To Bartholomew's horror, Blake had leaned in close to whisper in his ear about where the 'Awk' was sitting. Bartholomew had watched the unshaven face with its black stinking mouth and rotting teeth come close to his ear and had barely suppressed a shudder of revulsion. He feared Blake had picked up on his dislike and it was quite possible he was now feeling offended.

'I know who the thieves are,' rumbled Matheus, forcing Bartholomew to lean in across the table to hear him. 'I know where they were, and I know where they're going,' he leaned in even closer to Bartholomew, obviously, because he knew it was upsetting him. 'I also know that this is more than a common petty house theft. I need to know what was in your safe other than the money.'

Bartholomew mopped his brow again and gathered his thoughts. His main concern had been, and still was, the money and papers.

'There were papers, some old books, deeds and contracts, er... some trinkets... *Oh I don't know!*' he spluttered. 'I want my money back and the papers too! Why can't you just get them, I can pay you, then we can put this whole sorry story behind us and move on?'

Matheus smiled. 'Unfortunately, Mr Bask, it's not that easy. You see... my friend here believes that you had something else in that safe of yours, something extremely precious. There was a knife in there, and a book, and my friend wants those two things very badly. In fact so badly does he want them that he's willing to help me find your thieves and even get your money back.'

'What friend is this, is he here?' Bartholomew glanced around uncertainly, seeing only the same group of rowdy drinking parties he'd seen moments earlier. He noticed Blake staring across at him and he quickly broke eye contact. 'Who is this friend of yours? If he can help us I want to meet him. I care little for the knife; if he can help, then it will be his.' Bartholomew was now extremely uncomfortable and was becoming more and more desperate to end the meeting and be away.

Matheus glanced to his side and Bartholomew noticed for the first time that another figure was seated at the table with them. He was well hidden in the shadows of the nook, but even so, Bartholomew was sure that he hadn't been there moments earlier.

This was all becoming too upsetting for Bartholomew. He was a merchant of standing in the community, and here he was meeting with trackers and cutthroats in the seediest drinking house in town. Where had it all gone wrong? Hildy! He was sure that damn cleaning woman had something to do with this.

Hildy's departure had left Bartholomew in a pickle and no mistake. The house had run down quickly after she had left and Bartholomew wasn't having any luck replacing her. None of the normal methods of employing a maid had turned up anyone suitable - it was most distressing.

Bartholomew jumped, as he realised that he was being spoken to, and noticed also that the stranger had moved closer into the candlelight.

'Merchant Bask, may I present my good friend and acquaintance Mr Belial.' Matheus indicated the shadowed stranger. A nervous twitch appeared in Bartholomew's cheek as he studied the figure that was slowly raising hands to remove the hood of his cloak. A mad impulse to run filled Bartholomew, his hand with the scented hanky came unbidden to his mouth and he chewed on his knuckle.

'Bartholomew Bask, what a pleasure to meet you at long last, I know so much about you.' The stranger spoke in a smooth velvety voice and his features, when the hood was lowered, were ... beautiful!

This wasn't a term that Bartholomew used often, especially to describe another man, but this man wasn't handsome... he was beautiful. Bartholomew reached across to shake the stranger's hand in nervous relief. He had expected anything, anything at all... but not this, this incredible person.

'A real pleasure, Mr...I'm sorry, your name again?' asked Bartholomew, smiling and plainly relieved.

'Belial,' said the stranger in a voice that promised trust, friendship and understanding all at once.

Please call me Belial or Mr Belial, whichever you feel most comfortable with,' he smiled. 'For we shall be friends and I shall aid you in any way that I can.'

Bartholomew positively beamed. 'Oh, Mr Belial, I can't tell you how relieved I am to meet you and find you're working with Mr Hawk here. As I'm sure you know, I have been wronged and rightly seek regress.' Bartholomew felt he had at last found a sympathetic audience and relaxed. 'Belial, that's not a Freyan name, nor is it from Sterling or Minster if I'm not mistaken; may I ask where you're from?' Bartholomew picked up the tankard of ale that had, until then, remained untouched in front of him. This was turning into a far more pleasant occasion than he had ever thought possible.

'Oh Belial is an old name, Mr Bask, a very old name. I am in fact a king in a place far, far from here, but have also played the part of ambassador to courts and parliaments before this in many lands. Until recently I was regretfully imprisoned, but our good friend Mr Hawk here came to my rescue and...well here, as they say...I am.' He smiled a beautiful smile across the table at Bartholomew.

'Splendid, splendid, can I buy you an ale or a brew or some such thing?' returned Bartholomew happily as he cast around for a serving maid. A king and nobleman! Now this was the kind of person Bartholomew had dreamed of meeting. A career could be made on meetings such as this, and in Blake's of all places! Bartholomew smiled to himself at the irony of life.

'A king no less. My goodness, Mr Hawk, where have you been travelling to in our service?' Bartholomew smiled good-naturedly while Matheus Hawk stared back at Bartholomew, a thin sneer breaking his lips.

'Why I have travelled down to the deepest depths of hell, Mr Bask, for this is the great Demon Lord, Belial. King and commander of eighty legions of demons and second only to Lucifer himself. *That* is where I have travelled to on your behalf, and *this* is whom I have brought to our cause.' Matheus sat back in triumph, having played his trump card, and regarded Bartholomew with keen interest.

Bartholomew gazed at the two people across the table from him and a strange croaking noise came from his open mouth.

'I-I-I am sorry, gentleman, but I could swear by the Source that you said...'

Belial winced at Bartholomew's words.

'I would be awfully obliged if you could possibly refrain from swearing by the...well, no swearing if you please,' said Belial good-naturedly, and then added as if as an afterthought. 'Or I may have to roast you over a fire pit for all of eternity.' The Demon laughed and a deeper timbre seemed to enter his voice.

The tankard Bartholomew was clutching clattered noisily on the table.

'Only joking, Mr Bask, only joking,' he added. Yet his eyes showed that he might not really be joking at all.

'I think I'm going to be sick,' mumbled Bartholomew, and he was; much to the delight of Matheus Hawk.

Chapter 8

The Towers

Inside the darkness of the doorway, it was dry, and the wind reduced to a low ominous moan of anguish at their escape. Remains of a great archway were strewn about the entrance, a few rotten scraps of timber the only evidence of a door, the rest having long since rotted or blown away, along with much of the surrounding stonework.

As their eyes became accustomed, the crew of *The Griffin* could see they'd arrived in a large entrance hall. A flash of lightning illuminated everything for a moment as they shook water from their cloaks and they were left with the impression of two huge staircases sweeping in graceful curves from both the left and right-hand side and meeting in the darkness of unknown levels above. In the centre of the hall, under bits of stone and more remains of the wooden door, they could just make out what had once been an ornamental fountain. An old chandelier was perched on top having fallen centuries past, scattering its crystals across the ground, leaving the hall sad, cold and decayed.

With nothing dry between them they had no chance of making torches, so it was left to Loras to provide the light. He proudly muttered a few words and sent two glowing blue globes ahead to light the way; shadows flickered about them as they started to climb.

'The lower levels were where the students, servants and soldiers lived,' explained Mahra. 'But I think our search should begin above with the masters' levels and the towers. The council occupied the four towers, and as we're looking for the skull that links to Magician Pew we should head to his tower first, which is the East Tower.' The gloom fled back upon the approach of the globes and they could see that where paintings and tapestries had once been hung in decoration, now only strips of mildewed cloth and broken frames remained. Loras led, with Mahra pointing out things as the memories returned to her. The two flights of stairs finally met at a wide landing in front of large closed doors.

'As a student, this was as far as you could come without a master. It feels strange to be here now. I would ring on this bell,' she held out her hand to where a chain was hanging from the wall then pulled it; a bell tolled inside making everyone shuffle nervously. They all stood for a while, staring at the door.

'I don't think we're going to get a master to come,' pointed out Pardigan nervously, 'shall we just go in?' they waited patiently for Mahra.

'Yes, I think maybe we should,' said Mahra, reaching for the handle.

'*Stop!*' yelled Tarent, running forward. Mahra froze hand outstretched. 'Something's not right,' Tarent pushed to the front. 'I can sense some sort of energy coming from the handle. I can feel it as if it were glowing, yet my eyes tell me it isn't, I think it must be a trap of some sort.' Mahra withdrew her hand and they all stepped back.

Tarent crouched down peering at the doorknob. 'I think it's some sort of spell that's sensitive to heat - can you tell anything, Loras?'

Loras shook his head. 'No nothing, but if it's sensitive to heat, maybe I can use magic to turn the knob.'

Retreating down the staircase several steps, they watched while Loras muttered some words then turned an imaginary knob in front of him some distance from the real one on the door. The knob rattled, the door creaked and then swept open with a waft of ancient learning and decay, but without anything exploding or going wrong. Tarent reported that the strange feeling had vanished; the spell must have dissipated as soon as the door opened. The glow globes slipped inside and the group followed one by one.

'This is the main corridor of the masters' area,' whispered Mahra, indicating the long straight hallway that the globes were illuminating. It was cold, dark and as still as a grave. Lurking in the shadows, either real or imagined, was an ominous presence, as if something was biding its time, content to wait through eternity for the moment it could awake - they could all feel it.

Mahra shuddered. 'Chambers and other corridors lead off all over the academy. Over fifty masters led their lives here with their sleeping quarters, laboratories and libraries all on this level.'

They set off down the corridor, their feet making strange crunching sounds as they went.

'What is that?' exclaimed Pardigan in disgust. With the globes ahead of them it was hard to see what they were treading on, it sounded like eggshells or sticks or...

'They're bones,' said Loras staring down. 'Thousands and thousands of bones...I don't like it here,' he added in a small voice. 'Something is...evil.' They peered down as Loras lit a smaller, brighter globe to show them.

The hall was indeed covered in bones, human bones, and not in small skeletal piles where someone may have died, but evenly scattered all along the corridor, giving the impression of a long narrow crypt where the dead had been disturbed as they lay at rest.

'No skulls,' pointed out Tarent in a hushed tone. 'There are lots of bones of all sorts, the larger ones broken, but there aren't any skulls.'

'Are you all right, Mahra?' Pardigan asked quietly. Mahra was making small mewing sounds and tears were gently sliding down her cheeks.

'These were my friends,' she said gazing at the floor. 'It's not as if I can recognise them, but I remember them now after forgetting them for so long. Some homecoming, isn't it?' She sniffed back her tears and wiped her face with the back of her hands in an extremely cat-like way. With a shudder she pulled herself together. 'Come on, let's get on with this.' She strode off, crunching along the corridor.

'Go slowly and let me keep to the front,' warned Tarent pushing forward. 'If there was one trap, it stands to reason there'll be others.' He and Mahra walked side by side down the corridor.

As they passed open doors they peered in. The globes revealing the remains of furniture, pots and bottles all covered with a thick layer of dust and ancient cobwebs. Other rooms held row upon row of books, desks and chairs; time had stood still. Loras tried to pick a book up but it crumbled in his hands.

'So much knowledge gone,' he moaned. 'Unless I can somehow stabilise them? I wonder...' he walked on, lost in thought.

'Come on, Loras,' Pardigan hurried his friend along with a nudge. 'Let's get this skull thing and get out of here - this place is creepy.'

As Tarent moved on, slowly scanning for more traps, his hands were playing with his staff, constantly twisting it open and closed with a click. Pardigan began absently tossing a knife in the air and Quint walked with a scowl, his hand on his sword ready for anything. Loras was the only one not on edge and having a wonderful time. He walked along in his own little world muttering about stabilising paper and peering with interest into every room.

'You'll get your nose blown off if you're not careful, Loras,' warned Tarent. 'Stay with us.'

At last they reached the bottom of the corridor where it split into two directions.

'That way leads to the West Tower and this way leads to Magician Pew's rooms in the East Tower,' explained Mahra leading them east. They passed more and more rooms before a sharp snapping sound brought them to an abrupt halt. It echoed along the passages and the group glanced around wide-eyed.

'What was that and where's Loras?' hissed Quint. Distant shuffling sounds were coming from both ends of the corridor, accompanied by something like a long drawn out sigh - the vibrations of which were sending up little white clouds of dust from the bones at their feet.

'He was behind me a moment ago,' whispered Pardigan, peering around in the gloom. 'But now...he must have wandered into one of these rooms; he's been poking around all over the place.' Moving towards an open door, some way back down the corridor, he peered inside, Tarent started checking further on.

'Go carefully,' warned Quint, pushing to the front again. The sounds were getting closer. It was the same crunching of bones that they had been making, but the sigh had changed to a strange rustling sound. They glanced at each other nervously. 'I think we're going to have company,' muttered Quint reaching for his sword and drawing it clear with a loud ring.

'He's in here!' yelled Tarent, from one of the rooms. They ran over and gathered at the door. Quint and Pardigan took a quick look in at the hapless Loras, before turning back to guard the corridor from whatever was about to emerge from the dark.

Loras was trapped inside a large bubble. He didn't seem to be hurt, and was actually smiling and waving happily at them from inside. They could see him moving his lips, talking, but couldn't hear anything he said.

Mahra groaned. 'It's a bubble trap. The magicians would often use these to discipline students or to do exactly what this one has done and trap unwanted intruders. They're really hard to...' a loud pop echoed round the room and Loras was standing beaming at them.

'Wasn't that fantastic, thousand year old magic and still working; amazing? I wonder what it was guarding.' He started to move further into the room before Mahra brought him up short.

'Loras, I don't know how you got out of that thing, but we have company, we have to get going, its best we explore later.' She pulled at the sleeve of his robe, 'Please, Loras, come on!'

'Too late!' they heard Quint yell, as the clash of metal upon metal echoed in the corridor. Dashing out of the room, they found Quint and Pardigan furiously fending off attackers from both directions. Quint was slashing his sword from left to right in the confined space, keeping three skeletal warriors at bay, while Pardigan faced the other direction with a knife in each hand. He was facing two skeletons, keeping them back with his blades, whilst also managing to send bolts of lightning crackling through the air at the same time. Unlike the skeletons that had attacked them on the boat, these were armed with swords and axes and were fighting in a strange disconcerting silence; their sightless eyes, flickering windows to a world of horror. Further along the corridor, more skeletons were approaching accompanied by small black creatures, walking on their hind legs. They resembled large rodents with pinched, rat-like faces filled with evil yellow teeth. They squeaked and chattered amongst themselves as they scuttled along. Metal armour covered their chests and gripped in human like hands was an array of wicked black knives.

'Oh Source!' yelled Mahra. 'They're Ratten - creations of Magician Bleak. Loras, heat their armour and don't let them get close.' A black knife came flashing past Pardigan and one of the Ratten screeched in triumph as it found its mark in Quint's arm. He let out a yell and fell to the ground, writhing in agony.

Tarent moved in to fill the gap, twisting free the two halves of his staff and cutting a skeleton in two with his first strike. A Ratten launched itself over the backs of its brethren, and gave a shrill cry as it fell down towards Tarent's unprotected back. At the last moment he spun and sliced the creature in two, each half falling to the floor with a sickly thud. He glanced down to be sure it was dead then turned back to the horde still streaming down the corridor.

Quint was fighting the pain, clutching his arm. 'We have to find somewhere safe,' he managed to gasp, pushing himself up.

'We can try to make for one of the towers,' said Mahra. 'We'll find fewer creatures towards the West Tower, let's make for there.' Quint staggered to his feet.

'All right, I'll help hold the east side with Loras - the rest of you move on as fast as you can - preferably before I faint.' He held his injured arm to his side, gritted his teeth, and swung one-handed at the attackers as Loras sent bolts of energy, heating the Ratten's armour, sending them shrieking and spitting in retreat. Mahra returned to the shape of the Panther and leapt at one of the rat-like fighters, shaking it viciously before pinning it to the ground to tear at its throat while it tried to stab a small knife repeatedly but ineffectually into her neck. It died quickly, before it could do much damage and she was swiftly up and smashing a skeleton to pieces with the swipe of a huge paw.

'I'm going to move behind them,' said Pardigan, sighting further down the corridor, before quickly place-shifting.

A huge whoosh filled his ears followed by a moment of feeling unsteady then realised he'd successfully shifted behind the attacking creatures. He let fly with two knives into the unprotected backs of the closest Ratten and they fell squealing and twitching to the floor. Pulling free his knives, he ran in to attack the few remaining skeletons. The combined force quickly dealt with the smaller group of creatures as Loras sent a ball of fire towards the larger group, driving them back. With the few moments of time that this bought them, they turned and fled for the west end of the corridor, and their departing friends.

Returning to her human form as she reached a large oak door, Mahra forced it open and yelled for them all to get in. Loras was last down the corridor, helping the staggering Quint. The door slammed shut as soon as they were in and a heavy metal bar was brought down with a *clunk* to secure it.

They slumped down to the floor panting and gasping, their senses straining to hear sounds from beyond the door, but the Academy was silent once again. Tarent moved to Quint and examined the blade lodged in his arm.

'This thing is heavily barbed and is emanating some kind of evil, I can see it glowing red; we have to get it out.' He studied Quint's pain-racked face. 'This is going to hurt my friend, so brace yourself.' As he poured in healing magic, Tarent slowly worked the blade loose. Thankfully Quint gave a small cry and fainted at the first touch. The blade came out and Tarent flung it into the corner in disgust before continuing his healing. When the wound stopped bleeding, amazingly it showed signs of healing until finally it became less angry and inflamed. Tarent stepped back exhausted and sank down next to his patient. 'We should let him rest for a while. Mahra, how about you and Loras going up into the tower?' He pointed towards the spiral staircase in the corner of the room. 'Pardigan, you may as well go with them, I'll stay here with Quint. Don't worry; I'll call you if we have any more visitors.'

'Is he going to be all right?' asked Pardigan. 'He looks very pale.'

'Quint will be fine, he just needs rest and a little more healing.' Tarent yawned and closed his eyes. Realising they could do nothing, the others moved off towards the staircase, leaving Tarent and Quint in the light of their glow globe.

The stairs were damp and slippery in places and their breath turned to white clouds in the chill air as they went up in an ever-tightening spiral. They began to feel giddy as it twisted and turned. It was a strange experience, almost like being a mouse running on a wheel going round and round. They were working hard but seemed to be going nowhere. Just as they were discussing if this was some magical illusion that would have them climbing without end, they came to a small landing and a large closed door.

'Well this is it. It's silly but I feel I should knock,' said Mahra. 'This was Magician Clement's tower; he was such a nice old man.' She took hold of the large metal handle and pushed, and with a creak of stubborn protest, the door slowly opened.

Moving inside they gazed around the chamber of a magician, dead for over a thousand years. The room was large, and round, with several small windows lit with the flashes of lightning and the more animated violent points of the storm raging outside. Around the edge of the chamber, illuminated in the light of the glow globes, were bookcases and shelves with jars and bottles holding different coloured powders and liquids, and row upon row of books. A central desk was strewn with papers and even more books and ledgers. Cobwebs and dust covered everything including a body sitting slumped forward onto the desk.

'Magician Clement,' cried Mahra, moving forward. 'Oh poor, poor Magician Clement.' She reached out to gently touch the frail shape in front of her while Loras and Pardigan gave her some privacy and walked around inspecting the variety of objects that were lying around.

'Don't touch anything,' hissed Loras.

'Me!' said Pardigan indignantly. 'It's not me that's the problem, Loras old friend, it's you. Don't *you* touch anything, all right?'

'Yeah, yeah all right, neither of us touches anything,' said Loras, reaching out to pick up a glass jar with what appeared to be blue liquid in it.

'Loras...' warned Pardigan.

'*Eeeeek!*' Mahra jumped back from the table. 'He moved!' The boys spun round and studied the dusty form still slumped headfirst on the desk.

'What do you mean he moved?' said Pardigan with a frown. 'That's one dead magician, Mahra. He has to have been dead for hundreds of...'

The figure at the table coughed.

Mahra jumped back. 'See, he's alive!' Sure enough, the head started to lift and they heard the bones in his neck cracking as dust fell to the desk. The strange figure sat upright and gazed around, pale blue eyes peering out at them from behind a filthy mask of cobwebs. Blinking at the three figures before him he sneezed, sending up a cloud of dust and several startled spiders.

'Oh, Mahra, it's you,' the figure croaked in a dry brittle voice. 'I'm awfully sorry, I must have dozed off.'

'Magician Clement, you're alive!' Mahra was weeping. 'But how can you be alive?' The old magician peered around confused and lifted a hand to pull aside the veil of cobwebs from his face.

'Oh bugger!' He tried to stand but fell back into the chair.

'Oh bugger, bugger, bugger,' he whined. 'I suppose that Bleak thinks this is funny. Bugger!' He thumped a bony fist onto the table sending up another cloud of dust which made him sneeze again. Gazing at Mahra, he smiled. 'You wouldn't make an old man a nice cup of brew would you, dear? My throat is feeling rather dry.'

Chapter 9

A Walk in the Dark

They had nothing to make a brew with. After more than a thousand years, anything that had once been edible or drinkable was nothing more than dust and memories now. Mahra helped the old magician to stand, his knees knocked a bit and he stood quivering, gazing about through blue watery eyes.

'The bugger spelled me!' he spluttered. 'Bleak didn't have the decency to believe I could ever be trouble for him, so he just spelled me to sleep without a second thought.' He started to hop about testing his legs; clouds of dust flying up from his robes as he muttered about dark Magicians of Chaos and how they should 'bloody well watch out!' He made a comical sight and Pardigan and Loras weren't sure whether to laugh at the old boy's antics or feel sorry for him.

In the end Pardigan couldn't help but chuckle when, with robes held up to his waist, the old magician was hopping up and down from one leg to the other screaming out, 'Bugger, bugger, bugger,' in a shrill angry voice. He turned to the laughing Pardigan. 'Better watch yourself, boyo! I might have been asleep for a while but you shouldn't mess with an angry old man who could very easily come up with an interesting curse or two!' the last part was shouted right into Pardigan's startled face.

Mahra shot Pardigan a nasty look and took the old magician by the arm, steering him away. 'What happened Magician Clement, how did he trick you?' The dusty old man sighed and fixed Mahra with a sad gaze.

'Oh, I was an old fool who didn't really take much interest in the politics of the Academy. Pew tried to warn me. Then we did that spell...' he waved his arms in the air. 'Well, after the spell...I came back here and continued with my studies.' He gazed around and gave a little harrumph. 'Now my studies are dust and that bugger spelled me. Just put me to sleep.' He sat at his desk and absently doodled in the dust with his finger. 'You were part of that spell weren't you, Mahra? I mean...I remember that I taught you how to change into...' he thought for a moment. 'Some sort of bird and a cat too, if I remember rightly.'

'An owl, a cat, and I taught myself how to become a Black Panther,' said Mahra.

'A Black Panther! Really.' He patted her sleeve, smiling, then glanced over to where Pardigan and Loras still stood, too frightened to move. He raised an eyebrow and whispered, 'These are the heroes? They don't look like heroes.' He peered out of the rain-streaked window at the sky as it boiled over the rolling storm-lashed ocean. 'Although it looks very much as I suspected the end of time would look,' he muttered, pulling thoughtfully on his beard.

Mahra smiled, 'Yes, welcome to the end of time. These are two of the heroes, and now we have another...you!'

He gathered a few things as Mahra filled him in on recent events and with an appraising look at Loras, after hearing he was a fellow magician, he passed Loras a wooden staff, similar to the one he picked up for himself.

'Heartwood, boy, holds magic and can give a nasty headache if you *wop* someone with it,' he cackled, swinging his own staff about experimentally. 'I'm going to *wop* Bleak with mine if I find him. Won't catch me napping again, he won't.' He danced a little jig and held out his hand towards the staff that Loras now held. 'Here...first spell's on me.' A blue glow filled the staff and Loras nearly dropped it. 'Calm down, boy, calm down, it won't burn you. Throw the staff over there,' he pointed to a spot under the window. Loras happily threw the staff and it clattered to the floor. 'All right, well done, now what's its name?' Magician Clement's face loomed close to Loras who was wondering if the old boy had woken up as loopy as one of those crazy drunks in Market Square.

'S-s-sorry? Its name, sir?' Loras stammered.

'Yes its name, it's *your* staff now, so you've got to name it, then call it to you!' He turned to Mahra shaking his head. 'Didn't his master teach him anything?' He raised a dusty eyebrow, 'Bit dim, is he?'

Loras blushed and raised his voice in command.

'Staff, here!' The staff leapt off the ground and flew into his outstretched hand. Loras grinned while Magician Clement gaped at him open-mouthed.

'He called his staff…Staff! Well I never.' He headed down the stairs and Mahra winked at the delighted Loras as they followed.

* * *

Once at the base of the tower, introductions were made as Magician Clement sat down heavily on the floor, staring back at the door he'd just stepped through.

'By the Source I think Bleak added a few more stairs to my tower. I don't remember there being that many.' He glanced at Quint who was still sleeping deeply. 'What's the matter with this lad?' He held a wrinkled hand over Quint's face. 'Ah, the fighter of our heroes.' He smiled with recognition. 'Stabbed, and yes…partially healed, I believe. Where is the blade now?' Tarent walked over and gingerly picked up the black blade from where he'd tossed it and brought it back to the old man. The magician held out his hand to take it, but stopped short, drawing back. 'A Chaos blade,' he whispered. 'Very well, Chaos is balanced by Order, so to heal this Chaos wound we must cleanse it with energy of Order. Which you started to do quite successfully I see.' He smiled at Tarent. 'Would you mind if I finish your healing, young man?'

Tarent shrugged. 'Of course not.'

'If you place a hand upon my shoulder, and concentrate, I can show you how to increase your healing powers.'

Tarent did as he was bid and was joined by Loras. They started to feel what the old magician was doing and within seconds Quint was awake, staring up at them with a shocked expression. Loras introduced Magician Clement.

'Good day to you, fighter, it's good to see that little harm has come to you.' Mahra helped the old magician to his feet. 'Thank you, dear. Come, let's be off, I'm eager to see Pew's tower and to help in your tasks, for it looks as though I'm to be one of you heroes myself.'

They moved carefully out into the gloom once more, the old magician chuckling happily about being one of the heroes. Halfway along the second corridor he asked them to wait and disappeared into a doorway. He appeared a few moments later carrying a shining shirt of chain mail.

'Here, put this on and we may be able to keep you out of harm's way a little longer,' he passed the shirt to Quint. 'It was ancient when I was a student here. Legend claims it was made by some long-forgotten race and would stop any blade, or indeed any arrow. You'll have to let me know if that's true in a few weeks' time,' he added, amused again by his own wit. 'Oh I am enjoying being awake again.' His face creased in a frown. 'Or at least I would be if I could get a nice cup of brew to set me up.'

Quint slid the mail over his head and was surprised at how light it was. Pardigan helped him tie it in place.

'Very nice,' said Pardigan. 'Now if those rat things come back we'll be able to push you right to the front then all hide behind you.' Quint cuffed him around the head.

They continued down the corridor, eventually arriving at an identical door to the first tower. Stepping inside they bolted it then started up the narrow staircase. Quint led, and Magician Clement took up the rear, claiming that after a thousand years he would probably be slower than the rest of them.

Once again, the climb seemed to take forever, but then, as they neared the top they began to hear murmurs and talking coming from within the tower's chamber. A loud ringing filled the air as swords and knives were drawn then Quint opened the door and sprang through with the others close behind ready to do battle. However, the scene that greeted them wasn't one they had expected. The talking abruptly stopped and a hush descended as the group took in their surroundings.

Skulls covered every available surface in a variety of different sizes and colours - most were bone, some were metal and a few were made of glass.

'Well, about time too,' said one of the skulls from its place on top of a shelf.

'We've been waiting ages for you!' said another.

The Griffin's crew stood in amazement, as every skull started to speak at the same time, trying to be heard above the rest. The noise soon became deafening.

'Could you please move me; I'm tired of this position?'

'This fool keeps babbling nonsense in my ear; desist! He's still doing it. Stop, I say!'

'As I was saying the other day...'

'Liquorice - did they bring liquorice? I've had a hankering for a nice piece of liquorice for ages.'

'You can't eat liquorice; you've no stomach for it, *haaaaaaaa haaa!*'

'I said it would be today, didn't I say they would come today?'

Some were moaning, some were singing, but most were trying to get the visitors' attention with questions and comments; the noise was unbearable.

'*Silence!*' bellowed Magician Clement who, after finally making the top of the stairs, had entered the chamber.

'Ooh, who's this?'

'Bit loud, isn't he!'

'Who does he think he is, eh?'

The noise returned, this time, with sounds of laughter joining in.

'I said silence and I *mean* silence!' Magician Clement banged his staff on the floor several times then walked around, peering closely at the skulls. 'Bleak's work this is, all stained with Chaos.' The noise reduced to a low murmur for a moment... it didn't last.

'He's looking at me.'

'He said you were stained, are you stained?'

'He was talking to you!'

'No he was not!'

The noise picked up again, becoming deafening as, once again, each skull fought to be heard above its neighbours.

'Don't let him get too close, we don't know him yet!'

'Well I don't think he's being very nice.'

The skulls' chatter ebbed slightly but didn't stop; it seemed they were unable to do anything else. Pardigan stepped forward.

'We seek the skull that links to Magician Pew,' he shouted.

'That's me, that's me!' cried just about every skull in unison.

'Nice try, lad,' murmured Magician Clement when the noise had once again abated.

They started searching for anything obvious that could help them. The shelves, desk, windowsills, the bed and a good part of the floor, were covered in chattering skulls.

'This is hopeless,' screamed Mahra over the noise. 'How are we meant to find the right one amongst all these?'

'There's one here that says he knows which skull we're looking for, and if we take him with us he'll introduce us,' shouted Pardigan, but he didn't sound very convinced.

'Yes and there's one here that claims it's the one we want, but it keeps trying to bite me, so I think it's lying.' Tarent dodged back from its snapping jaws.

'There it is!' shouted Loras, pointing up to the top of a shelf. He started to clamber over several chairs and shelves pushing skulls out of the way as he went, apologising profusely to the complaints and gnashing teeth that followed his progress. The others stood back and watched his efforts, hoping he was right. As Loras touched a glowing blue skull, the others stopped whatever they had been saying and froze mid-sentence; hundreds of jaws clicked shut at the same time; the silence was deafening. Loras looked down at his friends. 'Well I think this *must* be the one if it shut that lot up.' He carefully picked up the skull and brought it down to the table. It was crystal and pulsating with a steady blue light. 'It was the only one,' he explained. 'Everything else, like the knife and the book has done the same thing with a strange blue light, so it was a fair guess that it was the magician's skull.'

'Well I don't know about being Pew's actual skull,' said Clement. 'But I do think it is the one we were looking for.' The skull glowed brighter. 'Clement is that you?' The skull's jaw didn't move but a voice came from it sounding muted and distant.

'Pew, are you alive in there?' the old magician dropped to his knees to be level with the strange skull.

'Alive yes but in here no, as my heroes will tell you, this is the skull that links to me, not my actual skull, I'm still using that.' A deep throaty laugh came from the glowing skull.

'I just explained that to them! I'm not daft, Pew,' grumbled Magician Clement.

Mahra pushed forward and gave a little yelp of joy. 'Master it *is* you!'

'Mahra, oh, Mahra you've done so well. The heroes are together and Bleak left us one hero extra, I hear. Clement will be of great help to us.

'Let me give some small explanation if I may.' The skull glowed even brighter. 'The great spell was conceived and wrapped around three crystal skulls of the kind you see before you. By uniting the skulls at the correct time, the spell will be activated. All of this, the creation of the spell, your Quest, Mahra's long vigil, is to counter the ultimate threat of the balance swinging to Chaos with no expectation of return. You must find the three skulls and bring them back to me and we can complete the spell; you cannot fail. The book will show you more when this first skull is placed with it, now flee this island as quickly as you can, there is nothing more for you here except trouble. May the Source speed you.'

A Walk in the Dark

The glow returned to normal and Loras placed it into his bag. Taking a last look around at the rows of silent skulls, Mahra and Clement offered up a prayer to the Source for the souls of their lost friends, and they left the tower, trailing down to the bottom of the stairs.

When Magician Clement finally arrived, Quint made to open the door to the corridor and lead them all out.

'Hold fast, young man!' cried Clement as he hobbled forward holding Mahra's arm. 'I am afraid we have a problem. One of my gifts is to sense the presence of Chaos. Sometimes, as with that knife, I must be close, other times as now, I can sense the presence from some distance away.' He sighed. 'I'm sorry to say that there is a demon in the academy, and it must be that it searches for us.'

* * *

Belial sat, as his rank demanded, higher than anything else, human or demon, on a platform made from a hastily cut-down table. Beside him to his right, stood Matheus Hawk and to his left, stood a demon. The demon had simply arrived, saying nothing before moving to Belial's side, where it now stood with its head bowed.

The room above the inn was stifling hot and Bartholomew suspected the smell that filled the air was emanating from this latest visitor. He eyed the demon from where he was crouched uncomfortably on a small wooden stool at Belial's feet. The new demon was hooded, but Bartholomew could still make out the twisted features of a bestial face. The sound of its coarse, laboured breathing was all that broke the silence of Belial's frequent meditations, and he couldn't be sure, but it felt like the demon was watching him as he fidgeted uncomfortably.

Things had taken a decided turn for the worse for Bartholomew. It was only a few blissful hours ago that he had been happily without any inkling that demons actually existed, and now here he sat in the presence of two of them. One apparently, almost set to eat him and the other was a king of demons no less. He was becoming somewhat desperate to get away, but had no idea how.

Belial had been in this latest meditation for some time, with his head propped upon his hand and his face set in a slight frown of concentration. At last he came back to them, his expression turning to a broad smile that was at once both beautiful and terrifying.

'Mr Bask, I am sure you will be as delighted as I, to know that one of my agents is closing in on this '*rabble of Order*' even as we speak. We shall soon be able to question them and return your goods to you.' He smiled down at Bartholomew. 'Which of course, shall make you beholden to me, but we will discuss my fee upon completion.' Bartholomew felt like a mouse being toyed with by some giant cat. He scowled up at the Hawk. Didn't that fool know the trouble he had gotten them both into?

Belial's features clouded once more as he communed with his agent. 'Excellent, oh yes excellent,' he murmured. 'The prey is in sight and the game underway.' The beautiful face split once more into a broad smile and a deep rumble of laughter erupted, echoing around the room.

Bartholomew started to feel sick again and once more sought for some means of escape.

* * *

'It walks the halls now searching for us.' Magician Clement slumped to the floor as he concentrated. 'We will have to face it, my young friends, and I'm afraid I'm not up to facing it alone. I am already tired and wouldn't last long. I can, however give some advice for when you do meet in battle.' He took a deep breath. 'Magician, do not attempt to use any magic of fire upon it, for it comes from a realm of fire and it would only enjoy the sensation. For the same reason however, it may dislike the feeling of cold.' He gave Loras a smile of encouragement. 'Use your staff. It will increase the power of any magic you choose to send through it, Source be true.' Next his gaze found Tarent and Quint. 'Do not slash at it with your swords or shoot at it with any normal arrow. Unless I am much mistaken, a demon of this kind and power has skin tougher than you could ever imagine, you will not be able to harm it.' His features glazed over.

'It comes closer and we have not much time. Pass me your arrows, boy, and you your knives, lad. I shall attempt to enchant them with what little energy of Order I have left, for that is the only thing I know that can stop it.' He passed his hands over the arrows that Quint held out, as well as the knives that Pardigan produced. Each pulsed with a fierce bright blue light of Order, before returning to normal. 'Aim for its eyes, they are its only vulnerable part.' He held Quint's arm. 'I know there are precious few arrows here, fighter, but would you humour a very old man and allow me to keep one?' Quint nodded his agreement and the old man smiled his thanks. With an effort he pulled himself to his feet. 'It is time to meet it.' He held the gaze of each in turn. 'Are we ready?' He saw the group of young anxious faces around him, these heroes of the balance, and added a small prayer.

'May we be blessed today with courage and with skill,
May our luck hold true,
And may the Source preserve us all.'
'The Source,' they echoed in return, raising their weapons.
Quint threw open the door.

Chapter 10

To Battle a Demon

The glow globes were first into the corridor, closely followed by Quint and then Tarent. Light from the globes' movement sent a confusion of shadows dancing on the walls and doors to either side. The crew watched nervously as a large dark shape about halfway down slowly came into view, the globes' dim light gradually exposing the demon's features. It was huge. Its head almost touched the ceiling and its massive shoulders were brushing the walls to either side, dragging plaster and old hangings down as it lumbered forward. It was completely black except for the deep red smouldering glow of its eyes, which were set above large flaring nostrils. Pardigan pushed through to join his friends. His first thought on getting a good look at the creature, was that it resembled the features of a giant bat freshly drawn from the worst of fevered nightmares. Wings could be seen above its shoulders, folded now, but flexing from time to time as it crunched along the bone-strewn corridor towards them.

One taloned hand held a long, heavy blade that dripped an evil, pungent mixture in a steady green flow, hissing as it landed in sticky lumps onto the floor. The other hand was empty, but was flexing, ready to rip and tear at anything that came close. As it approached, it opened its mouth and let out an ear-splitting screech, almost deafening them with its intensity. Without hesitation, Tarent strode forward to meet the creature, closing the distance between them quickly, his twin blades unsheathing in a blur.

Quint watched Tarent's attack and strained to draw his bow back before quickly letting fly two arrows - the first bounced from the creature's head, a little above its left eye, the second was snatched from the air and flung to the ground in contempt. The demon lurched into action, its huge sword swinging high and Tarent quickly found himself being pushed back into the others. Unable to do much against the creature's sheer size and strength in such a narrow space, he battled to keep fear, as well as the demon at bay.

Mahra, now in the form of the Black Panther, ran forward and leapt using her weight and speed to push the thing back. In the confines of the corridor it wasn't possible for them all to charge at once, so Tarent and Mahra fought from the front with the others striking from behind. Mahra was really unable to do little more than distract it; her claws doing no damage even when she was able to strike at it. Magician Clement had been whispering to Loras who now also joined in sending spears of ice flashing at the demon from the tip of his staff. The demon screamed in pain as ice spears struck and then enveloped it. Enraged, it broke the ice and struck out making Mahra leap back with a yelp as the black blade carved a path along her side, peeling her skin back with a deep red flow of blood. She sobbed in pain and fell whimpering, as Magician Clement shuffled to her side attempting to find a little more energy to heal her.

Light from one of the globes briefly lit further back down the corridor. Pardigan snatched the opportunity and place-shifted behind the demon. He immediately turned and sent electrical charges into its back that struck with loud cracks sending sparks flying, diverting its attention, forcing it to turn and try to swipe at him. As it did so, he sent a knife spinning into the demon's face.

'Eat that!' he screamed in triumph as the blade entered the demon's eye, striking with a meaty thunk before sinking to the hilt. It howled and snarled in agony as it faced him, enraged, half blind and seeking revenge. The knife fell from its eye and black blood and gore oozed down its cheek as it ran towards him screeching.

From behind it, Quint fired arrows while Loras continued to cast spells, freezing the air around the demon's feet to hinder its movement. It stumbled but didn't fall as it continued its assault on Pardigan. Tarent moved back in and stabbed repeatedly at its back trying to make it turn around, then Pardigan let fly his second knife. Before it could find its mark it was snatched from the air and flung back at him with demonic force. It struck him in the leg and he collapsed to the floor with a scream of agony. Forcing himself not to be beaten by the pain, he glanced up, and then pushed himself back from the evil vision lumbering towards him. Fear entered his soul like a blade of ice.

Sensing at least one of its prey was now vulnerable, the demon closed in for the kill, bringing its sword up for a stabbing stroke to Pardigan's head. The sword destroyed the ceiling on the upward stroke, showering the demon with plaster, and then swept down meeting nothing but air, exploded into the tiled floor of the corridor as Pardigan place-shifted back to his friends.

Snarling and shrieking in frustration, the demon spun around shaking its head as Quint let loose another volley of arrows. Raising an arm it managed to deflect most, yet one got through and struck it heavily in the same eye socket as Pardigan's knife. Its scream almost deafened them, yet it continued to stagger forward, forcing the group to bunch against the tower door.

They knew that if they retreated into the room, they were doomed. They would never all make it up the staircase, not with both Mahra and Pardigan wounded; they had to make their stand here and now.

Out of arrows at last, Quint drew his sword and leapt forward alongside Tarent and for a few moments they drove the huge beast back. It then appeared to gain new resolve, as if goaded forward by some unseen presence, and began to press them even harder.

The arrow imbedded in the bloodied eye-socket was hissing and spluttering as black blood flowed over the glowing blue shaft. The demon was dying, but it wasn't happening fast enough. Its new attack sent Tarent spinning and one of his blades clattered to the stone floor. Sensing victory once again, the demon roared and moved forward. A clawed foot struck Tarent in the chest throwing him backwards into Pardigan's arms.

Quint blocked its advance, facing the beast alone. His sword flashed as he repeatedly struck the demon, with all his failing strength. If victory was to be decided upon skill and courage, then Quint would have triumphed again and again; yet skill and courage simply weren't enough. His blade bounced from the demon's skin doing little more than delaying the inevitable blow that would fell the tiring fighter. It wasn't long before he was staggering, fighting exhaustion as well as the demon. Unable to do much more than deflect the demon's attack and make a half-hearted defence. Sensing triumph at last, the demon rose to its full height, its head brushed the ceiling and plaster fell about it as it uttered a screech of triumph and advanced on Quint, its black blade poised to deliver the killing strike.

Staring up at the towering figure, Quint lifted his sword for what he knew would be the final time; and then time seemed to freeze. A robed figure dashed from behind him and leapt up at the demon.

Magician Clement was clutching the arrow Quint had given him and, using the force of his own momentum, he drove the arrow deep into the demon's remaining eye. It cried a long agonised scream that echoed down the corridor into every part of the old Academy and finally fell down, dead. But as it fell, its heavy sword fell with it, striking the old magician a mortal blow, cutting him deeply from the shoulder down into his chest. He fell silently to the floor.

The Griffin's crew witnessed this final scene in a helpless daze with tears coming unbidden. Mahra changed back into a girl and ran forward to cradle the old man's head in her lap. She stroked his long white hair and carefully wiped the demon's blood from his face.

'Oh, Magician Clement, you shouldn't have done that. It was the bravest thing I've ever seen, you saved us all.'

The old man's eyes opened and he tried to speak, his words coming in a soft whisper. 'Do not confuse courage with necessity, my dear.

When a person only has one choice, it's not just a matter of bravery. I simply did what we all did. I did all that I possibly could. You gave an old man the chance to do battle with evil and I thank you all for that.' He peered around him and coughed, blood dribbling from the corner of his mouth. 'It's been a very strange day,' he glanced back at Mahra and smiled. 'Thank you for waking me, Mahra, thank you for today.' The magician's pale blue eyes fluttered and he died in her arms, the soft smile still upon his lips as she hugged him to her chest, weeping gently.

* * *

Belial leapt from his chair with a roar, his face no longer a beatific picture of calm.

'Children!' he kicked out, sending Bartholomew scuttling back to lean against the wall. 'Children and an old man stand against a demon lord... and triumph? How is this possible?' He paced the room attempting to regain some control. 'You!' he pointed to Matheus Hawk. 'Take the fat one and journey by sea. Find them and follow them, learn of their movements. I shall ride with my brethren and meet with them personally. It is time for us to end this farce for I tire of the game.' He stopped and took a deep breath to gather himself. 'The time of Chaos is almost upon us. They will not be allowed to thwart what has always been written in the halls of time. The world has turned and will soon belong to my people; it is *our* time, for the balance has rightly swung to our favour. We hunger for the feast that has been promised us and no mere gaggle of children will stop us.'

Matheus Hawk needed no further prompting. Grabbing Bartholomew by the collar, he half dragged him out of the door as the demon continued to rant. The pair made their escape down the stairs and pushed roughly through the drinking hall, eager to be out of Blake's and into the fresh air. Once on the waterfront Bartholomew dropped thankfully to his knees, sucking in air noisily while trying to make some sense of what was happening to him.

'Are...you...in...sane?' he gasped, staring up at Matheus's white face. 'You have us in league with a Source damned demon!' He climbed to his feet, only to be slapped down again by Matheus.

'You keep a civil tongue, you fat fool. I'm well aware of our little problem in there, but events got out of control. The demons are on the same path as us, so we have nothing to fear from them, at least not at the moment we don't.'

'Nothing to fear!' squealed Bartholomew only to be silenced with a look from Matheus. 'Well I want nothing more to do with any of this. I'm the victim here, but I'll not deal with demons to get my property back.' He started to walk away, only to be stopped by Matheus's laughter.

'Are you really that stupid? You're involved all the way, my friend. We have to get your trinkets back and destroy any link between us and that demon, the book, the knife and whatever else there is. He's hunting those children; you don't want to be next on his list, do you?

'Do you have a boat, Mr Bask, because it looks like we're going sailing, and that would be easier if we had a boat, would it not?'

Bartholomew's lip began to quiver, he was crestfallen, he'd been delighted to be out of that room and hadn't even minded Mr Hawk handling him so roughly, just as long as he was leaving. Now he was being told he had to continue, and to sea no less. Bartholomew had never once taken to sea and he wasn't excited by the prospect now.

'Why can't *you* go? There's no need for me to be there, I'm a merchant not a sailor or soldier. I can supply you with a boat, but I'll not go to sea myself.' He attempted to look defiant to Matheus Hawk's smiling face.

'Oh, you'll be coming, Mr Bask, you'll most certainly be coming to oversee your investment so to speak. An' if you don't,' he moved in closer; his breath rancid in Bartholomew's face. 'You'll wake up with yer throat cut from ear...to ear.' His dirty fingernail described a slow cut across Bartholomew's neck.

Bartholomew started to sob. 'Oh mercy, mercy me, what have I, an honest merchant, done to deserve all this?' He slumped to the ground outside Blake's, a pitiful sight, not caring who saw him now, as Matheus laughed at his distress.

'Don't you worry, Mr Bask, we'll get the upper hand here and turn a profit to boot. Or my name's not Matheus Hawk.' He helped Bartholomew up and they walked off into the night in search of a boat with Bartholomew still crying at the injustice of it all.

* * *

Before leaping at the demon, Magician Clement had performed enough healing on Mahra to allow her ease of movement. Using the lesson Magician Clement had given them; Loras then healed it further, and closed the wound properly after cleansing the Chaos corruption that the demon's blade had left bubbling there. Tarent had administered healing to Pardigan, who now limped, but would be able to help if something attacked the group.

'We can't just leave Magician Clement here,' sobbed Mahra, 'Not in this horrible place, it isn't right.

'I know, but we have to, he would understand.' Tarent placed a hand on her shoulder and drew her away.

At last, they made it back to the entrance hall where the dim light of another dawn filtered through the broken doorway.

'The storm has stopped,' said Loras in awe as they emerged. It was far from a pleasant day, but it wasn't the storm-lashed centre of Chaos that it had been when they'd arrived.

'I think we're already making some difference to the balance,' said Mahra, smiling. 'We've found the first skull and the spell is beginning to work.' They ran to the cliff and carefully descended the treacherous path, eager to be on board *The Griffin* for a hot brew before leaving for wherever next the book would send them.

It was long past dark again when they did get to the book, gathering round as Quint slotted in the knife, changing the ragged pile of papers into the now familiar Book of Challenges.

To Battle a Demon

'Let's see where we're off to next then,' said Quint as he turned the pages. Sure enough, a new page had appeared and Quint read out the passage with the others listening eagerly.

> *The Tree of Truth.*
> *The second skull you now must find,*
> *With Minster's woodland Hidden kind.*
>
> *The skull has lost all memories,*
> *Of any life but as a tree.*
>
> *Beneath a branch where land meets sun,*
> *You shall find the crystal one.*
>
> *Beware now heroes, listen to me.*
> *The Hidden folk must all agree,*
> *To give the skull away to thee.*

'Well that would appear to be simple enough. We head for Minster and go searching for some people that are well hidden,' said Pardigan laughing.

'Who are the Hidden kind, and if they're hiding, where do we look?' asked Loras, ignoring Pardigan with a frown.

Mahra became thoughtful, biting her lip nervously as she stared at the page. 'Well...there are several old legends about the Hidden, but I thought they were just that, legends. I didn't think they were real...maybe they are.' She sat down on her stool, licking the back of her hand in a typically cat-like way, then realised what she was doing while still in human form and sat on her hands. 'Magician Pew did once claim to be in contact with them, I didn't believe him. It's like saying you saw fairies or elves; they were never real...until now I suppose. People tell stories about the Hidden to frighten each other on stormy nights.

'The legends say they remain away from the world of man cursed, they believe, to guard great secrets, not trusting a soul and shunning all contact. There are all kinds of horrible stories - none of them good. The ones I remember most are where they steal babies from their beds and eat...cats.' She shivered at the memory of being told stories as a child. 'Never leave a window open at night; it may let in the Hidden. I remember being told that.'

'You don't believe that though do you, Mahra?' asked Quint with a frown.

'I don't know what to believe. Up until now they were simply childhood stories, but now they're becoming real. They're supposed to live deep in the forests, so if they are real, and we have to find them, we might well find them in the forests of Minster.' She didn't appear happy. 'And don't forget, the book says they must agree to us taking the skull, we can't just steal it.'

'We'll have to worry about that at the time,' said Tarent. 'We have the Minsten trading permit that Pardigan took; we'll just have to hope it's not been reported stolen. We will need something to trade, but it still won't be easy to get into Minster harbour. I suggest we go via Sterling Port and find some cargo.'

As the wind continued to moan outside, the crew sat and talked, allowing the tension of the last few days to melt away, until one by one they went to their bunks and slept.

Chapter 11

Gathering Skulls

They departed Skull Island without any problems, but the crew remained cautious and vigilant. Loras was noticeably nervous. Quint sent Pardigan forward to the bowsprit, where he guided their progress out between the rocks. It proved difficult as it was still raining and he was soon cold and soaked through but after manoeuvring, shouting and the occasional touch of the rocks they made it into open sea.

A morning's sail saw them a good distance from the island and by early afternoon the clouds had parted and the sun shone down upon *The Griffin* for the first time in days. Spray flew back over her deck, washing away the taint of Chaos that had permeated everything on Skull Island and the crew began to relax.

The two days it took to get to Sterling passed quickly: no storms, no strange scratching noises and, thankfully, no demons to disturb their passage. It was late afternoon when *The Griffin* sailed into Sterling Port, escorted by a cloud of cawing gulls, dipping and whirling in an aerial ballet that had Mahra transfixed, pawing the air in frustration.

Once moored, Mahra, Tarent and Loras went into town for fresh provisions while Pardigan and Quint went in search of suitable goods to take to Minster. They walked along the quay perusing the various offerings scratched on slates outside each portside warehouse, discussing which would be the best cargo to take. As a forested island with few natural resources other than wood, the list of possibilities was endless.

They finally decided on several bolts of cloth, some crates of tools and all the barrels of fire pitch available. Fire pitch was always sought after in any port, and would be especially well received on the island province of Minster. It was useful for a number of things, from waterproofing boats and roofs to refining down into lamp oil. The seller promised the barrels would be rolled down to *The Griffin* straight away, and even gave them the name of a contact in Minster Harbour who, he promised, would buy it all for a good price. Quint slapped palms with the warehouseman, paid the coin and then he and Pardigan walked off to see what else they could find before they went to sea again.

The back streets of Sterling were an incredible hive of activity with crowds streaming among the shops, taverns and teahouses, the vendors eagerly competing for their business. The cries of merchants and barrow boys filled the air and brew sellers walked the streets with kettles and glasses slung over their shoulders adding their call to the general hullabaloo. The air was heavy with the aromas of brew, spices and wood smoke and the boys were soon caught up in the wonderful atmosphere of it all.

Sterling was a centre of commerce for the whole kingdom, and several wagons and trading caravans were being loaded in the stables and marshalling yards ready for their long treks to far away cities across the kingdom. The Dhurbar, who made up most of the caravans, were from the southern deserts and had a rich flamboyant culture coupled with a fearsome reputation that kept all but the most desperate or determined robbers away. The colourful fabrics they wore set them apart, contrasting heavily against the dull stone of the city. Pardigan and Quint watched mesmerised as the Desert horsemen skilfully managed their beasts. The Dhurbar were readying for departure, tying huge bundles, crates and barrels to their camels as the animals shifted and complained under the weight, filling the air with strange moaning cries.

Without warning, Quint gripped Pardigan's arm and pulled him back into the doorway of a small tavern. 'Look, over there, it's the merchant!' he hissed. Pardigan followed Quint's gaze. It was the merchant all right. Merchant Bartholomew Bask and here in Sterling Port!

'Maybe it's coincidence, maybe he's trading with the Dhurbar or something, he is a merchant after all.' They watched him talking with one of the horsemen, questioning him at length, obviously exasperated with the answers he was getting. He appeared dishevelled, hot and uncomfortable.

Quint poked Pardigan in the ribs. 'Trying to get some of that money back, I shouldn't wonder,' he said, laughing. 'He's probably forgotten all about his midnight visitor by now.'

'Oh I wouldn't say that,' said a deep rasping voice. 'Merchant Bask hasn't forgotten anything. You caused him no end of trouble and he's actually here searching for you.' Matheus Hawk's hands came down upon the boys' shoulders in a grip of steel. 'Merchant Bask,' called Matheus, 'look what I've found!'

The fat merchant swung around at the sound of his name, his face still caught in a frown of concentration. Seeing Matheus Hawk with his hands on the shoulders of two scruffy louts, it obviously dawned upon him that these might well be the thieves themselves.

'Hold them!' He hurried over towards the tavern, pushing people out of the way in his haste. Several passers by noticed a scene was unfolding and watched with interest as Pardigan struggled in the tracker's grip.

Quint, in contrast, was standing quite still, taking in the situation without panicking, his newly acquired instincts already planning his move. In one fluid action, he stamped down hard, scraping his boot down their captor's shinbone and onto his foot, causing Matheus to let both boys go with a howl of agony and rage. In the same movement, Quint kicked out at the nearest table, sending it spinning across the narrow street, and a jug of sweet red berry juice flying into the air, all over the approaching merchant.

'*Run!*' bellowed Quint, pushing through the crowd.

Pardigan didn't need to be told twice; he slapped down the hands of the person trying to hold him and chased after Quint, down the street and into the labyrinth of passages that made up this quarter of the city. They could hear the sounds of laughter from the crowd and the merchant shrieking, 'Thieves, thieves, stop them!'

Footsteps echoed in pursuit.

'We've got to get out of here and fast,' said Pardigan. 'How were we recognised? I was sure I wasn't seen going into the house and I've never met that tall ugly fellow before, have you? I would have remembered him all right, he was scary.'

'Stop talking and keep running, we have to get to the boat,' panted Quint. They dodged their way across town and down to the harbour where the last of the barrels were being loaded under the watchful eye of Tarent. Mahra was curled up asleep in her favourite spot on the hatch top, her tail flicking lazily in the sun.

'The merchant's here,' Pardigan gasped as they came alongside. 'Almost...got us...got to go...now!'

'Where is he?' Tarent glanced towards the warehouses, but life appeared normal up there.

'Is this the last of it?' questioned Quint, looking at the barrel a labourer was guiding over to the hold, the wooden crane creaking with the effort.

'Yes, only a few more barrels then we're loaded. Loras is below deck so we can leave just as soon as...' his words were left unfinished as a crowd of people entered the harbour bunched around the familiar figure of Merchant Bask, who let out a loud roar when he spied *The Griffin*.

'There they are!' he bellowed. 'Stop them, hold them, I demand justice!' His waddling gait increased, limping at his side, the tall man was snarling and the crowd was still with them, eagerly anticipating entertainment.

The crane deposited a barrel in *The Griffin's* hold and swung back for another, the two workmen looked to each other and then at the young crew.

'Wos going on 'ere? That fat chap seems to want words with you lot.' The workman held out a hand to hold Pardigan but Quint leapt up and pushed him back.

'We're leaving right now, and it would be a good idea not to try and stop us.'

Tarent had already cast off the mooring lines and Pardigan followed him onto *The Griffin* leaving Quint alone on the quayside. The little boat began to ease out into the harbour under the power of its small foresail.

The workman eyed the sword at Quint's waist and shrugged. 'Good luck to you, boys, I'll not be a trouble to yer as I think yer got trouble enough.'

Quint jumped onto the deck and nodded in thanks, then, fishing into his pocket, he flipped over a gold coin. 'We'd really appreciate it if you could delay them somehow.' The man glanced down in surprise at the coin; it was more than a month's pay and he smiled.

'Maybe I can think of something, maybe I can.'

The Griffin drifted further out towards the harbour mouth as the crowd came level. Bartholomew was red as a plum and screaming curses at being so close to his hated quarry, while the tall hunter muttered a spell under his breath with an evil look in his eyes.

'Get Loras up here,' called Quint. 'I think that tall one is up to some sort of magic.' As he said this, a ball of fire darted from the Hawk's fingers towards *The Griffin* and exploded on the mast close to Quint's head.

Pardigan sent an electric charge back at the group on the quayside where the crowd all jumped and started to disperse as it crackled and spat amongst them. Another ball of fire hit the deck setting it aflame and Mahra reverted to her human shape to help put it out. Merchant Bask had already set off back down the quay towards a large ship, shouting instructions to get underway.

'If that ship gets going, it's going to catch us in short order,' said Quint, eyeing the powerful looking vessel with its crew efficiently casting off lines, ready to navigate from the harbour.

'Well, we'll have to slow it then, won't we,' answered Loras coming up beside him. He muttered an incantation, his fingers fluttering in the air and with a jolt; the merchant vessel leaned heavily to one side. Merchant Bask, who'd just arrived back onboard, lost his footing and disappeared from sight and several crewmen, caught unawares, slid yelling from the deck and landed with a series of splashes in the murky harbour. What had been an orderly efficient vessel a moment before, became floundering confusion with the boat listing to one side so badly, it appeared like it might even sink.

'Oh Source, well done!' said Quint in admiration. 'What did you do, Loras?'

Loras cuffed away a fireball thrown by the cursing hunter. 'I simply enhanced what was already there. I made their anchor about a thousand times heavier than it already was. They won't go anywhere until they think to cut it loose!'

They heard a scream and a splash and turned to see the hunter floundering in the water. The workman that Quint had flipped the coin to was running off down the quay after giving their attacker a hefty push.

Matheus was having trouble in the water. His cloak was weighing him down and he was madder than a sack of bees.

'The demons shall have you...this doesn't end here! You young...you have not heard the last of Matheu...' The last was finished in an angry rush of bubbles as he bobbed under the water again, his hands splashing the surface trying to grasp something or maybe he was still trying to shake his fist at them with a last ball of fire.

A small boat left the stricken merchant vessel and struck out towards the drowning man, one sailor shooting arrows at *The Griffin*, while another rowed. Bartholomew Bask was standing in the small boat, giving animated directions that were causing the boat to rock violently. He was slapping the back of the man rowing and cursing the efforts of the archer as his arrows fell short. *The Griffin*, now under full sail, passed the seawall leaving behind a harbour filled with a mixture of cursing and laughter.

They headed out to sea until losing sight of the land, then turned south once more, bound for Minster, *The Griffin* sailing fast, as if it knew trouble was close behind them.

'I don't think they'll work out the problem with the anchor for a while,' said Loras grinning happily.

'All the same, we have to make good time to Minster and keep an eye out for pursuit, but how did they find us?' puzzled Quint. 'The merchant was asking questions, looking for us, but the strange thing is; how did that nasty looking tall fellow end up behind us? Was it a coincidence? Maybe it was, but then again, maybe not.'

Mahra sat up from where she'd been sleeping again. 'There's no such thing as coincidence. These were soldiers of Chaos, hunting us. Chaos aids them; the balance is alive and well. We have three skulls to find. One we already have, one we know is in Minster and the other is in an, as yet, undisclosed location. There will almost certainly be a further destination to complete the spell. This is going to give our enemies ample opportunity to stop us.'

'Well thanks for all the good news, Mahra,' muttered Quint, 'but whatever they throw at us we're going to throw it right back and go gathering skulls, eh Loras?'

'Absolutely,' agreed Loras happily.

'Hmmm,' murmured the cat settling down to sleep once more.

* * *

'What by the great demon's toenails were you doing, man?' Bartholomew Bask screamed down his frustration at Matheus Hawk's wallowing figure. 'Some kind of help you turn out to be. That lad was swatting down your magic like it was...uurghh.' A bony hand with fingers like talons had erupted up from the water and fastened themselves around the fat merchant's throat. The boat wobbled precariously as Bartholomew thrashed about and the two sailors did what they could to keep it from capsizing.

'*Uurghh*, get...off, damn riff-raff...tracker, gutter...snipe,' gasped Bartholomew, as he thrashed at the water where the arm indicated Matheus must be. He was abruptly dragged down to the edge of the boat, his chin cracking on the side as Matheus used Bartholomew to pull himself above the surface.

Ignoring Bartholomew completely, except as purchase to stay afloat, Matheus addressed the closest sailor. 'Help me out, you fool, don't just sit there.' He cast a look at the harbour mouth but *The Griffin* was nowhere to be seen. '*Damnation!*' he cried and tipped Bartholomew into the water as he clambered aboard. 'Get us back to the ship and hurry.' He sat down and wrung water from his sleeves.

The sailors began to drag Bartholomew back into the little boat, which wasn't easy as the merchant weighed as much as three normal men put together and he wasn't doing much to help the effort. Matheus glanced over at the merchant ship as it listed heavily to one side.

Sailors were running around the deck, clambering over the sides and rowing around the boat in an effort to see what was causing the problem as the ship's captain bellowed orders from the wheel.

The two sailors helping Bartholomew finally managed to pull him into the boat and he landed with a huge flop like a fat heavy fish. He lay unmoving and silent; a wheezing sound the only indication that he still lived.

The little rowboat got underway and, at the Hawk's direction, headed to the shore rather than the ship. Matheus needed to contact Belial and tell him of the mess the merchant had got them into after he, the tracker, had successfully located the quarry. He stared in disgust at Bartholomew lying prone in the bottom of the boat, completely spent by the recent ordeal, and almost felt sorry for him. But then, on reflection, decided that maybe he didn't.

* * *

Three days later and *The Griffin's* crew were once again looking out for sight of land. Finding the small island in this huge amount of open water was a formidable task, but the crew had faith in their captain, especially after finding the Isle of Skulls, which hadn't even been on any charts. By Quint's calculations they should sight Minster within two turns of the glass.

The crew were eager to get to shore. Mahra was certainly not made out to be a ship's cat; she didn't like *The Griffin's* rolling motion. Several times over the last few days she had taken the form of an owl and flown alongside merely to get off the boat. The rest of the crew however, were contented sailors, eager to continue their Quest. They were taking their roles as heroes seriously now; Magician Clement's death had affected them all deeply. If he was willing to give up his life for this cause after only just getting it back; then they had become willing to give everything possible to see this strange Quest through; they didn't want anything that had happened so far to have been in vain.

Chapter 12

A Rude Reception

The Island of Minster was sighted mid afternoon and Quint was congratulated once again on his navigation abilities. He tried to hide his relief at getting them there, as with great excitement, the crew looked on.

Minster was overwhelmingly green. A thick blanket of trees covered the island, growing right down to the edge with branches overhanging the shallows, regularly trimmed to an even height by the rise and fall of the tide. It gave the impression, as they got closer, of a huge neatly manicured bush from some merchant's pampered garden. It was bigger than they'd first thought and appeared to be without any beaches, moorings or settlement of any kind, simply an unbroken green barrier to an unknown interior. Staying a good distance off, they sailed east in search of the harbour.

The sun was hot, the wind was light, and they moved gently through a sea so smooth, only the barest ripple hinted at the breeze that fluttered the sails. Birds and chattering monkeys called from the island and thousands of fish milled around the boat and the reefs beneath, sending Mahra and Tarent rushing to find fishing rods.

As *The Griffin* sailed slowly on, they finally started to notice signs of occupation. Several small canoes were sighted paddling in the shallows, but the occupants ignored their greetings and scuttled quickly back into the forest of branches when they got close. Mahra flew off

A Rude Reception

over the island, returning a short while later saying that nothing was visible through the thick forest canopy, but they were getting close to a harbour.

A Customs boat eventually came out to meet them and a stern official stepped on board as soon as the two boats came together and demanded to know what business they had on Minster. He rudely harrumphed their story of being traders and seemed ready to order his armed marines to force them to turn *The Griffin* around, but when Tarent produced the contract of trade he hesitantly apologised.

'A contract for business in Minster is hard to come by and I didn't expect to be seeing one on this...' he studied *The Griffin*, and its young crew, '...this fine vessel.' he finished with a sneer. 'May I ask how you came by it?'

'You may, but it *is* a contract legally entitling the bearer to conduct business here, is it not?' queried Tarent.

'It is,' replied the official.

'Then we are the bearer and wish to proceed into the harbour, we have business to conduct.'

The official regarded Tarent suspiciously. 'Are you refusing to tell me where you got this contract?'

'Well unfortunately, you came onto this boat acting in a rude and unprofessional manner. If a real official of this harbour wants to question us, in a polite way, then we'll be happy to answer any questions. Tell me. Who should I send my complaint to? There's a guild of Merchants in Freya, isn't there?' Tarent took up pen, ink and paper ready to write any details down.

'Complaint?' queried the official uncertainly.

'Yes complaint, what's your name?'

Sniggering could be heard coming from the Customs boat; evidently the marines were enjoying the exchange.

'Young man, please!' hissed the official, now worried. 'I'm sure you came by the contract legally, I'm not questioning that. It's just that we get so few, new traders here... you and your crew are most welcome.

We shall guide you in and I shall personally show you to your berth.' He pushed Tarent's pen aside and walked over to Quint at the wheel.

'Run this flag up your mast, it shows you are a legal trader here and can be admitted into the harbour.' He handed Quint a blue and white flag then shouted across to the Customs boat to get underway. After an oily smile to Tarent, whom he obviously took for the captain of this strange boat, he walked to the side rail and stood with his back to the crew, silently watching the island as it slipped past.

'What by the Source were you doing there, Tarent?' whispered Quint, 'He's going to make our lives a misery in Minster. We've got our first enemy and we haven't even arrived yet!'

'If he was to question us freely and look closely at that contract, a contract that Pardigan stole, don't forget, we may not even have got into Minster. We may have an enemy but at least we're getting into the harbour, aren't we?'

Quint shook his head and sighed. 'I suppose so, but you gave us all a fright.' He smiled at his friend. 'Well done.'

As they headed towards the harbour, Mahra hung over the side, mesmerised by all the fish swimming around the coral heads. When a turtle popped its head up above the water to watch them glide past, her hand was reaching out like a cat's paw, dabbing at the empty air in frustration, it was all Pardigan could do to hold on to her and stop her jumping in. The Customs official pretended not to notice.

Finally, as they passed around yet another forest-covered headland, Minster harbour came into view and the crew gazed at it, spellbound.

It was only as they got closer that they realised what it was that was so different. All the buildings, in fact everything, was made with trees. Not cut wood, but living trees. The jetties, the warehouses that lined the quayside, the whole town behind and houses over the hills, were all built from living trees with vines and flowers growing through them all. It wasn't so much that the forest had been cleared and a town built, but a town had been grown in, around and among the forest; everything was alive and beautiful.

directed into the harbour and up to a good mooring, close to the merchants' warehouses, and finally bid good day to their unwelcoming host who tipped his hat to Tarent, ignored the rest of the crew completely, and strode off into the town.

'I'd like to think we've seen the last of him but I very much doubt it,' said Quint. 'Let's go ashore and explore; we can unload the cargo tomorrow.'

The air was heavy with forest smells, rich and earthy, yet also sweet and perfumed from the many flowers. The flowers in turn were home to bees, humming birds and honey fishers that darted about competing for the abundant supply of nectar. Birds sang happily, clouds of butterflies hung in the warm air and groups of small monkeys chattered from branches, their community alive and flourishing amongst the townsfolk.

'What a beautiful place,' said Mahra in awe. 'This is a stronghold of Order, it has to be.'

'Well we met the agent of Chaos earlier, so the balance is alive and well,' said Tarent with a grin. 'It's a very strange place and no mistake. I wonder how they go about growing a building like this.' He was examining the corner post of a warehouse, that as well as supporting the roof also had branches coming out to form the large doors and several of the windows. Other trees were growing to make the other walls and beams and a thatch of branches and leaves formed the roof. It was hard to tell where the forest stopped and the town began.

It wasn't only the buildings that were strange, the inhabitants of Minster were an odd lot as well. For a start, the majority of people were no taller than Loras. Quint and Tarent towered over everyone yet they weren't being stared at, so traders must be fairly common here. Everyone they met seemed polite, and several offered an 'Evenin',' the men touching a finger to their hats and the women dropping in a small curtsy. All the menfolk had beards, with all but the youngests' being fluffy white. Below their beards they wore tight waistcoats over white lacy shirts and most were trying to balance tall black hats on their heads, many of which being almost as tall as the wearer. The Minsten women had their hair in plaits and wore long flower-patterned dresses, buttoned high to their necks, and all the Minstens had bright red cheeks, making it seem as if the entire population was walking around slightly embarrassed.

The crew of *The Griffin* ambled on past the last of the warehouses and on into the main town. There didn't seem to be any order to the streets with buildings springing up where you might expect a road to continue. All in all it was a magical mixture of life that appeared to get on perfectly.

They bought hot honey filled pastries wrapped in large leaves from a shop, and sat down to munch them as they studied their surroundings. Several non-islanders walked past, most seemed to be heading towards a large building built in and around a massive, and clearly ancient, oak tree.

Quint stood up, sucking honey from his fingers. 'I think we've found the local version of Blake's, my friends. Let's mingle, and try and find out as much as we can about Minster and any reference to the mysterious Hidden.'

Tarent handed them each a few coins and he and Quint walked over to the inn where a large sign hung from a branch of an old tree, proclaiming it to be 'The Acorn Forest Inn.'

'Well I think it's been a fair few years since this was an acorn,' observed Tarent. 'This thing looks like it's been growing forever.' They gazed up through the mass of branches, many of which grew into the building to help make up the beams, walls and roof. Other branches went off in other directions, aiding with the construction of several neighbouring buildings and providing the chattering monkeys with a highway in the sky.

'She's an old un is The Acorn, that she is,' cackled a little old Minsten through his thick white beard. He blew out a stream of smoke drawn from a long-stemmed clay pipe. 'Why, the Acorn is the centre of Minster life and folklore. Any story about Minster worth telling will either start or end at the Acorn. Indeed, the very best stories start *and* end at the Acorn.' He giggled at his wit and took a long gulp from a tin mug of ale, and then drew several times on his pipe to get it glowing good and hot before blowing out another huge cloud of smoke. 'Why then I suppose it must follow that the very, very best stories start in, end at, and are all about the Acorn, stands to reason really... if yer get ter think'n about it much.' He drained his mug of ale and upended it, looking at the bottom as if another drop may be holding on in a corner. He gazed over at Quint and Tarent. 'Now if you young gents would like a tale of the Acorn, I would be right happy to oblige... if yer could see yer way to fillin' me mug agen.' He smiled hopefully.

'We'd love to hear about the Acorn and all about Minster,' said Quint. 'We've only just arrived and know nothing about it. What are you drinking?'

'Why Elder ale of course, tis the very best ale in the known world and that's a fact.' The old fellow smiled happily. 'The name's Feneggin. Now, you get me that ale and let's get acquainted.' He held a chair out which Tarent took while Quint went in to get the drinks.

The interior of the Acorn was gloomy and it took a few moments for Quint's eyes to become accustomed to it. Daylight was trying to come in through several small windows, but a thick curtain of green leaves was hindering it. Small flickering lamps were set on every table and others were attached to the walls adding to the 'twilight' feel of the room. Smoke rose from the lamps as well as from the long pipes that many of the drinkers were puffing on and Quint held a deep breath before walking in further through the gloom.

A long serving bar ran along the far wall with several people standing and talking over the music, played by a motley assortment of musicians in the corner. The music was unlike anything Quint had heard before. Three Minstens were blowing horns of some kind, stuffed onto lips lost in waves of fluffy white beard. Each was given to standing up once in a while and blowing an especially complicated mixture of noises. As they did so, their cheeks puffed out and their faces creased in concentration. The one standing now was blowing so hard it seemed to Quint that there must be a bee stuck in the horn which the player was furiously trying to dislodge with every breath he could muster; the sound that filled the room was high pitched and wailing.

The drummer, who played an assortment of drums, gongs and even bottles filled with different amounts of liquid dangling on a frame, was too tall to be a local. He had long scraggy white hair, was dressed head to foot in black and wore a sombre expression. He in turn was given to mad bursts of drumming that didn't really seem to be part of what anyone else was playing. After each eruption of sound he would go back to a steady rhythm and stare straight at the wall, as if the outburst hadn't happened at all and he'd deny any knowledge of it if ever asked.

The final member of the band was another Minsten. He was standing up on a stool, his eyes closed in concentration while playing a large heavy wooden instrument with strings. He hugged it close to his body, the fingers of one hand flying up and down the neck pressing hard on the strings while the other hand plucked furiously lower down, coaxing deep thrumming sounds from within. Unfortunately, while the little man played, he was getting his beard tangled up and was constantly stopping to untangle himself mid tune.

Quint walked over to the bar and was joined a few moments later by Pardigan.

'What a weird place, eh? Have you seen the band?' Pardigan was doing all he could not to giggle at the efforts of the musicians. 'They're rubbish!'

'Tarent and I are outside with some old man who's going to tell us about the island,' said Quint. 'Where are the other two?'

'I saw Tarent as we came in. Loras is watching the band over there,' Pardigan indicated a table that Loras was sitting at, watching the antics on stage. 'While Mahra is with me over at the table by that group of younger Minstens, at least I think they're younger, it's hard to tell when they've all got beards.'

'Well good luck, see what you can find out and have a good time. Oh, and look out for Loras, will you?' Quint's last words were drowned out by the drummer playing a long solo on the glass bottles ending with a smash as one flew to pieces sending liquid all over a horn player.

A Rude Reception

The drummer faced the wall again and continued tapping out a slow rhythm as if none of this had happened. Loras turned around and grinned over at them in delight.

Clutching a tray of drinks, Quint made his way outside to the table.

Tarent glanced up as he set the tray down. 'Feneggin here was telling me about the Hidden folk, they've all apparently gone from Minster now but he was saying he remembers them well.'

'Oh, I remember the Hidden all right,' said Feneggin, accepting his ale. 'Call themselves that but they weren't hiding much back then. Was about twenty summers since we saw the last one here at the Acorn.' He sucked noisily on his pipe. 'See this has the makings of a good story already, cos we started at the Acorn see.' He smiled. 'They used to come in and trade in those days. You had to keep your eyes on them, funny little things the Hidden, smelt strange and were filthy dirty. Anyhow, one night an awful fight broke out. Two local boys got to drinking and there was an argument with one of their traders. Well, they're only little people the Hidden, so these two strapping great Minstens shouldn't have done what they did, should they?'

Tarent glanced at Quint; neither could help but smile at the thought of this little Minsten calling anyone else small or calling any Minsten strapping for that matter.

If he noticed anything, Feneggin didn't say, he simply continued. 'The Hidden may have a nasty reputation but it's just talk n' rubbish really. They used to get accused of just about anything that went wrong, from stealing babies to cakes getting burnt, never any proof of course, and this one was minding his own business apparently.' He sucked noisily on his pipe and gazed up at the tree remembering.

'So what did they do to him?'

'Well they hung him by his boots from the tree here.' They glanced up at the branches to where Feneggin was pointing his pipe.

'And?' asked Quint.

'And, ain't no *and* about it,' said Feneggin frowning. 'Just hung him up, don't rightly remember why. The landlord cut him down a little while later and he skulked off back into the forest. But none of the Hidden came back into Minster again after that, reckon they was insulted. Just faded right back into legend they did.' He stared into his pipe and laid it on the table. 'Nobody really misses them mind, quite horrible to look at they were.' He gave an exaggerated shudder. 'They're the ones used to bring the Elder ale.' He looked down at his mug, a frown creasing his face. 'My sister's cat went missing a few summers back, never gave it much thought really, but that could have been the Hidden. I mean, they say they eat cats, don't they?'

'Well if they don't come into Minster now, how come you're still drinking Elder ale?' asked Quint, ignoring the mention of cats.

Feneggin glanced up. 'Good question, but I don't rightly know, youngster, don't rightly know at all, but got me to thinking you 'ave. Best you ask ol' Drabert the landlord 'bout that.'

They sat talking with Feneggin for some time then Pardigan and Mahra came out to join them when the music inside became too much to bear.

'Loras actually likes it,' said Pardigan incredulously. 'He's really getting quite into it.' Quint disappeared for a while to talk with Drabert the landlord, and after more drinks and plates of fish stew with crusty bread, they made their way back to *The Griffin*, quite content with their evening.

The sun was well down by the time they got on board, with Loras remembering at the last moment to cancel the guard spell and mutter 'Griffin Griffin Griffin,' as they walked up the gangplank. Sitting around the table they talked about their day and what they'd learned. Drabert, the landlord, had said someone called trader Jack brought in the Elder ale, and he was next due in two days, so the best thing to do was probably to wait for his arrival.

They chatted for some time, then as they all began to yawn, Mahra offered to watch over the boat through the night. The gangplank was pulled in as a precaution against intruders, and they turned in ready for an early start. With a stride towards the hatch, Mahra transformed into the familiar shape of the owl and flew out and up, into the night towards the stars.

A Rude Reception

Watching her go was a black raven, its beady eyes glowing red as it watched her fly off, silhouetted against the moon. It glanced down towards the boat and cawed, its head leaning from one side to the other. Its eyes flashed red once more before it flew off towards the open sea and a distant speck of light briefly flashing on the horizon.

Chapter 13

A Minsten Tale

The next morning the crew once again rose early. Pardigan and Loras went straight off for bread, milk and buns while Tarent and Quint went in search of the warehouseman that their contact in Sterling Port had said would be a sure buyer of their goods. True to his word, the trader in Minster was excited to hear they carried fire pitch and quickly struck a bargain with Tarent, making *The Griffin* a tidy profit. He took the other goods in with the deal and sent two of his workers along with a portable wooden crane to unload.

'The name's Maginty,' he said, shaking hands enthusiastically with both boys in turn. 'If you want a regular run, just bring me ooh, say fifteen to twenty barrels of pitch every three months and we could all make a tidy packet.' His eyes sparkled and his big red cheeks pushed out in a smile, not quite concealed, behind the usual fluffy white beard. They agreed to return in three months with a new load, then questioned him about the island. Maginty was happy to chat.

'Most trade goes on here in the harbour. There are one or two outlying settlements, and a native tribe or two, but the fire pitch is for use in this harbour. Maybe one or two shops will sell it in smaller amounts, but only once it's been refined down to lamp oil.'

'What about the Hidden we've heard about, does anybody trade with them?' asked Quint.

Maginty's smile dropped and he fluffed his beard nervously. 'Now who's been toying with you, telling you old stories of the Hidden, eh? Course there *are* stories that long ago a race of little people lived on Minster, out in hiding, guarding some great dark secret. Supposed ter be that if one touches you, bad luck will follow you all day long, but it's only stories boys, really. That ain't the reason we got a fence all round the town, not the reason at all.'

Quint glanced at the little man who appeared to be getting more uncomfortable all the time. 'So why is the fence there then?'

Maginty frowned. 'The one to talk to is Trader Jack if you want to know about the island past the town limits.'

'He's the trader that brings the Acorn its ale, isn't he?' asked Tarent.

'That'll be him.' Maginty glanced back behind his warehouse to where a tall fence separated the town from the trees. 'Brave to walk the island, I don't envy old Jack much...not that I believe in the Hidden of course, just ain't right thas all.'

'Haven't you ever been around the island?' asked Quint in amazement.

'No I have not! Nor would I, nor would any Minsten for that matter. There are strict rules as to who can go where and do what, been in place thousands of years.' Maginty appeared shocked that anyone would be so stupid as to suggest roaming the island and busily stroked his beard to calm himself.

'Well who would stop you?' asked Quint.

'Well first commonsense, and then there's Customs,' said Maginty, as if that ended the matter. 'Now if you young gents don't mind I've got to get on, I've got a business to run.' He started to go then turned back again. 'See you in three months with more fire pitch then?'

'Surely you will, Mr Maginty,' replied Quint, 'and thanks for your time this morning.' Maginty left them with a wave and the boys walked on.

'Well I can guess which Customs man stops people coming and going on the inland path, can't you?'

'Yeah, that would be our friend from the welcoming committee.' Tarent shrugged. 'So what are we going to do?'

'Well tomorrow we're going to try and find Trader Jack and see what he has to say. There's not much point trying to form a plan until we've met him.'

They spent the day exploring and picking up a few of the local goods to sell back in Freya and Sterling. The local craftsmen made wonderful furniture, toys and wooden boxes, and the boys stocked up to help with their cover story. Bringing goods in was obviously a profitable run, but there didn't seem to be much to trade back out again; nothing in Minster was in demand back on the mainland.

They spotted the Customs man several times, snooping about, possibly spying on them, but when Tarent waved at him and made to walk over, he scurried off in another direction to annoy someone else. Boats came and went in the harbour and they kept a watchful eye for the big merchant vessel. They knew it was close behind them, but their luck was holding and nothing arrived to upset their day.

The crew had a great time exploring Minster town. The people were extremely pleasant and hospitable, but when they asked anyone about the Hidden they were either laughed at or the subject was changed as quickly as possible. They rounded their day off once more at the Acorn Forest Inn, chatting with Feneggin and some of the other locals. The musicians were playing inside, but it was only Loras that sat watching them.

'I can't understand what you can enjoy in that din,' said Pardigan when Loras finally came out and joined them. 'They're all playing different tunes, it's horrible.'

'The drummer's playing three different tunes all on his own,' joined in Tarent. 'I'm only glad there isn't a singer with them, and I'm sure that the bass player has really just discovered a complicated way to pluck his beard.' This drew laughs from the rest of the table and Loras blushed.

'Well I like them. Haven't you noticed that they all sort of play together, then one or two may stop and allow one of the others to take the music in a new direction? That's really clever.'

They all stared at him, somewhat lost for words. 'Is that what you really hear: one song with lots of directions, not a mad jumble of nonsense?' said Pardigan in a shocked voice.

'Give it a go,' said Loras, standing and heading back to the door.

'I think I'd be scared to go and listen now. I'd hate to think I could actually start liking that noise. I'm quite comfortable disliking it.' Pardigan settled further into his chair.

'Don't you worry, young'un, just you be staying right there and I'll go and get the next round of drinks. I'm not a big fan of the Acorn's band mind, but they work hard, and I reckon I'm brave enough to listen on the way to the bar.' Feneggin smiled at Pardigan through his beard. 'Course, if you were going in there in the first place, you would still be wanting to pay, wouldn't you?' He stood and held out his hand.

Pardigan stared up at Feneggin in amazement and before he knew what he was doing, he was passing over some coins. Feneggin closed his hand and marched inside before Pardigan could come to his senses.

'I would swear I wasn't about to go in there at all,' he whispered to Quint. 'I think he just tricked me.'

Quint put his arm around Pardigan's shoulder. 'Maybe it's magic, my friend.' He was trying hard to keep a straight face, which Pardigan saw and poked him in the ribs.

'You know Quint, I think we should trade here when all this is over, this isn't such a bad life. That contract will still be good. We could trade between here and Sterling, then back to Freya before returning here. We'd have a real business and a good life.'

'Well we could as long as we were a step or two ahead of Merchant Bask all the time. He knows it was us that got his stuff and he didn't look that friendly the last time we saw him, did he?' Both boys glanced over at the harbour, but no ships were coming in.

'Oh yes, I forgot about him,' said Pardigan, grimacing.

'Well I doubt he's forgotten us,' replied Quint. '...unfortunately.'

*\ated**

It had taken the best part of two days to figure out and then fix the problem with the *Esmerelda*, Bartholomew Bask's proud trading vessel. Bartholomew had seethed with fury the whole time, making life for the captain and crew miserable. Comments and jokes had been constantly hurled from the group of locals that had been in attendance ever since the entertainment had begun. No amount of threatening and glaring from Bartholomew had shifted them and he'd spent the entire two days taking the brunt of their humour and ridicule personally. That, of course, had delighted the crowd and the insults had become more and more personal. Bartholomew had risen to their baiting as the jests were once again aimed at him, rising to a peak when they eventually worked out that the problem was with the anchor so cut the chain, the boat righted itself and everyone on board was flung to the deck.

'Finally moved yer dinner plate from that side of the boat did yer, porky?' shouted a youth and the crowd howled with laughter.

'Old fatso must have been drying his undershorts and they just fell overboard, ain't that so, blubber butt!'

It had taken Bartholomew most of the two days to realise that when he shouted and threatened the crowd, it only made things worse, so he was now trying to restrict his fury to the captain and crew. Once the anchor chain was cut, he glared at the captain and yelled, 'Get us out of here and underway immediately, you incompetent fool,' then returned to glowering at the crowd, ignoring the captain's efforts to say something.

'The diet worked I see, you must be hungry again, have a bun.' A stale cinnamon bun was hurled up, falling short of Bartholomew and bouncing along the deck, accompanied by laughter from the crowd.

'Damn and blast you all, I'll see yer all in irons before I'm done. I'll remember you…and you …and you…and…' He took some time pointing and shouting to the amusement of the crowd until, finally spent; he turned and sat down heavily on the deck. It was then that he noticed the captain.

'Begging yer pardon, Merchant Bask, but we can't go to sea without an anchor, it would be completely foolhardy. And an anchor for a ship the size of the *Esmerelda* will mean going ashore to get one made...' He saluted, waiting hopefully for Bartholomew then edged back into his First Mate as Bartholomew's trembling face became red enough to explode.

'Anchor! What do I need with a Source-damned anchor when I can use you!' Leaping to his feet, which was no easy feat for such a large man, Bartholomew grabbed the captain by his collar and leggings, lifted him over his head, and threw the startled seaman over the side. The crowd on the dockside rolled around slapping their sides in mirth and for once, none of them could muster the breath to hurl more abuse at him. Bartholomew glared down at them then at the spluttering shape of the captain splashing in the water below and sat down again with his head in his hands.

By contrast, the last couple of days had actually passed fairly pleasantly for Matheus Hawk. His initial fury at being bested by a group of mere children had subsided as he'd watched the antics of Bartholomew Bask and his crew. Matheus had taken a room at a small boarding house close by and taken great delight in watching Bartholomew being baited and teased. He was almost disappointed when he saw them cut away the anchor allowing the boat to spring upright. He had worked out what the magician brat had done a few hours after *The Griffin* had slipped port but was enjoying the entertainment far too much to enlighten the crew himself. He knew where *The Griffin* was heading, and they would catch up soon enough, meanwhile the entertainment was simply too good to pass up.

He checked out of his room and made his way through the crowd to the boat where he passed the ship's captain making his way back on deck after his swim.

'Out of my way, yer weasel,' growled Matheus, brushing past the wet seaman. He'd watched the man bullied and abused since they had first boarded the *Esmerelda* back in Freya, and had no respect for anyone that wouldn't or couldn't stick up for themselves. The man was a sorry excuse for a captain. Matheus glared at him. 'So are we getting underway?'

'We are,' responded the captain, tugging on his shrinking jacket and attempting to pull himself together.

'And to where are we bound?'

'I haven't been advised of our next destination. I only hope it is to some harbour and not an anchorage as we currently have no anchor,' said the captain, unhappily wringing water from his lace sleeves, as a crewman handed him the sodden remains of his hat.

'We're heading for the Island of Minster, and we will indeed be required to anchor.' Matheus made to walk off, then turned back to the dripping man. 'For the sake of this voyage and the Source, pull yourself together man, get dry and start acting like a captain.' He threw his bags to a sailor and strode over to Bartholomew who was intently studying a chart. Matheus stabbed a finger down and indicated Minster. 'We're going there, because that's where your thieves went.'

'How do you know?' Bartholomew's face was sweaty and fatigued. The last week had taken its toll on him yet he still remained cautious and somewhat polite with the Hawk.

'Let's just say a demon told me.'

The *Esmerelda* slipped out of Sterling Port shortly after sunrise, three days delayed, but once again on the trail of *The Griffin* and its crew. As Bartholomew Bask and Matheus Hawk stood with the captain on the wheel deck, a black raven came flapping down and landed on the wheel, making the helmsman jump. It hopped across with a *'kaauww'* and sat on Matheus's shoulder drawing a cursory glance from Bartholomew while the captain, quite sensibly, kept his eyes forward. Matheus reached up to stroke its black feathers and it nipped his finger. He uttered a curse but let it alone - it wasn't actually his bird.

* * *

A Minsten Tale

The arrival of Trader Jack was obviously a cause for celebration. The trader headed a small caravan of three clonking wagons piled high with all manner of goods and products. They halted and made a camp cum market outside of the Acorn and were immediately surrounded by a small crowd of eager onlookers. One wagon was filled with barrels that were destined for the inn while the other two held a mixture of the trader's possessions and marketable goods. Trader Jack himself was not a Minsten, which was the first thing that struck *The Griffin's* crew as they watched from a table outside the Acorn. He was taller, and appeared to be from the mainland. The second thing that struck them was that he wasn't apt to doing much work himself. He had three helpers with him who drove the wagons, cared for the oxen that pulled them, as well as unloading the barrels and setting up the stalls to display the goods.

More townsfolk began to emerge wearing their best clothes and Trader Jack set to doing what he did best; he sold. His patter was fine, his delivery perfect. He flattered the ladies and complimented the men, gave sweets to the children and had a roving eye, searching out the buyers from the crowd.

'Ladies and gentlemen, boys and girls, I come here today with news and goods from the far distant corners of this island of ours.' He beamed at the crowd. 'We have fine fabrics from the north, fresh fruits from the east, precious stones and jewellery from the west. What we don't have isn't worth having, which is why we don't have it. So step up and treat yourselves, you just know you want to.' Again, he stopped and beamed at the crowd, many of whom had been saying the words with him; they'd heard them so many times before.

'Four Corners of the island! How big do they think this place is?' Pardigan smiled at the trader's antics. 'We sailed around most of it in less than a day, didn't we?'

'Don't forget what that warehouseman, Maginty said, most of these people haven't been outside of this town their entire lives, they have no idea how big the island is,' said Tarent, watching the trader intently. 'Trader Jack is a salesman, and salesmen like making deals. I think

I'll have a word with him later; maybe we'll be able to come to some arrangement.'

Barrels of Elder ale were rolled into the Acorn and then a good business was transacted from the stalls with the local people. After some time, the crowd thinned out and Tarent managed to draw the trader to one side and a discussion was started that had both of them smiling, frowning and gesturing wildly at various points, until Tarent abruptly turned on his heels and walked back to his friends at the table.

'What's the matter, is he pretending the Hidden don't exist or something?' asked Quint.

'Oh he says they exist, and that if we're crazy enough to want to go, then he'll take us. He just doesn't want to be seen doing it, case he loses his licence to trade.

'If we can get out and meet them further up the path, he'll take us for five gold pieces.'

Pardigan spluttered into his mug. 'Five gold pieces...is he mad?'

'No, he's a salesman, and that's a very good deal for asking him to do something highly illegal and, in his mind, incredibly stupid. It's up to us to get out of here and meet him on the other side of the gate. The problem is, the gate is locked, and guess who has the key?'

'Your friend the Customs man, of course,' muttered Pardigan. 'Don't worry I'll get the key, leave it to me.'

'That's what I hoped you'd say,' said Tarent. 'Our other problem is we have to move *The Griffin*, or it'll be obvious we're not here. If *The Griffin* is still at anchor and we're not seen around town, they'll know we've gone past the gate and we'll have problems when we come back.'

'Well maybe there's some way that we won't have to move her,' said Loras drifting off in thought. The others left him to it, enjoying the afternoon's entertainment, trusting in Loras's ability to do whatever was necessary with *The Griffin*.

Trader Jack and his wagons left for the interior two days after arriving in town and that same morning *The Griffin* was also seen to leave, heading for open sea. The Customs man was greatly relieved. He hadn't liked the scruffy little boat and its young crew and had sent letters to Freya asking for verification of the trading contract but wasn't expecting a reply for weeks. All in all it was best they were gone and no longer his problem. What he didn't see was one of the Minsten fishing boats limping back into port some time later, well before the rest of the small fleet, and tying up in a far corner. It was *The Griffin* having been disguised both physically and magically.

The crew had sailed east a short while then anchored up and changed the look of the boat, not in any great way, but enough so that it appeared to be different. Loras had added some spells to help make people believe that it was one of the normal fleet and they had sailed back in with only Quint on deck. The spell worked so well that even the harbourmaster ignored them as Quint tied up. They then sat below deck spending a hot and uncomfortable day out of sight, waiting for nightfall and an opportunity to move.

Chapter 14

Finding the Hidden

The moon had long risen, bathing the island in a soft magical light, the harbour and streets long deserted. Even the band at the Acorn had gone home before *The Griffin*'s crew finally chanced to walk into town.

Mahra flew ahead, ready to warn of any late-night wanderers, as Pardigan practised his invisibility, from time to time flickering into view with a curse as he struggled to hold the spell. So it was three, then sometimes four people that headed past the Acorn and on towards the gated path.

The gate, when they reached it, was over twice the height of any of them and was inevitably made of wood. Wrapped around the two central poles was a thick metal chain and padlock with a sign that none of them could read. A small black and white house stood close by, a lamp burning in an upstairs window.

'He's still awake,' hissed Tarent.

Pardigan peered up at the window. 'No problem, I'll see you later.' He blinked out of sight and crossed the road. The others crouched down in the shade of a tree, out of the bright moonlight, watched over by a large owl, its eyes blinking and its head swivelling as it peered all around.

Pardigan skirted the house and saw his way in almost immediately; a downstairs window had been left slightly ajar allowing air into the pantry. He pushed up the latch with his knife and slipped over the sill.

Landing softly he stopped, listening, every sense tingling as he waited for sound, but the house was silent. He allowed himself to relax a little, stood and looked around the small pantry. A large cheese sat under a mesh dome and Pardigan cut a slice and stuffed it into his mouth as he moved to the door. It creaked as he opened it and he froze. A ginger cat had lifted its head and was staring at him. His last encounter with a cat had turned out to be Mahra, so he didn't take this one's presence for granted, especially when it followed his invisible progress across the kitchen as if it could see him. The kitchen opened out onto a small hallway with a staircase going up to bedrooms above and two other doors, one of which he carefully opened and slipped through.

A writing desk covered with papers stood centrally with two cabinets to either side. Glancing out of the window, he could just make out the shapes of his friends by the tree opposite and he stifled the impulse to hold back the curtain and wave. He had been hoping the key would be lying on a desk or hung on a wall, but after a brief search, it was obvious that there were no keys in the study at all. The next room, a small sitting room was quickly searched and no keys found; it must be upstairs.

Mahra returned from a short flight and landed on a branch above the boys' heads. 'Have you seen him yet?' Her voice was strange and hooting as an owl.

'No, no sign, he's been in there for a while now but he'll be okay.' Quint sounded confident in his friend's abilities. 'Did you fly up the path and see if the traders are there?'

'Oh they're there. The wagons are all grouped together and they're playing music.' Her head twisted to stare at Loras, her eyes blinked. 'It's much better music than that awful noise in the Acorn.'

'Oh and an owl is going to know good music when it hears it,' retorted Loras with a grin, his teeth white in the moonlight.

Mahra ignored him and took off; gliding across to the house she landed and peered into the upper window.

The Customs man was sitting upright in his bed; his glasses propped on his nose and a huge pile of papers in front of him. He was working in fits and starts. Waking from sleep he would push his glasses back up his nose, take a few pages, enter some figures in the ledger then sleep would reclaim him, his head would slump and papers would fall.

Pardigan was watching from the bottom of the bed, waiting for his moment to take the keys he could see on the bedside cabinet. He was invisible but could see Mahra peering through the window and became visible for a moment as his concentration dropped and she jumped back in a flurry of feathers. Fortunately for Pardigan, the sleeper continued to sleep and missed what would have been a scary moment for all three of them.

The Customs man awoke once more and scrabbled about, spilling some papers onto the floor in the process. Pardigan decided to sit down with his back to the base of the bed and wait for a better moment to make his move.

The decision came when the hard wooden floor had finally made his legs feel numb. He stood and peered over the bottom of the bed. The Customs man was asleep again with his head flopped to one side and a thin line of dribble falling from his mouth. Pardigan smiled and whispered, 'Hide.' He flickered invisible and crept around to the bedside cabinet. Making sure not to step on the fallen papers, he gently picked up the large bunch of keys and with a last glance at the sleeping form he crept carefully out of the room.

He only became visible again when he was standing in front of his friends, making Quint fall back and all three of them jump in surprise.

Pardigan held out the keys, a grin on his face. 'Let's go find the Hidden.'

Grabbing the keys, Quint slapped Pardigan's arm. 'Nice job, but don't go sneaking up on us like that, eh. I almost wet myself.' He walked to the gate and peered around. Seeing that Mahra was perched on the house keeping watch, he tried several keys in the lock, found one that fit, turned it and the lock sprang open easily. He waved them over and they silently slipped through to the other side. Pardigan stayed and beckoned for the key.

Quint held it out. 'Silly question maybe, but how do you plan to get over?'

'Don't worry,' whispered Pardigan, 'I've got that covered.' He re-looped the chain, clicked the lock back into position, and then blinked back to invisibility.

Returning to the house he made his way back to the bedroom and was glad to see its occupant still fast asleep. He replaced the keys on the bedside table and, feeling rather smug, made for the door. Unfortunately, the perfect burglary came to an end as his foot disturbed the fallen papers and the sleeper awoke with a start. Pardigan froze less than an arm's length away, the sound of his heartbeat loud in his ears.

'Who's there?' called the Customs man in a frightened voice. He sat up and felt around for his glasses.

Pardigan stopped breathing and didn't move a muscle.

'Is somebody there?' Swinging his legs out of the bed, the opposite side to where Pardigan was standing, he walked to the door. 'Hello?' he gingerly peeked into the hallway before venturing further out.

Pardigan let out his breath and lifted his foot from the papers. The constant effort of holding the invisibility spell, and the tension of the ordeal, was beginning to tire him. He was feeling faint and was sweating freely. I've got to get out of here soon or I'm going to blow this, he thought. He took a couple of deep breaths. Hold steady now... get a grip, not long and we're out. The self-encouragement helped and he started to regain control. Noises were drifting up from below and he decided to take his chance on the stairs. They creaked a little in several places but he made it to the bottom without being discovered.

The Customs man was in the kitchen making himself a sandwich, talking to the cat as it brushed up against his leg, purring for a saucer of milk. Pardigan slipped past into the pantry without a problem.

Once out of the window he slumped down, becoming visible then wiped his face on his cloak and finally allowed himself to relax.

'Are you okay?' whispered Mahra. She was standing over him in her human form, calmly scanning for observers.

'I think so, or I will be as soon as we get to the other side of that gate. I have to be somewhere high to shift across. I need to see where I'm going.'

Mahra helped him to his feet and they walked around to the side of the building. It felt good to be outside even if it wasn't much cooler than inside the house. She helped him climb to the top of an outbuilding, which was an easier and less noisy climb than the roof of the house. Once on top, Pardigan could see his friends standing in the moonlight watching anxiously for his arrival. With the last of his energy, he place-shifted, appearing so fast in front of Quint that his friend once again found himself sitting on the ground staring up at him with a shocked expression. Mahra landed softly beside them, changing once more from an owl to a smiling girl. She stared down at Quint.

'Are you still resting?'

Quint glared up at her then at Pardigan, who murmured an apology.

'Sorry, Quint, I didn't mean to make you jump this time.' He slumped to the ground exhausted and Quint's anger turned to concern for his friend. Helping him up, he half carried him down the path until they rounded a bend and were able to rest without being seen from the gate.

After taking a drink and receiving a little healing energy from Loras, Pardigan began to feel better and was soon able to walk unaided. The forest was dense and oppressive, but the path in comparison, was wide and clear of obstructions making it easy to follow in the moonlight. Night birds sang and an occasional monkey chattered at them, unseen in the trees.

Quint led while Mahra remained at the back, padding along silently as a Panther, a low growl sounding from her every now and then as she sensed something watching from the gloom. The camp came into view fairly quickly and one of the helpers who had been keeping watch rose warily to greet them. He was a small man even by Minsten standards, coming not much higher than Quint's waist. His lank hair almost covered his eyes and he was smiling, or leering, at them through a mask of dirt. His clothing was little more than animal skins crudely stitched together. He was absently pulling at what passed for a shirt as if it itched. Rubbing his hands together, he licked his lips and readied himself to greet them.

'Greetings...visitors, come in come in,' his said in a voice that was thin and whining. His teeth were crooked and pointed, and his pink tongue flicked nervously between thin lips as he gestured for them to enter the camp. 'I've been anticipating your arrival,' he simpered. 'You're the first travellers that have...requested to visit my people in many years, interesting, yes very interesting. You weren't scared by the stories? We know all about the stories.' He began mumbling as he assessed the crew with critical beady eyes. 'Nasty stories...not true...poor Hidden,' he wiped his nose with the back of his hand then reached out and squeezed Loras's arm, only to scuttle back as Loras pulled away.

'Oh where are my manners, I am Groober, partner of Trader Jack.' Thin bony hands darted out to clasp Quint's in an attempt at welcome, then quickly moved back to Loras. 'I like you,' he smiled, his tongue squeezing between his teeth.

'You're one of the Hidden! You keep away from me!' said Loras stepping back, amazed that he hadn't noticed the helpers were Hidden when the caravan was camped outside the Acorn. Now that he realised, the differences were more than apparent. The Hidden were much thinner than the Minstens who were almost as short, but more stocky in comparison. Groober was beardless, very dirty, and had a longer narrow nose; his lips were thinner than the Minstens as well. The little creature's eyes were darting nervously about him and he was shuffling his feet uncomfortably as if worried that they might attack him at any moment.

'I won't harm you! The Hidden are good people, not like the stories, nasty stories. For some reason Trader Jack makes us wash and change clothes before we enter the town,' whined Groober unhappily as he tried to explain the difference in his appearance. 'We do not like to bathe because the trees do not bathe, nor do the animals. This we know appears strange to outsiders, so Trader Jack makes us wash.' His nose crinkled in distaste. 'But it's perfectly natural and is the way the Source intended us to be, but you're right, I am indeed proud to be one of the Hidden. Come into our camp and be seated.' He ushered them towards the fire area.

'We've been waiting for you and now that you're here we can leave at first light. Trader Jack is sleeping and I wouldn't wish to wake him. We Hidden need only a little sleep and can go days without the need to rest,' he explained. 'He is human and not as young as he used to be so needs his sleep. My friends Serik and Char are about here somewhere looking for food.' He tried to smile at the group before him, but it appeared to make them even more uncomfortable, so he stopped and decided to try a little bow. 'We are the Hidden, do not fear us, we simply remain...a little different perhaps than others you have met. We are an ancient race, both noble and peaceful. Do not judge us until you know us...please.'

'Now, are you in need of sleep or maybe refreshment of some kind?' He pounced upon a bag and started to dig around, bobbing up a moment later to offer a hunk of something brown and greasy wrapped in a large leaf. All eyes fell on the offering as Groober held it out, his hand shaking as he saw they weren't going to take it. 'Woodcake...it's made of all the very best things in the forest...it's very good.' He bit into it and tried the smile again, which was a mistake.

'Er, thank you...but no,' said Pardigan tearing his eyes away. He untied his bedroll as the others dropped their bags around the fire. 'I'm going to sleep but I'm sure Loras will stay up and chat with you, and I bet he would like to try woodcake.'

Loras tried to decline but Quint whispered in his ear. 'Someone has to stay up and keep an eye on these...people. I'll relieve you in a turn or two.' Loras nodded unhappily but waved away the proffered woodcake with an apologetic look. 'I am not eating that...stuff,' he whispered. 'It looks like there might be worms in it!'

Pardigan lay down and Quint and Tarent began unrolling bedrolls close by. Loras and Mahra both stayed with Groober by the fire as the little man glanced about him nervously. He appeared sad and was pitifully shy, but brightened a little when two other Hidden, supposedly Serik and Char, appeared out of the forest without any warning clutching armloads of roots and fungus. They skirted around the seated figures keeping their eyes downcast, only glancing over timidly as they stored their finds in the back of a wagon. When Groober finally plucked up courage and asked Loras about life outside of Minster, the two other Hidden quietly crept over and all three cuddled up together to listen.

Loras began by telling them of Freya and Sterling, of the bustling cities made of stone and Sterling's great colourful Dhurbar caravans. When he told them of The Isle of Skulls with its perpetual storms and the cold solemn Academy, the little Hidden held each other closely. Seeing their reaction he refrained from any mention of demons, skulls or skeletons.

Mahra listened and watched. She wasn't sure what to make of the Hidden, they were strange creatures, with their toothy grins, greasy dirty hair and dark beady eyes, but the more she observed them, the more she felt they couldn't be the monsters that legends described. They were behaving like three small children, not three small monsters.

Loras finished his tale, and the three Hidden reluctantly told stories of Minster Island and their people who had lived in hiding since time began. They told of how, many generations ago, the Hidden were charged with the sacred duty of remaining in seclusion, cut off from the outside world, never to mix with the world of man. With pride they told of how their little caravan was the only exception as it travelled around the island.

'The humans live in Minster Port and we trade with them for goods from the outside world. We make or grow all the things we really need and don't crave many things that we can't produce ourselves, except certain... exceptional items, but those can usually be found in Minster,' said Char smiling.

At least Mahra *thought* it was a smile.

They explained how they were ruled over by a king and that they would take *The Griffin's* crew to meet him. 'Anyone who comes into the lands of the Hidden has to meet the king,' said Groober rubbing his hands together happily. 'You'll be the first outsiders to meet him since he met Trader Jack many, many years ago. *He* wasn't scared by the nasty stories of us, and now neither are you.' He appeared delighted by this.

'Which stories?' asked Loras in a worried tone.

'Oh you know...stories...there are many. They are horrible...horrible. We Hidden are a noble race, we eat only roots and what the forest provides; we don't eat birds or squirrels or...or...babies and cats!'

Char reached an arm around her friend to comfort him. 'Just stupid nasty stories to scare little children; they will see the truth of it.' Groober nodded, then his face lit up and he jammed more greasy woodcake into his mouth, offering some to Loras again. He appeared disappointed when Loras shook his head again.

'But they don't believe the stories, do you?' Bits of brown, half-chewed woodcake dropped from his mouth as he started to giggle. 'You visit the Hidden, the Hidden will like you.'

'Oh they will,' confirmed Serik, pouring some brew for them, he patted Char's arm.

'We were told something happened at the Acorn?' asked Loras.

'Loras!' hissed Mahra. 'Maybe you shouldn't be talking about that.'

'No, it's all right,' replied Char, 'we can speak of what happened. Many years ago, Cahlrik our King travelled in with us, posing as a helper on the caravan. He wished to see for himself these people that spoke evil of us. Unfortunately, he didn't understand the nature of the humans as we do and there was an argument. Cahlrik was ridiculed and insulted, which would have been a terrible crime to any of the Hidden, but to the King it almost meant war. Fortunately we're not a war like race as I have said, it was just one more cruelty that the Hidden have had to endure.'

They chatted happily for some time until Loras felt a hand on his shoulder and Quint sat down to relieve him.

'You are keeping a guard?' said Groober sadly. 'But you are safe now in the lands of the Hidden, you will find the monsters are all on the other side of the gate.'

Loras undid his bedroll and lay by the fire, as confused as Mahra. The monsters he had been expecting certainly looked the part, but they didn't act like monsters, far from it. They were shy, intelligent and in a funny way, really rather sweet. As he lay staring up at the stars, it took him a long time to fall asleep while he tried to make sense of his first meeting with the Hidden.

* * *

Bartholomew Bask beat repeatedly upon the door of his agent's house. His mood was foul, having had to convince every official he'd met since entering Minsten waters that he should be allowed in, despite the fact that he carried no contract of Trade.

'It's been bloody stolen, you imbecile,' he'd bellowed at the poor fool on the boat that had come out to meet them. 'Do you have *any* idea who I am? Are yer deaf, man? Maybe Mr 'awk here can wash yer ears out so you can hear me better!' He had cuffed the petty official around the back of the head sending him flying into the spectral figure of Matheus Hawk. The terrified man had taken one look at the hunter's leering face and scurried back over the side and into his own small craft.

'I'll take that as permission to enter the harbour, shall I?' Bartholomew had bellowed over the side at the retreating boat, his face flustered and red.

Similar problems had happened on two further occasions before arriving at the small house by the great gate of the island; so at this point, Bartholomew was feeling less than pleasant.

'*Wakey, wakey*...Yer lazy slob...knock, by the Source, *knock!*' he barked, pacing outside and glaring up at the windows above. 'Shift yer bones and let me in!'

The sounds of a flustered panic were heard from inside and the white sleepy face of the Customs agent peered around the door.

'Merchant Bask...is...is that truly you?'

'Yes, it is I,' Bartholomew peered at the face behind the door trying to remember what his agent looked like. 'Now are you going to invite me in? Or do I have to push the damn door in?'

The agent shrank back, his face at once pleading and pained. 'Please, please come in, Merchant Bask. It is indeed an honour to have you visit our humble island and indeed my very humble home.'

He ushered Bartholomew into a small sitting room where Bartholomew plumped down heavily into the only comfortable chair. Peering around with some distaste Bartholomew picked up a small vase from the table by the chair and, appraising its value as very little, set it down again with a bang.

'I'm searching for a boatload of brats.' He scowled across at the grimacing official who was still trying to make some sense from this visit.

'A scruffy lot that stole something from me, got a cat with 'em...have yer seen 'em?' Bartholomew leant forward.

The agent drew up a chair and offered Bartholomew an oily smile and a plate of biscuits. Bartholomew snatched the plate and started feeding his face with biscuits one after another, still staring at the agent.

'As it happens, I have seen a boatload of young hooligans who could possibly be the ones you seek, milord; they did have a contract but...now let me see...'

Bartholomew listened as he heard a description of *The Griffin* and its hateful crew and how they were still one step ahead of him. He stuffed biscuits into his mouth, snarling and spitting crumbs, the plate shaking in his hand.

* * *

Finding the Hidden

The woodland city was incredible. Minster town had been a wonder of tamed nature but the city of the Hidden was nature in harmony with its inhabitants. The city existed inside, beneath and on top of the trees and was very hard to see. When *The Griffin's* crew first arrived, they had seen the Hidden scurrying amongst the huge trees along dark woodland paths that were touched by little of the sunlight that shone through the canopy of green and gold high above. A mist still clung to the base of the trees and a strong musky smell of decomposing leaves and moss filled the air. It was only when they saw one of the Hidden vanish into a tree, that they realised something was a little different about this particular part of the forest.

'Where do they keep disappearing to?' Loras asked Groober as around them, more Hidden emerged giving shy toothy smiles before scuttling out of their way to watch from the damp shadows of the forest.

'What's that you say? Who keeps disappearing?'

Loras glanced down at Groober. 'Hidden, that's the third one I've seen walk into a tree and ... look there went another one!'

Groober grinned. 'They're not disappearing, you're with the Hidden, this is our city, look,' he pulled Loras over to a tree and showed him a fold in the bark. 'It's a doorway, most of the bigger trees have shops in the base and homes above; others contain stairs to higher levels. Below us are the warrens, tunnels beneath the earth where others live and shelter from the heat of the day.' His nose was twitching as he held the fold aside. 'It is very important to us that our lives are at one with the forest, the trees... with the Source.'

Loras peered inside the tree and was surprised to discover a small dark musty room and stairs leading to both an upper and lower level. Sitting at a table was one of the Hidden, stitching some of the familiar animal skins, already filthy, making what passed for clothing. He glanced up and waved at Loras who pulled his head out with a start.

'Very good tailor, you may want to get yourself a nice new coat or something,' said Groober walking on. 'He's very good with squirrel and rat skins taken from the dead animals we find.' He stopped and gazed intently at Loras, 'We don't...kill...animals, the Hidden are nice.' Loras smiled a little uncertainly. Groober nodded then carried on. 'Up above us are...well let me show you,' he glanced around and strode over to a large elm. 'Come on, follow me,' he called, before disappearing into the tree.

They walked over and saw a narrow staircase. It was a little cramped, especially for Quint, but they managed to climb up until it opened amongst the topmost branches of the forest and into another, quite different, part to the city. It was lighter up here and the smell of mould and decay was gone, replaced by fresher air and the scent of life rather than the stagnant deathly aroma that filled the forest floor. Here walkways of branches and covered platforms nestled amongst the leaves stretching as far as they could see into the forest.

The Hidden still preferred the shadows even up here. As they moved around they were making every effort to avoid the soft green light, darting across any sun-splashed areas as quickly as possible. They were shy, preferring to observe from the shadows but several waved and gave them toothy smiles as they made their way along the walkway.

'Down below it's so damp and depressing, but up here it's beautiful,' said Mahra, echoing everyone's thoughts. Groober gave her a strange look then ushered them along a narrow walkway of woven living branches, proudly pointing out different parts of the city, the homes, shops and even a small factory with rows of Hidden busily hammering away. They stopped at a school with a group of tiny children who threw things at them and shrieked until the teacher clapped her hands and they reluctantly returned to the lesson.

'I am sorry, they are young. We are taught to fear and avoid outsiders...people less fortunate than ourselves,' simpered Groober by way of an explanation as he led them on.

'It's a long way down from up here,' observed Tarent peering over between the branches, 'best keep an eye on Loras, if anyone's going to fall over the edge it'll be him.' Loras glared at Tarent for a moment before continuing after Groober. They walked on for some time then stopped as Groober announced that the King's home was up ahead.

'Please be careful when speaking to King Cahlrik. It is a delicate matter to bring outsiders into our city and we all wish this meeting to go well.' He became a little hesitant. 'I'm sorry, but would you mind leaving your weapons by the door? I will of course vouch for your safety.' He offered his best and most rehearsed smile, which was so awful it actually made Loras wince. 'As I've already said, we are not a violent people, and it would be a bad start for an armed group to enter the King's hall.' They exchanged glances then unbuckled their swords and left them with their bows by the door, secretly however, they were each keeping a weapon well concealed.

'Very well, my friends, let us go,' said Groober marching to a screen of branches and pushing them aside; a strong unpleasant smell rushed out to greet them.

Reluctantly, they entered, emerging into a large, gloomy room where they could just make out the twenty or more elderly Hidden that made up the King's council, gathered in attendance. The smell of mould, decay and...Hidden filled the stuffy space; the rank air held in by a thick curtain of vines and leaves that made up the walls and roof of the room. It really did allow little air or light to enter. A fire crackled in the centre, but it was belching mostly smoke offering little in the way of light.

As their eyes eventually adjusted, they saw Cahlrik himself seated on a wooden throne talking with an ancient advisor huddled over a stack of parchments. He was dressed the same as the other Hidden, in animal skins, and was every bit as dirty as the rest but had a small brass crown upon his head, held in place by large prominent ears; it was the only indication that he was king. As the group walked forward into the room, the talking stopped and the King looked over to see what had made everyone go silent. He gazed across at the group of large strangers standing by the entrance, stood up and began tugging on his short jacket. His tongue flicked out to dampen his lips and his eyes darted over the group once more before he flopped down on his throne.

'Have they come with an apology?' he asked inspecting them, searching for their leader, his eyes finally coming to rest on Quint, the largest member of the group. 'Haven't you heard the stories of the Hidden...boy?'

'They heard...but chose not to believe them,' they heard Groober whisper behind them.

Chapter 15

The Tree of Truth

The demon King Belial came out of the trance and studied his four fellow demons carefully as they waited for his command. They had been standing silently, unmoving for the long duration of the dreamlike state and, accustomed as they were to inactivity, they were now eager to be away.

'Our prey has reached the Island of Minster and, as the Hawk and his fat friend can't find them in the closed port, they must be with the Hidden. I tire of waiting; it is high time we joined the hunt, my brothers. There are some things that demons do *better* than humans.' A low murmur of agreement came from the four hooded figures; none would be stupid enough to actually voice an opinion to their king, but the news that the time for action was now at hand, made them rash enough to show this slight sign of approval.

'Find me the fastest ship available. I shall summon three more of our brethren and then we will leave for this Minster Island at once.'

One of the demons dropped to the floor, his face touching the rough boards, his hands outstretched in abasement. 'My King,' his deep, rough voice rattled against the floor. 'There is a ship in the harbour that may be worthy of your presence; we can leave at your convenience.'

'Very good.' Belial closed his eyes as he sought the calm necessary to invoke the required spell.

Shortly after, a tearing, screeching sound tortured the air and a small hole appeared in the fabric between dimensions. An arm was forced through, straining black muscles exerted in effort. A head followed, spitting, roaring and angry at the strain. The demon gradually made the hole wide enough and landed in an exhausted steaming heap upon the floor, gasping and drawing ragged breaths into its lungs. Some time later, by the time three new demons lay on the floor, Belial was himself close to collapse from the exertion.

It was, therefore, seven demons that accompanied their king as he marched down the stairs into Blake's drinking hall.

A blanket of silence descended upon the room as all became aware that something strange was in their midst. The drinkers parted as the demons, standing head and shoulders above the crowd, pushed their way through. A woman screamed but was ignored by both demons and humans alike.

Once through the inn and out onto the harbour, the demons sniffed at the thin air suspiciously while several passers-by scuttled for cover. They scanned the line of boats tied up at the quay and seeing the one they needed, headed straight towards it, lurching along, huddled protectively around their leader, shading their eyes against the unaccustomed glare of the sun.

The boat the demons had chosen was a large 'Ship of the Line' with a compliment of sixty crew, plus a detachment of marines. It had entered the harbour only two days previously on its regular patrol of the coastal waters and sat proudly flying its many pennants in a show of naval strength. As the demon party boarded, the crew soon realised they had intruders and started to react, several marines ran forward. Unfortunately, the strange group that was boarding the ship was not the ordinary bunch of thugs and cutthroats that they'd been trained to deal with, this was an entirely different problem and the marines stopped in a horror of confusion, gawping at the invaders.

The demons were a hideous assortment of nightmares made real. The only racial similarities amongst Belial's honour guard was jet-black skin and large gaping mouths set beneath red soulless eyes, any further demonic likeness ended there. Of the demons now climbing the gangplank, three had long white hair, hanging in clumps, the others had little that could be called hair, rather scales or horns sprouting from faces that promised nothing but torment. They were huge intimidating creatures, clad head to foot in dark metal and leather and carrying a gruesome assortment of weapons.

Before they could do anything past recovering from the shock, the defenders were tossed over the side of the boat with little ceremony as Belial, surrounded by his escort, made his way to the bridge. He judged the boat worthy and smiled as several arrows bounced off his skin. He brushed them away like a small swarm of mosquitoes. Addressing the closest demon and ignoring the efforts of the boat's captain to talk to him he started to issue orders.

'We'll require twenty of the humans to help sail the boat, keep them on board and remove the rest.'

Hearing this, several crew, including some of the ship's officers, leapt over the side and into the waters below. Others, not fast enough, were captured then dragged to the ship's hold and hurled down without any care for injury. Seeing this rough handling, Belial stopped the closest demon.

'Twenty will not be sufficient, try to keep thirty or so whole, these humans are fragile creatures and there will be breakages.' The demon nodded, giving a snort of understanding and went back to capturing crewmen. The ship's captain finally got Belial's attention, which he promptly regretted. 'Ah, an eager volunteer I see.' Belial picked up the screaming seaman and, lifting him over his head, tossed him half the ship's length, through the open hatchway and into the hold. 'Yes I think that one broke as well,' he muttered thoughtfully. 'Let's get underway; I have a hankering to eat children for lunch.' He closed his eyes and slowly raised his arms into the air. Around him, the ship trembled and demons and humans alike struggled to stay standing as the great ship rose groaning into the air with water streaming from its sides. Several seamen still aboard took this last chance to bolt for the relative safety of the water, where they watched in awe as their ship rose above them.

With an agonising creaking sound, the ropes binding the great ship to the harbour wall strained and then began to snap one after another, lashing back with a series of loud cracks to the boat, now moving above and still streaming water from its bilges. The massive ship, against all normal laws known to man, continued to rise out and over the harbour wall and away across open sea.

* * *

Tarent stepped forward and dropped to one knee. 'Your Majesty, we are from a land far from here and are on a Quest in the name of the Source. We're not Minstens and have only been on this island for a few days. We travelled here to the home of the Hidden, because this is where our Quest directed us.' Behind him the others were also kneeling at eye level with the little king. All waited for the king's response.

'You look like Minstens,' murmured the king looking them over carefully. 'Maybe a little taller and you don't have beards yet, but you're not of the Hidden, are you?'

Groober shuffled forward, once more wringing his hand unhappily. 'These travellers were visiting Minster town when we met them,' he whined, 'Their boat is docked in the harbour. I hope I have not displeased my King, but they paid Trader Jack good gold to come here and they weren't...' he turned to Tarent smiling his horrible smile, '...scared of us at all.' The room was silent for a moment as the crew fingered their hidden weapons wondering where this strange conversation was heading. Finally the king stood and banged on the floor with his staff before returning his attention to the crew.

'We Hidden are aware of the evil stories told about our people, how most would shun us believing us to be evil. These stories have saddened us greatly, but as we have sought to remain away from the world, they have also helped to maintain our seclusion. You, however, saw past the legends and came in search of the real Hidden and for that we welcome you amongst us.' The Hidden shouted their agreement with King Cahlrik, their feet drumming on the floor. After a moment Cahlrik raised a hand to bring back quiet. 'Tell us your story and how you believe the Hidden may help you. If we can, then we will...if not...' he offered a toothy grin, making his crown wobble forward and he casually pushed it back. 'Well...if we can't then we can at least show you the real hospitality of the Hidden.'

Tarent stood and with a nod of approval from Quint, told of their Quest so far; of sailing storm-lashed seas, fighting creatures from a nightmare realm and the seeking of crystal skulls. The room was rapt and mostly silent as the tale unwound. When all was finally told, the council of the Hidden leapt to their feet stamping, hooting and applauding Tarent's story-telling abilities. The weaving and telling of a good story was a talent prized by the Hidden, and this story had kept them thoroughly entertained. The hall was humming with excited conversations, questions were thrown all around and it took King Cahlrik to stand on his chair and bang his staff loudly upon the floor again to bring some semblance of order back to the room. Reluctantly the talk subsided and everyone resumed their places.

'As you can see, the Hidden are supporters of your Quest,' he waved his hand at the gathered council members to quieten them. 'But weren't you scared by the horrible stories about us? Most are. Some may say you're extremely brave...others would call you extremely stupid. According to some stories we've heard, we may well have eaten you!' This drew laughter from all around the dark dingy room as Cahlrik returned to his chair. 'I am afraid we don't have any crystal skulls.' Around the room heads were shaken in agreement. 'If we had found one...we would probably have sold it,' laughter followed this and several calls of, 'The Minstens will buy anything!' came from the darkest corners, which caused Cahlrik and the others to erupt in laughter and chatter.

Tarent raised his voice above the noise. 'The Quest brought us here to find a very special tree, which is where we're told we'll find the skull. Do you know of this tree?' The laughter turned to shrieks and excited shouts at the mention of the tree. Several times the name 'tree of truth' was mentioned. Again, the king beat his staff upon the floor to restore order.

'We know of this special tree that you speak of, yes. It is because of this tree and its incessant chatter that we are cursed to remain Hidden.' He held up his hands to ask for quiet as voices had begun to rise once more, then craned forward frowning. 'What do you want with the tree?'

'We mean to find it, then find the crystal skull, and then finally restore the balance. We politely ask for the aid of the Hidden and permission to visit the tree.' The little king glanced from Tarent to the group behind him, then around at his chattering council.

'I am sorry but the council of the Hidden must discuss this alone,' he said attempting to regain some control. 'This matter goes to the very heart of the Hidden.' He returned his gaze to Tarent and the others still seated, 'Please... leave us. Groober will show you to a place of rest and we will meet again after the sun has risen tomorrow morning.'

The crew left the council and spent the rest of the day exploring. Everywhere they went the people met them shyly, but obviously delighted with the strange guests to their city. Tarent and Pardigan discovered an armourer and bought protective mail similar to Quint's. It was light, yet they were told it would be a barrier to any arrow or blade. The little old Hidden was thrilled to see Quint's original vest, confirming it to be crafted by the Hidden, but from a far distant time.

The armourer showed all his teeth, something Quint was beginning to recognise as a smile. 'Guard it well, young man, for it will certainly guard you. It is extremely precious.'

Much to her dismay, Mahra was pelted with rotten fruit by a group of tiny children and spent the rest of the afternoon cleaning herself and vowing to fly off as soon as she could. As she sat feeling miserable, three Hidden women quietly came and sat with her apologising for their children's behaviour.

'You are strange to them, too... clean; they wanted to help make you... one of us.' Mahra sat in amazement as the children were brought in and they muttered their own apologies. I judged them wrongly, she thought as the children departed in fits of giggles; just as the world has judged them wrongly.

Much later, when they left the forest floor and began the climb up through the trees, the moon was shining brightly through the leafy canopy and any fears or mistrust they may have had of the Hidden had been long forgotten.

The sleeping area that had been set aside for them was a simple platform covered with a thatch of woven leaves and a rail around the edge to stop them dropping the terrifying distance down to the woodland floor. Lying down on beds padded with fragrant grasses and moss, the crew experienced the best night's sleep they had enjoyed in days.

* * *

The sun was just touching the uppermost leaves of the tallest trees, making them look like large clusters of stars in the still dark sky when Groober, bearing a tray of hot brews steaming in the chill air, gently woke them. The birds and squirrels were already up and active and it was the chatter of forest animals that welcomed them to another day on their Quest.

Pardigan sat up and rubbed the sleep from his eyes. He glanced about and saw that Mahra's bed was empty and that Loras and Quint were still trying to stay asleep. He sipped at his cup of brew, blowing the steam off to cool it, happy to stay in his bed and look around. Tarent was talking quietly with Groober in hushed tones so as not to wake the others. He glanced across to where Loras slept. A squirrel was sitting close to Loras's head and it appeared to be contemplating a nibble on his ear. Pardigan laughed and tossed a twig at it and it scurried away, Loras slept on, unaware of his narrow escape. Sitting up, Pardigan pulled his cloak around his shoulders and hugged the hot cup with both hands enjoying the warmth.

The light began to improve and he noticed activity on other platforms across the city. The smell of newly baked bread wafted up to him from somewhere down below and his stomach rumbled, reminding him that he was hungry.

'What's happening?' he whispered across to Tarent who had finished his conversation with Groober and was sipping his brew with a frown on his face.

'Apparently the king's council was up most of the night debating what to do and Groober says it may not have gone well.' Placing his cup to the side, he stood up. 'Come on, let's wake the others, Groober's invited us to break our fast at his house and says Serik and Char will be there as well. After we've eaten we're to go back to the king's throne room to meet with the council and hear what they've come up with.'

'Well at least we're going to eat first, that's a blessing from the Source, I'm hungry enough to eat one of these squirrels.' Pardigan pulled himself up and shook Loras's shoulder. He had to do it several times before Loras finally propped himself up on one elbow complaining of the cold and the early hour, but he soon cheered up at the sight of the hot brew and talk of food.

Groober's house was on ground level in the base of a huge sycamore tree, the light didn't reach this far to the forest floor and it smelt damp and earthy. Inside, Serik and Char were in fine form, chatting happily as they pulled fresh buns out of a small oven.

'We were eating with friends last night and they were asking all sorts of questions, some of them very silly. You have to remember that most of the Hidden haven't seen outsiders ever before. That's the problem really, that so much has to change if we're to trade over the seas as we would like.' Serik laughed out loud at the notion, the sound emerging as more of a strange barking sound than a laugh.

'These two would be building a huge ship the likes of which no Hidden could ever sail, then vanish off to see if they could trade with the Source itself,' said Groober.

They chatted happily but breakfast was over all too soon, and the crew, escorted by their Hidden friends, made their way to the king's throne room.

When they arrived, it smelled just as awful and as dingy and smoky as before. There was a hush as they walked in and a hurried scuttling as the council members returned to their seats. King Cahlrik waved them to the front and council members moved to the side as they made their way through. Groober followed, quietly apologising to all he disturbed, and sat close by.

Cahlrik stood. 'Friends, we welcome you back here to the heart of the Hidden people and wish you to know that when you leave here, you are welcome to return whenever you wish. This has not been said to any outsider in many years and it is with joy that I say it to you now.' The council members all clapped their hands and stamped their feet in agreement, accompanied by many calls of support. Cahlrik continued when the noise had died down. 'The council has been in discussion all night and debated your Quest back and forth but we keep returning to one problem. Should you find the skull you seek, will it take the magic of the tree away with it? We believe that it would, and in doing so it would not only rob all reason from the lives of the Hidden, but it may give life to the ancient curse. Should the rest of the tree be disturbed, then a time of eternal night shall descend upon everything, the trees will die and the night-walkers will inherit the forest. It is because of this tree and its continual chattering about life, love and all kinds of stuff, that we are cursed to guard it, to keep it hidden. We can't just let you all wander off with it now, can we? It has therefore been decided that you cannot visit the tree. If there is any other way that we can help your Quest we would gladly do so. I am truly very sorry.' The king did indeed appear sorry and it was obvious that the decision had not been easy in coming. The Hidden waited for some kind of response. At last Tarent stood up and addressed the gathering.

'King Cahlrik, council members, I don't think that anyone knows what to say or do next. We know you don't want to give away the one thing that you have been guarding for so many years, we wish we didn't have to ask for it, but we believe you've been guarding it for a reason, waiting for the time when it would be needed. The night-walkers as you call them may already be here; I think *they* are what we call demons. We search for the skulls to defend the earth from these agents of Chaos.' He glanced down at his companions, and drew a deep breath.

'We've told you how the balance has swayed back and forth, a universal battle between Chaos and Order since a time before humans and the Hidden existed. How everything and everyone is a soldier for one side or the other and how those sides switch backwards and forwards as the years slip by. But Chaos has been getting stronger and we're now on the brink of the balance; the world is sinking lower and lower into instability, hostility and fear... into chaos and the darkness you speak of. A group of magicians saw all this happening a thousand years ago and a great spell was forged. Three crystal skulls formed the key to this spell, which when activated, would correct the balance, allowing the world to live in harmony. We have to find those three skulls and bring them together at the right time, in the right place, for it all to work. I believe your ancestors were charged to remain in hiding by these magicians, to become the Hidden, so that one of those skulls would be safe until we could...'

'*Kaboom!*'

A huge explosion ripped the air and Tarent along with half the council was flung to the floor. Screaming and shouting could be heard from outside and the smell of sulphurous smoke filtered into the room. The king picked himself up from where he'd fallen and addressed a council member struggling up beside him.

'Go and find out what's happening.' Another loud explosion came, rocking the room again, followed by the creaking scream of a tree and the terrible crashing sound as it fell to the ground. The shouts and cries from outside increased and panic started to spread in the throne room, a crush developed round the doorway as everyone tried to leave. *The Griffin's* crew hadn't moved during all this, but stayed in a group waiting until a direction opened for them and some sense could be made of what was happening.

The council member returned. 'We're under attack by something from above us; it's causing terrible damage in the city, my King. A tree has fallen.' He stood trembling, waiting to be told what to do.

'Chaos it seems is visiting us,' muttered the king. 'Come this way.' He pulled back the curtain behind his throne and headed down a dark passage followed by everyone else who wasn't already crushed round the door.

The passage led out to a lower level and onto a walkway amongst the trees. Above them, through the trees, they could see a huge wooden shape drifting past, dropping things that were exploding in the city. Several trees around them shook violently forcing everyone to cling to the swaying walkway.

'What is it?' asked Quint.

'I have no idea,' replied Tarent. 'From here it could be anything, I've seen flying things before, huge bags filled with hot air and a basket hanging underneath, but I don't think that's what that is.'

'It's a boat,' said Pardigan. 'Look, it's got an anchor dangling underneath.'

'Funny boat, why is it attacking the Hidden and how did it know where to look?' As Quint finished speaking the boat changed direction and started to turn towards them.

'I'm going to see who's on it,' said Mahra leaping from the walkway. Several of the Hidden stepped back in alarm as she shimmered into the shape of a large snowy owl and flew away.

'It would seem your stories were true, several of my people had you for liars.' King Cahlrik tugged on Tarent's sleeve. 'So why is our city being attacked?'

'I really don't know, but we've been attacked by all kinds of things recently, I'm sort of getting used to it, which is a bit worrying,' said Tarent as Mahra returned, swooping down and changing back into her human form.

'It's a ship with demons on it. They're hurling down clay pots filled with something explosive and there's one demon on there that's wielding magic sending all kinds of spells down onto the city.'

'But why?' asked Pardigan.

'At a guess I'd say they're looking for us,' said Tarent, 'maybe trying to flush us out. King Cahlrik, I'm sorry we've brought this to your city, but this is Chaos. These demons, or night-walkers as you call them, are trying to stop the great spell from being completed and this is the world they would have us all live in, a world filled with demons, misery and fear.'

Cahlrik stared at Tarent, then out at his city falling around him, the screams of his people and the dying groans of the ancient trees as they fell. He took Tarent's arm. 'Come,' was all he said as he headed off at a run.

'You go,' said Loras. 'I'm going to help; at least I can fight magic with magic.'

'I'm going to fight as well,' said Quint. 'But I need to get on that ship somehow.' Groober pulled his arm, 'I'll get you on.' They ran off together as Loras walked towards a stairway.

Pardigan and Tarent followed the king as he led them down to ground level via a winding series of stairs and walkways. When they were on firm ground they started to run through the trees, away from the devastation. Cahlrik stopped a few times to offer encouragement to his subjects but then quickly moved on.

'I'm going to take you to the tree,' he shouted behind him to the two running figures. 'If the night-walkers want to stop you getting that skull, then I think the only way I can save my people is to help you get it. Maybe you were right and it's time we were rid of it.' Tarent glanced at Pardigan but said nothing as they jogged on after the figure of the small king.

Quint could clearly see Loras standing on a platform. The magician was sending pulse after pulse of energy at the strange ship, which was now slowly turning towards him. Fires were blazing on its deck and he could see it was going to pass close to where he was, but wasn't sure if it would be close enough. Mahra was standing beside him.

'Fly over and see if Loras can make the ship come towards me here, I have to get onboard.'

Mahra pitched forward and the snowy white owl flew out through the trees towards Loras. A few moments later he saw her land close to his friend and resume her human shape. After a brief conversation, Loras stopped the energy bursts and held out his hands differently, gently moving them from side to side. Quint couldn't see what he was doing, but sure enough, the huge ship started altering course to come closer to him. He could see the black hooded shapes of the demons, distracted from dropping explosives; they were clustered around their leader offering him the protection of their bodies as he continued to spin his magic. His arms lifted and a red ball of energy went spinning towards Loras's platform. Loras flung his arms to the side and the red ball dipped harmlessly away towards the forest floor, Quint could just make out the smile on Loras's face.

The ship was getting closer now, Quint grabbed Groober's arm. 'Go and help your people, get them away, because we're going to bring this ship down or die trying.' With that he raised his bow and fired off three arrows one after another to distract the demon group then took a mighty run along an outstretched branch and leapt, half flying and half falling, towards the massive boat as it passed about three spans below. He landed with a thump, rolled into a ball, and came up slashing his sword. It sliced down the back of the closest demon which spun with a shrill scream, flinging its cloak back to show a black twisted face. It hissed at him, mouth agape with row upon row of needle-sharp teeth. Quint's sword flashed past and went deep into its eye, its only vulnerable spot, and with a new scream, this time of pain, the demon threw its hands up, gripped the sword, and fell to its knees in a spreading pool of sticky black blood. With a wrenching twist, Quint withdrew the sword and sought his next demon. It had all happened in an instant and the rest were still ignorant of the danger in their midst, allowing Quint to dispatch another before he found himself facing three new demons, now very aware of his presence. This time, they wouldn't be caught by surprise. Two others were hurrying their leader to the front of the boat as he continued to battle magic with Loras.

The three demons spread out around Quint, slowly drawing massive swords from their scabbards. They hissed and growled as they closed in.

Okay, Loras, this would be a really good time to throw something in this direction, thought Quint as the first of the three demons launched its attack.

Chapter 16

Different Paths

The path was long and winding, taking them well away from the sounds of battle.

'I hope your friends can help my people,' puffed Cahlrik. 'We never expected to be attacked by anyone.' He slowed to a trot, allowing Tarent to catch up.

'I'm sure Loras and Quint will give them something to think about. The demons' attack will probably be focused on them by now.' Tarent glanced around him as he ran. 'How much further is it?'

'It's just a little way up here, on the cliff... see, you can just make out the clearing.' Cahlrik pointed up along the path and sure enough they could see the brightness of blue sky between the trees.

They emerged into an open area on the edge of a cliff and fell to the ground panting. The Tree of Truth stood before them, the sound of the sea crashing some thirty spans below on the cliffs. The tree's great trunk was twisted with age and its heavy branches hung low to the ground casting great shadows around its base. Massive roots gripped the earth like old gnarled fingers, as if it were aware that one day, as the cliff eroded, it would drop to the sea below but would cling on to the very last moment.

'What sort of tree is it?' asked Pardigan staring up in awe.

The air around them calmed and the sound of the sea became much softer. 'This is a place of tranquillity, an island within the realities of life. I am the skull you seek, named The Tree of Truth by the Hidden people. My gift to the Hidden has been to see into a soul and call forth a being's destiny; *that* is the sort of tree I am.' The voice they heard was deep and dry; it was as if they were being spoken to from a distant, ancient time.

'Oh, Source, I think I'm getting used to speaking things, 'cos that hardly shocked me at all.' Pardigan grinned, then glanced back and saw King Cahlrik holding back, apparently unhappy to be this close to the ancient tree.

'What truth would you know? What secret shall I call forth from your soul? You, Cahlrik, do you once more seek your destiny? A time ago we spoke at length, now you rarely come at all.' The voice sounded sad and a feeling of great loss and remorse filled them all. The king took several steps further back.

'You are troubled, Cahlrik, your soul reveals all to me. I know today is not a good day for your people but remember, it is only one day in many, and the pain you receive today is the price the Hidden pay in the whole scheme of things. I am aware of why these young people are here, I know what they seek and why they seek it; my own destiny has been revealed to me at the right time, as was intended. I am needed now for a greater task. The burden placed upon your people has now been lifted; you will no longer have to hide from the world of man.'

The tree gave what sounded like a giant sob. 'Heroes, take the skull.'

At the base of the tree the ground started to swell and a blue glow lit the shadows. Little by little the crystal skull was forced to the surface until it rested on the grass, lit by a thin ray of sunlight. Leaves began to drop from the branches and tears fell from the king's eyes. Around them, smoke from the burning city was now clouding the sky and it was becoming much darker.

Pardigan picked up the skull and wrapped it in a fold of cloth before slipping it into his bag. 'What do we do now?' He coughed as the smoke swirled around them.

Different Paths

Tarent covered his nose and mouth with his sleeve and shrugged. 'I'm not sure, have you got the book?' The king watched as the two heroes took out the tattered book and slipped the knife into the spine.

'There's a new page!' exclaimed Pardigan excitedly. Cahlrik came over to see what they were studying.

'What's that?' he asked.

'It's *The Book of Challenges*, it's sort of like the guide to our Quest,' explained Tarent. 'Each page opens only after the last part has been completed.' They studied the now visible page.

> *The City of Sand*
> *Two paths are taken by our band,*
> *The heroes seek a city of sand.*
> *Half shall fly, half shall sail.*
> *Beware the mudlarks, beware the flail.*
> *The skull you seek is guarded well.*
> *A sultan's daughter she will tell.*
> *And then she'll guide you down through hell.*

Cahlrik made a snorting sound. 'Well I don't like the sound of that! Mudlarks, guided down through hell, and I'm not sure what a flail is either but I'm glad I won't be finding out any time soon. Seems as though I'm not the only one having a bad day, doesn't it?' Pardigan and Tarent both stared at the little king.

'I thought you were in deep mourning for the loss of your tree and the devastation of your people?' said Pardigan glancing towards the sad sight of the tree. It had already lost most of its leaves, its old, once proud branches drooping sadly to the floor.

'Oh I am, I am, but the curse has been lifted and we Hidden can't stay down for long.'

'You were down for years when...ouch!' Tarent elbowed Pardigan in the ribs and gave him a glare before studying the book again.

'It's fairly clear. We're to leave in two groups, probably to keep the skulls separate. One group will fly,' Pardigan shrugged. 'Okay, well that's not us, is it? But two will sail. Do you think we're meant to go back for the *Griffin*?

Tarent shook his head. 'We have the skull. I think it would be too risky to return to the port. King Cahlrik, do you know of a boat we can use?'

Cahlrik nodded. 'Follow me.'

The king led them down a small sandy path towards the sounds of the sea, and eventually, to a small boat a little over half the size of *The Griffin*. It was in fair condition and would get them to Freya as long as they could work out which direction to point it in. They said their good-byes to the king and he helped them cast off.

'Please ask Mahra to come and find us; tell her we can explain what the book is saying.' Cahlrik agreed happily and waved them goodbye.

'Hope you find a good name,' called Pardigan. 'Now that you don't need to hide anymore I mean.' The sails were set and the little boat glided out through the overhanging trees and away towards open sea, picking its way carefully between the reef heads.

With the wind in their hair once more, Tarent and Pardigan smiled at each other then Pardigan gave a whoop of joy.

'Let's just hope the others can get out of there without getting hurt and meet us somewhere.'

'Dhurban, I'm pretty sure the book is talking about that huge city in the middle of the desert, Dhurban.' Tarent twitched the helm past the last reef and Pardigan went to haul up the forward sail. He stopped and glanced back as the little boat carried them out and away from the Island of Minster. The smoke seemed to be lessening and he wondered how the others had got on.

* * *

The sword that flashed past Quint's unprotected face was so close that he felt the soft breeze of its movement kiss his cheek as it passed. He was facing two demons, having finally dispatched another a few moments earlier. He was tiring now and it was taking a lot of effort to keep the sword raised and in a position to deflect the heavy blows from the demons that towered over him. Because they were so much bigger than he was, he couldn't block their swords so was twisting and turning in a deadly dance, using their force and momentum against them whilst seeking an opening. After parrying yet another fierce strike, he glanced up and realised that he'd left his defences open. For an instant, as he braced himself to receive the blow he felt sure was coming, a flurry of feathers exploded onto the scene and a great white owl with claws outstretched, flew into the attacking demon's face letting out a terrifying screech as she did so. The demon mis-struck its blow and Quint quickly seized the opportunity to bury his knife deep into its eye, sinking the blade to the hilt as he deflected yet another assault from its companion. With a great howl the dying demon stumbled to the side of the boat, black blood splashing over the deck and, giddy in its confusion and agony, it fell over the edge; its scream falling with it to the forest floor. One demon still remained but it was holding back, cautiously seeking a weakness in Quint's failing defences.

The flying boat was fast approaching Loras as he continued to send bursts of magic at the figure on the fore deck. Belial's two remaining guards were unsure from which direction to protect him. They were all too aware that four of their comrades had now fallen to Quint's blade, and only one of their kind now stood in the way of him turning to attack them. Belial was oblivious to most of this and was still throwing everything he had at the small boy on the platform. He was infuriated that none of his powers had so far had any real effect on the young magician. He snarled and bellowed as his hands thrashed back and forth throwing lances of red power at his adversary, only to see them pushed to the side and a blue ball of hateful Order energy hurled back at him. It hurt when he reached out to deflect these blue spheres; it felt like ice creeping up his arm each time he touched one. His energy was almost drained and he was now searching desperately for escape.

The boat lurched dangerously underneath them and one of his guards stumbled. Glancing across he smiled to see the fighter was still aboard, then frowned as he saw only one of his demon guards still lived. He let go his magical grip of the boat and it dropped, falling down through the trees as gravity reclaimed its hold, crashing through the branches, battering itself to pieces in its rush to meet the forest floor. Belial watched the branches flash past and the boat disintegrate around him knowing that he and his fellow demons would survive such a fall and that the human fighter would not.

The boat hit the ground with an ear-splitting crash and a great cloud of dust and dirt filled the air. A few moments later Belial emerged from the wreckage, brushing bits of wood, rope and sail away and surveyed the scene; no human could possibly have survived that, the fighter was dead.

'To me!' he called and the three remaining demons pulled themselves from the mangled pile that had once been a boat and followed him into the forest, unseen amongst the confusion.

'Quint!' screamed Mahra as she stood on a platform glancing around.

'He's over there,' said Loras pointing. 'I saw him going down with the boat and managed to get a vine to him. Look he's on that branch, go and see if he's all right.' Mahra threw herself forward and the owl silently glided over to Quint's unmoving form.

He was still breathing, but had obviously used the last of his strength to get to the branch. Two of the Hidden were peering out of a stairway so Mahra called them over and they helped drag him to a less precarious spot. She checked him over for injuries and seeing no human blood, only the black blood of the demons, told the Hidden to leave him.

'I think this hero has earned a sleep,' she said, smoothing the hair away from Quint's dirty sweat-streaked face.

It was much later when Quint finally awoke and was brought over to a crackling fire; the light was flickering on the faces of his two friends as they sat talking to King Cahlrik.

'Quint,' said the king, standing up to welcome his guest. 'My people have told me of your fight on the great boat. You are truly a mighty warrior. If the three of you hadn't done what you did, who knows what would be left of our city, you will be long remembered by the Hidden.' Cahlrik went on to explain what had happened to Tarent and Pardigan and how he had led them to the tree.

'They're in a boat right now on their way to Freya,' said Mahra. 'I flew out to speak to them earlier, they have the skull.' She glanced over at Loras who was awake but didn't look like he would be for long. After fighting a demon all afternoon he was now fighting sleep and this was a battle he was losing fast.

Quint raised an eyebrow. 'They left on their own, why didn't they come back to find us?'

'The book,' said Mahra, and told him what it had said. When she'd finished, Quint still appeared confused.

'We still have to go back for the *Griffin*, how are we going to fly out of here? I know Loras is getting good but that's a pretty tall order even for him.' He glanced over at his sleepy friend.

'I'll think of something,' mumbled Loras. 'I just wish I had my books with me.'

'Come, sleep,' said Cahlrik with a toothy smile. 'My people will watch for the night-walkers tonight, you'll do no flying until you get some of your energy back.'

Loras curled up into a ball by the fire, followed not long after by Quint and Mahra.

Cahlrik studied the three heroes. Only children, he thought with a shake of his head, *big* children, but still just children. He looked out at the devastated city, mostly concealed by darkness amid the many flickering lights and fires. So many fallen trees that had been homes to his people for countless generations and several lives lost, fewer than he had feared but still too many. He sighed and reflected that a lot had changed in such a short time. With that thought he put blankets over the three sleeping figures and headed back into the tree to find his own bed and hopefully some sort of rest.

The next morning they said their good-byes to the Hidden. It was a tearful affair; none of the Hidden came and blamed them in any way for bringing such slaughter and mayhem to their city. The crew of the *Griffin* received nothing but thanks and gratitude for the part they had played in the battle against the demons and their ship.

The king pinned a golden acorn onto each of their cloaks, passing over two more for Pardigan and Tarent.

'You have started the process of reconciliation between the Hidden and the outside world and you've shown us there are indeed good people in the lands of man. We must now do our best to dismiss the evil stories and rejoin the rest of the world. May the Source guide your Quest and bless it with success. These golden acorns are the highest forms of honour and recognition that we can bestow upon anyone, human or Hidden, they are worn by few humans.'

They thanked him as they accepted the brooches.

'I'm glad we could help to reunite our peoples but I'm so sorry it had to be this way.' Quint raised his voice so as many could hear as possible. 'Such terrible destruction; you Hidden are a very special people when you're able to see the good amid such Chaos, and extremely special to have endured seclusion for so long. With people like you aiding the force of Order, I know we cannot fail.' The Hidden cheered and Quint placed his hand onto the king's shoulder then turned and Groober led them away from the large gathering of cheering Hidden and on to the path for Minster Harbour.

* * *

Belial and his three demon soldiers stormed onto the *Esmerelda*, the gangplank bouncing and swaying under their weight.

'Where are the Hawk and his fat friend?' hissed Belial to the two sailors in the unfortunate position of guards to the main deck of the ship.

'Mister Hawk and Merchant Bask are in the captain's cabin, my Lord. May I send them word that you're here?' The guard was trembling and perspiring heavily as he desperately tried to focus on the relatively human features of Belial, rather than the visitations of horror that accompanied him. Belial treated him to an oily smile.

'Why that would be just...' he brought his face close to the sailor's. '...*perfect!*' The sailor retreated towards the hatchway as fast as he was able. His companion, now alone, came under the scrutiny of the demon king. Belial was tired of humans after the somewhat humiliating defeat in the city of the Hidden; he'd walked all night and was in no mood to be nice. The sailor stared out at the Jungle City trying not to make eye contact with any of the demons. Feeling Belial's gaze he trembled and began to panic, unsure what to do. The clink clink clink of his armour rattling, the loudest sound on the boat.

'*Boo!*' shouted Belial pushing out at the hapless man, sending him flying up in the air and over the side of the ship where he landed in a heap on the harbour path. Several other sailors suddenly found other things they should be doing on a different part of the boat, and in only a few beats of a demon heart, the deck was clear of humans. Belial walked over and wiggled the ship's wheel from side to side then slapped the compass cracking the casing. '*Hawk,*' he bellowed. A sound of steady steps came from the hatchway and Matheus Hawk's head and shoulders appeared. Matheus glanced at the demons then around at the deserted deck before cautiously stepping out.

'And where pray tell, is our fat friend?' growled Belial.

'He is coming, do not fret, he moves a little slower than most men below decks. It gets somewhat cramped down there and he finds it hard to negotiate the ladder.' The Hawk smiled. 'And to what do we owe the pleasure of your visit?'

'I'm tired of your human bungling and decided to take control of this fiasco you call a manhunt.' Belial spat on the deck and a fleck attached itself to Matheus's boot.' Five children have bested you and I mean to stop them once and for all. They come now to this town and it is here that we will finish this charade.' He walked to the side of the boat and studied the variety of vessels around him. 'Somewhere in this harbour they have a boat and we have to stop it leaving. I shall be watching and giving my...' he came closer to Matheus. '...advice.' A fetid breath of pure Evil accompanied the softly spoken word causing Matheus to sway a little but he managed to remain on his feet.

'I'm sure that will be most constructive.' Matheus coughed, still wavering slightly as he fought the urge to vomit.

Belial slapped the back of his hand across the Hawk's face, sending him spinning across the deck. Matheus glared up at Belial, his eyes narrowing. Saying nothing, he waited to see what the demon king would do next.

But then Bartholomew Bask's wheezing form finally arriving from the cabins below broke the moment. He stopped and mopped his brow before noticing the scene in front of him. His eyes darted from Matheus Hawk lying supine on the deck with blood dripping from his mouth, to the hunched figure of Belial breathing heavily, watched over by three hooded demons. The thought of returning down the stairway briefly occurred to him, and his head did turn back towards the hatch, but he knew it wasn't really an option.

'Mr Bask how nice of you to join us.' Belial strode over and grabbed Bartholomew's cheek in a painful pinch, pulling the frightened merchant towards him.

'How can we be of service to you?' squeaked Bartholomew, standing up on tiptoes. Belial smiled and brought his lips close to Bartholomew's ear.

'Some children will be arriving here soon; they will get on one of these boats and together we will stop them,' he hissed. 'Get this boat ready to move the moment we sight them; they have something I need and then I want them dead.' He twisted Bartholomew's cheek even tighter then leaned closer and bit his ear.

Bartholomew let out a squeal. '*Eeeeek!* They have plenty of mine as well,' he danced up on his toes, sobbing. 'We're here for the same reason so why are you treating me like this?' His high-pitched voice carried over the silent ship.

Belial pondered the question. 'I think I've decided that I don't like humans very much, now get this boat ready, and come closer to the harbour mouth, I want to be able to see every boat that leaves.' He pushed Bartholomew away. Walking to the side rail, the demon king stood gazing out over the harbour without saying another word.

Matheus picked himself up, dusted himself down and cast an icy glare towards Belial. Bartholomew grabbed his arm but Matheus shook it off.

'What are we going to do?' hissed Bartholomew. His cheek and neck were both red, already showing signs of bruising. A single drop of blood hung from his ear.

'We shall stop those brats and deal with this...' Matheus waved a hand towards Belial's back, '...later.'

'Bartholomew's mouth dropped open. 'Later, later, what do you mean later? That... that thing, laid his hands upon me, beat you down and has threatened our lives. What do you mean deal with it later?' he hissed trying hard to keep his voice low while casting an eye towards the three silent figures.

'Just do what he says and ask the captain to move the ship. I don't think we'll have any more outbursts from our friend Mr Belial for a while. He was simply flexing his muscles, letting us know who's boss, that's all.'

Bartholomew stared at Matheus Hawk with something approaching pleading in his eyes. 'For the love of the Source, man, if you can do something... anything, then just do it. I don't think the boss likes us and I'm very sure I don't like him.'

'Tell the captain to move us, Mr Bask, everything will happen in its own good time; it always does.'

Bartholomew gave an exasperated sigh and headed for the hatchway, muttering to himself.

Chapter 17

The Flight Of The Griffin

Mahra flew silently over the gateway to Minster town, the moon casting her dancing shadow across the silvery pathway. She circled several times before returning to where Loras and Quint were hiding with the others amongst the trees, the snowy owl blurring into the shape of the girl.

'There's nobody in sight. The light is on in the Customs house again but I can't see him in his bed. Maybe we should wait a while?'

'No, let's just do it,' said Quint, 'but very quietly, let's try not to wake anybody, all right?' With a nod to Groober, four of the Hidden ran out dragging a hastily constructed ladder. They propped it up against the gate, braced the bottom and Loras ran up and gently dropped over to look back at Quint through the gate. Quint was about to move when he felt Groober tug on his cloak.

'What will you say when you hear evil stories of the Hidden? Will you be our friends when you return to the heart of ignorance?' Quint glanced up as Loras hissed at him, urging him to come quickly, then turned back and smiled down at the Groober.

'We shall tell the world to listen with their hearts when they meet you, and that the stories are all untrue.'

Groober tried hard to smile. 'Looks can be deceiving, can't they, the same as nasty stories. The Hidden have learned never to judge another by his looks. You're all so…ugly…yet we bid you welcome … and you showed us you were as honest and true as any Hidden, I'm glad that we did, I hope the world of man will welcome us.' With a wave he disappeared back into the shadows leaving Quint a little bemused. They thought *we* were ugly!

'Come on,' hissed Loras.

Quint dropped over the gate, the ladder was quickly withdrawn, and the last of the Hidden disappeared back down the path.

The two friends made their way through the twisting streets moving from shadow to shadow with the snowy white owl flying ahead, scanning for late night walkers - but all was still and silent in Minster town.

The harbour, when they got there, was also deserted. Only the gentle slap of water against hulls and occasional rattle of ropes against masts disturbed the silence of the night. It was only as they came within sight of the heavily disguised *Griffin* that a man stepped out onto the path in front of them stopping them short; a second and then a third quickly joined him. Quint and Loras spun around ready to run, but three armed men stepped out from behind them as well. A trap! Turning back towards *The Griffin* they saw yet another man had joined the others, the unmistakably stout figure of Bartholomew Bask. His grinning face lit up from the light of a smoky oil lamp held up in front of him.

'Well, well, well, I do think we have two of our thieves, boys. Where are your other shipmates, yer ragamuffin scum? I was hoping to hang you all together.' He waddled forward without waiting for an answer. 'You have some property of mine and I'd like it back. How about you return it and we just let you go?' He leered at them, his face unnaturally yellow in the glow from the lamp. One of the men sniggered and Bartholomew slapped the back of his hand against his chest to silence him. 'Well?'

'Close your eyes,' whispered Loras. Quint had scarcely done so when a bright flash filled the night between them. All but Quint and Loras were momentarily blinded and they quickly used the opportunity to push past the startled merchant and his men. They had made it halfway up the harbour path before a shout came and an arrow clattered on the stones ahead of them. Both dived for cover behind an upturned boat. The sound of Bartholomew shrieking in rage could be heard coming towards them.

'If you've got any other good ideas, please feel free to use them,' urged Quint. The voices were getting closer and Loras chanced a peek over the top of the boat. The merchant was beating the sailors ahead of him, urging them on as they searched the pathway with all its possible hiding places. Loras ducked back down again.

'Listen, there are several barrels a few paces in front of where they are, if you can burst one I can turn whatever's inside into steam and blind them to our escape again.'

'An arrow will just stick into the barrel, it's not going to blow it up, and what if it's fire oil inside, the whole harbour might go up in flames. We may even burn the whole town down!' Quint was fingering an arrow nervously as the need to fire it and start hurting people got closer and closer.

'They're not barrels of fire oil, Quint. We had fire oil on *The Griffin*. Those barrels are larger. They're something else. Whatever it is, I won't set it ablaze, I'm only going to turn it to steam, there is a difference.' Loras wrapped his hand around the arrow that Quint was holding and a blue glow enveloped it. 'There, now it will turn heavy upon impact and the barrel will burst open. Just be sure to put as much force behind it as you can.'

Quint stood up and in one fluid movement fired his arrow at the stack of barrels, still a little in front of the approaching sailors. The arrow hit one of the bottom barrels and it exploded with a dull thud then a crash turning it into splinters of wood and liquid, which quickly spread with a whoosh across the path. The arrow continued on, bursting another barrel behind it, and a third barrel fell from the top stack breaking on the floor. The sailors drew back in shock and Merchant Bask dived for cover, believing he was under attack.

'Protect me! Protect me!' he whined from behind a pile of crates. There was a strange whumping sound and the air immediately filled with a noxious smelling cloud. The sailors staggered in retreat, pulling their shirts up over their noses as Bartholomew got up screaming, 'Get your lazy cowardly carcasses back through that mist and find those brats.' Though it was no good, the path for the moment, was blocked.

From up on the roof of a warehouse, Mahra watched the antics of Quint and Loras and was relieved to see they hadn't, as yet, come to any harm. She could see several boats coming across from the large ship, anchored close to the harbour mouth, *The Griffin,* it seemed, was trapped. She took off with a beat of her wings gliding above the confusion and over to the dirty broken fishing boat that was the heavily disguised *Griffin*. Quint and Loras had just clambered down the hatchway as she landed changing to her human form; she followed them down, closing the hatch softly behind her. Inside, *The Griffin* was the same as they'd left it, both Quint and Loras were sitting slumped and exhausted at the table.

'What are we going to do now?' asked Quint glancing up.

'Well the book said we'd fly out, but I'm the only thing that can fly around here.' Mahra was as nervous as Quint. She peeked out of the porthole as the sounds of shouting and angry conversations could be heard getting closer.

Loras stood, his face creased in thought. 'Well whatever we do, we have to do it soon 'cos they're going to be searching all of these boats. Let's cast off from the harbour. At least, it'll buy us a little time while I think on this.' He headed for his cabin to look something up in one of his books as Quint and Mahra climbed up through the hatch.

'They're getting closer,' whispered Quint as he crept out keeping low. Slipping the ropes holding *The Griffin* to the quayside, he gave a push on the harbour wall and the little boat began to drift out. Moments later, a shout of alarm went up from the sailors in a rowing boat and Bartholomew's group on the harbour path began to run as arrows clattered onto *The Griffin's* deck. Quint quickly hoisted the mainsail and *The Griffin* pulled further away from the path, the sail flapping slightly as it caught on the weak breeze. He sent a few arrows towards the sailors on the path without trying to hit any. Glancing down he saw that Mahra, in the form of a cat, was rubbing against his leg. She peered up at him and meowed.

'I know, Mahra, I know. I'm worried too. Loras...*Loras?*' Quint watched as a ball of red demon fire came arcing towards them from the big ship that was slowly manoeuvring, blocking their only escape route. 'There are demons out here, Loras...hello, Loras can you hear me? I said there...'

'Yes I heard you, Quint,' said Loras, emerging from the hatch. 'Don't worry, we're going to get out of here, just give me a moment.' Loras bent down and stroked Mahra's sleek grey fur. 'Magic is a wonderful thing isn't it, Mahra?'

'What are you going to do, Loras? I mean do whatever you can but ...' Quint notched another arrow and let it fly at the fast approaching boats. Mahra decided that it was probably a good idea to be somewhere else and leapt over the opposite side of the boat, shimmered into the form of an owl and flew across to the far harbour wall.

The Griffin was heading directly towards the big ship and they were close enough now to make out the name *Esmerelda* painted on her sides as well as people and several large black demons standing on her deck. Another ball of red Chaos energy flew from the ship and Loras casually waved his hand and the red ball altered course towards one of the rowboats. The occupants saw it coming, and jumped clear amid a chorus of yells, just before the ball of fire exploded into the tiny boat, blowing it into a thousand splinters. Loras closed his eyes and began to mutter, then opened them and warned, 'Hold on to something, Quint, we're going flying.'

Quint just had time to take hold of *The Griffin's* wheel when he noticed a blur of movement, his whole world shimmered before him and he found himself holding on to a thick pelt of feathery fur. What had been the deck of the boat only a heartbeat ago was now a writhing mass under his feet. He sank down in shock and tried to get a tighter hold as his mind raced to cope with what was happening. *The Griffin* gave a loud shrieking cry and lifted clear of the water, the two figures holding precariously onto her back. With the body of a lion and the head and wings of a giant eagle, *The Griffin's* sharp talons clawed at the air and her huge wings beat as she fought to gain height and get away from the harbour.

From where she was sitting on the harbour wall, Mahra could see the full majesty of the creature that the old boat had become. She let out a raucous squawk of excitement. 'Now you're a magician, Loras, never have I seen such magic.' She watched as *The Griffin* launched into the air, the huge animal tearing itself free of the water, barely missing the top masts of the *Esmerelda*; the down draught of its wing beats flapped the canvas sails of the huge ship. Quint and Loras were far too busy holding onto the feathery pelt to glance down and see what was happening on the boat, but Mahra saw the looks of astonishment from everyone as they gawped and stared at the strange creature passing overhead.

The Griffin climbed higher and higher away from the island, thankfully leaving behind all chance of capture, at least for the time being.

* * *

A cry of rage and frustration erupted from Belial as *The Griffin* reared up out of the harbour, showering the deck and everyone on it with glistening droplets of water. He lashed out in frustration sending Matheus Hawk spinning across the deck and then kicked a sailor so hard, that his broken body lifted up, landing far out into the middle of the harbour with a distant splash.

'What magic are we up against here?' he stormed. 'These are no mere children, this is the Source playing games with us and I will not have it.' He rounded on Bartholomew Bask who scampered back towards the hatchway before Belial could strike at him. He then noticed Matheus rising from the deck and anger infused his features as the Hawk slowly walked towards him, the very one he had entrusted the simple job of catching these ragamuffin thieves.

'That was the last time you will ever strike me, demon,' growled Matheus Hawk. 'We could have done so much together, but you have turned against me too many times, and now it must end.'

'What are you snivelling about, little human? Hold your tongue before I draw it out and cut it from your head. I need my concentration, for this ship must fly, we shall chase that… thing and it is *I* that shall defeat them.' He raised his arms and the great ship began to groan as the weight was shifted and it began to lift from the water.

'No, we shall fly nowhere. We no longer need you, so I'm sending you home.' The Hawk felt satisfaction as Belial's eyes opened in… fear? Had he finally understood what Matheus was capable of doing?

'*La-i-leb*' shouted Matheus Hawk and Belial disappeared with a small pop, the call-back spell; Belial's own name pronounced backwards and cast so many weeks before, now having done its job. The ship crashed down the three full spans it had risen into the air, causing everyone on board to fall to the deck.

When Matheus regained his feet, the three demons had also disappeared, held in this dimension by nothing more than the magic of their demon King. He stared at the distant speck that was *The Griffin* and, making note of the course, ordered the shaken, but greatly relieved captain, to make for open sea.

* * *

In the first rays of early morning light, Minster sat amid a sparkling sea, a green jewel in a blue setting. Glancing back, they could only guess at the commotion their departure had caused as the steady wing beats of the mighty *Griffin* continued taking them further away.

'That was really impressive, Loras,' shouted Quint grinning. 'Any idea how we steer her?'

'Navigation and boat control I leave to you,' replied Loras happily. 'That was good eh, Quint, I bet old Bartholomew's really upset now.'

They were still laughing when Mahra landed next to them exhausted from trying to catch up and changed from owl to girl.

'They're making for open sea. The demons have all gone. I don't know what happened, they just disappeared,' she glanced back at the island, the wind ruffling her hair. 'Do we know where we're going?'

'We're heading for Freya and then we'll pick up the route to Dhurbar. We've got one more skull to find and according to the book, that's where we'll find it.' Quint leaned his body to the left pulling on *The Griffin's* fur at the base of her wings and was delighted when the great creature responded with a cry, banking towards the far distant city.

* * *

Belial found himself spinning blindly out of control, falling, falling, falling and as he fell he let out his frustrations in a long drawn-out wail. How could the human have tricked him so? He felt disappointment and confusion fused with a burning desire for revenge envelop him, then he finally landed with a colossal thump upon solid ground. Clouds of dust covered and surrounded him as he mentally checked his body for damage. As a demon he felt little physical pain, only the pain of his betrayal once again by human kind. He sat up, glaring around, but all was darkness in the realm of demons.

After so many centuries trapped here, he had no wish to be back amongst his kin. Even for a king of demons it wasn't a pleasant place to be. He tried to trace the patterns of the Magic that had brought him to the realm of man. He'd managed to summon his brethren to him once he was there. Couldn't he find his own way back? Maybe, he could.

A scampering sound echoed around him, but from what, a wall, a cliff? His eyes were becoming accustomed now to the dim luminescent glow. His hand shot out and he drew it back, peering down to see a small creature staring back at him with large saucer-like eyes. He slowly broke its neck with the pressure of his thumb and tossed it to the ground. No, he wasn't ready to start eating demon food just yet.

He crawled on his hands and knees, feeling his way to the cliff-face then leaned back against it to afford some protection while he started to chant. He had no plan to be here for long, not after the sweet air and fine food of the human realm. Now he had retribution to add to his list. Matheus Hawk and his fat friend Bartholomew Bask would die as surely as those brats and this time, he'd do it properly.

Chapter 18

Seas of Sand

Two days after setting out from the Island of Minster, the little boat made its way into the harbour at Freya and tied up at the far end of a long line of trading vessels. This boat wasn't as spacious as *The Griffin* and both boys were eager to be back on dry land after its somewhat cramped confines.

The subject of what they'd do when finally arriving, had been the centre of debate the entire voyage. A room at Blake's, a decent brew and some fresh cinnamon buns were at the top of the list. Tarent was also looking forward to a long soak and a snooze in a tub of hot water, a desire that Pardigan didn't share.

'We've washed lots lately,' he whined, sniffing tentatively at his armpits.

Tarent shook his head. 'If you're going to sleep in the same room as me, and then travel with me to Dhurbar, you're going to have to wash in a proper tub.' He cuffed his friend's ear and darted off with Pardigan hot on his heels calling him a scented dandy.

They got their room at Blake's and stowed their gear, being sure to leave the bag with the skull in with Blake downstairs. It was common knowledge in Freya that Blake, or one of his staff, regularly searched the guestrooms and helped themselves to things that took their fancy. If, however, you took advantage of the house's offer to guard your valuables in their strongbox, for a small price of course, then your belongings were in the safest place in all of Freya.

First stop after Blake's was the public bathhouse situated halfway up The Cannery. Reluctantly, Pardigan had his clothes washed while he and Tarent lazed about in hot tubs splashing water around. It was good to lie back and relax and even Pardigan felt better when a few hours later, they walked out in search of the bakery and the sweet cakes it offered.

Market Square was its usual buzz of activity with traders trying desperately to out-scream their neighbours and draw customers to their wares. Two traders, both offering similar cooking pans, were arguing heatedly and ignoring the protestations of the shopper who was trying to buy a pan from one of them. Tarent and Pardigan sat down outside a bakery and ordered glasses of iced lemon water and watched as the two traders started hitting at each other, accompanied by the loud *clunks* and *dongs* of the pans they were using as weapons. A crowd started to gather, jeering and hooting at the combatants and Pardigan noticed two of the watchers were wearing the colourful flowing robes of the Dhurbar horsemen. He nudged Tarent.

'We may be in luck; it looks like a caravan's in town. Let's go to the stabling ground, the caravans usually camp out there.'

'Sounds like a plan if ever I heard one,' said Tarent, draining his glass and standing up. Some of the onlookers had now been drawn into the argument and the whole thing was turning into a small scale riot. As Pardigan and Tarent walked away they could hear the high-pitched whistles of the city watch getting closer. They followed the two Dhurbars as they broke from the crowd and headed away in the direction of the stabling grounds.

When they arrived, they found the stabling grounds were indeed host to Dhurbar traders, lots of them. It appeared that either one huge caravan was in town, or possibly several smaller ones had met up. Whatever the case, the horsemen were using the occasion to celebrate. Corrals had been set up to hold their precious horses and camels, and brightly decorated tents, woven with a patchwork of bright colours, beads and tiny mirrors twinkling in between, had been put up all around. The smoke and smell of cooking meats, exotic spices and baking flat breads was thick in the air, mingling closely with the musky smells of the animals. Many of the locals of Freya were walking around, curious of their desert visitors and their stalls from which colourful clothes and Dhurban souvenirs were being sold to the milling crowd. No Dhurban liked to overlook a chance at making a profit.

After asking around, the boys found out that in fact two caravans were encamped, each going in a different direction. The one they would be interested in was the caravan of 'Azif Benhoudin Sharif,' who, they were told, could be found either in his tents, easily found as his flag of purple and gold would be flying from its top, or walking with his retainers.

'You won't miss him,' cackled an old Dhurban, his grey beard yellow-stained around a mouth totally devoid of teeth, giving the impression that his face was collapsing whenever he stopped speaking. 'Big fellow is Azif, and he'll have a large group of people around him, mostly cooks. Likes to eat does Azif, maybe he'll eat you, boy.' He stabbed a bony finger into Pardigan's chest.

'Go eat dung, you old goat,' snarled Pardigan, rubbing his chest. Tarent hurried him away leaving the old man cackling behind them.

'Pardigan, try and be nice, these people are all carrying knives; we'd be better off making friends here, not enemies.' They wandered on, thrilling to the sights and sounds around them, and found Azif's tent easily enough, but the large Dhurbar standing at the entrance informed them that Azif Sharif was not in residence. The guard had fierce eyes and appeared eager to draw the large curved knife he was fingering at his belt, so the boys retreated into the crowd.

'Maybe we should find another way to get to Dhurbar, Tarent. These aren't the friendliest people we've met lately, are they?' Pardigan pulled out the book and sat down close to a tent. He closed it a short while later and stood up, looking disappointed.

'Nothing else in the book so I suppose this really is where we're meant to be.' They continued walking, searching for Azif in the crowd. They eventually found him watching a camel dashing around a roped-off area, trying unsuccessfully to rid itself of the rider perched on its back. Seated on a pile of cushions, Azif was laughing hysterically and eating from a variety of plates being offered by a small group of animated men around him.

Azif Benhoudin Sharif was an extremely large man. The folds of cloth wrapped around him would surely have been enough to make one of the colourful tents if he hadn't been using them to cover his ample frame. He had a purple and gold cloth wrapped around his head in the Dhurbar fashion and under this, his great rubbery face was moulded around an extremely large powerful nose. The moustache beneath would be large enough to double for a broom if one were ever needed.

Tarent took one look at Azif and grabbed hold of Pardigan. 'Don't you let me down, Pardigan, if you start laughing at this man, we may well end up dead, the whole Quest would end and Chaos would reign. This is *very* serious.' He stared at Pardigan, hoping the message would get through. 'Do you hear me?'

'I'm not stupid!' retorted Pardigan. He had actually been about to make a joke, but decided Tarent was right. These people probably wouldn't take a joke too well. They walked closer and stood waiting for an opportunity to speak with the massive caravan master.

* * *

The Griffin swept lower and lower towards the distant city in the sand. They'd been flying over the featureless desert for far too long and were now exhausted from the constant buffeting from the wind, exposure to the sun and the necessity of holding on to the great beast beneath them.

It had been quite beautiful first thing in the morning, the dunes and cacti sending long shadows across the desert giving them wonderful scenery to look down upon. As the sun had risen however, the shadows had become fewer and fewer and they could see little difference in anything below, everything had blurred into a fiercely bright featureless expanse.

'How do the Dhurbar navigate in this?' asked Loras, peering down through his fingers to shield his eyes from the glare. 'One sand hill seems the same as another to me and I don't see how any road or path would last long down there.'

'They navigate by the stars and by landmarks that only they can see,' explained Mahra, holding her head close to Loras so he could hear her. 'Two similar-shaped hills may be called the brothers, or a large hill close to a small hill may be the mother and infant. What appears as a featureless landscape to you is a well-documented landscape to them. They would find it incredible that Quint was able to find his way over water, when no landmark at all is visible.'

'Mahra, I *also* find it incredible that Quint can navigate at sea, but I get your point about the desert.'

Mahra smiled. 'We each have our abilities which we find comfortable ourselves, but seem impossible for others to understand. I can change into other forms, Quint can navigate and send an arrow into a tiny target from a thousand paces, and you, Loras, can change boats into beasts. I still have no idea how you did that.'

'It wasn't actually that hard. Do you remember how you tried to prompt me when I wanted to make the fire hotter back on The Isle of Skulls? You had an idea it could be done. Maybe you'd seen it done before. When I read my books the answer was to increase something that was already there. In the case of the fire, it was easy; just increase the warmth that was already available. The change of *The Griffin* was really no harder than that. *The Griffin* was a *Griffin* in all of our minds, even though it was only a name. All I did was to expand on that and make the name grow... easy!' Loras grinned but Mahra remained silent, regarding him thoughtfully.

It was late morning when they spotted the desert city of Dhurban. At first it was an irregular feature in the bright desert, then later appeared as an extension to a range of crumbling mountains. As they got closer still, it gradually resolved into the ancient city.

They made long fast sweeping turns searching for a likely landing spot, the warm air rushing over them making it difficult to see through tear-filled eyes. Dhurban was about the same size as Freya but the two cities shared little in common. Dhurban was a walled city, with watchtowers and battlements all around as if expecting attack from an army emerging from the desert. A copper-domed roof, centred with a spike, topped each watchtower like outlandish hats worn by a desert merchant. The roofs of the buildings inside the city were either flat, or were similarly dome-shaped as the towers. A few of these also shone copper or gold and were flashing in the brilliant sunlight as *The Griffin* sped past overhead. The three flyers were excited about the city, if not a little nervous about what their reception would be. They could see several market squares and then what must be the sultan's palace in the north; it was the only building with green gardens surrounding it. Huge golden domes topped the building and as they got closer they could see fountains set amongst the lavish gardens; this seemed like the spot they should land in and Quint coaxed *The Griffin* towards the front of the largest building.

As they got lower they were spotted; armed soldiers began running around after them, peering up and shouting as they tried to anticipate where the strange creature would land.

Mahra raised her voice over the rush of the wind. 'Let's try and do this right, no arrows, and no magic unless we have to, all right?' They nodded their agreement and *The Griffin* descended with claws outstretched and wings beating fast, gently coming to a perfect rest amid a great cloud of dust. Folding her wings, *The Griffin* settled herself as soldiers, coughing from the dust, surrounded them. With spears pointing at the great beast, they gazed on, eyes wide with the wonder of this strange visitor. *The Griffin* ignored them and sat staring at the closest fountain, its head cocking from one side to the other, mesmerised by the play of light through the dancing water.

The soldiers wore burnished armour chest pieces over golden robes, and conical helmets similar to the roofs of the buildings. The same golden cloth fell down behind the helmets to protect their necks from the fierce desert sun; they looked very smart. A large man pushed himself to the front and marched forward brandishing a spear. He spoke rapidly in a language that none of them understood, then seeing the lack of comprehension on their faces, he changed to Freyan.

'Who are you that come uninvited to the great sultan's palace?' He saw they'd understood him and went on. 'Quick, tell me who you are before I kill this thing you sit upon and cast you all into the dungeons.'

Mahra slid down, followed closely by Quint and then Loras. The head soldier approached, once more ready to issue more orders.

Mahra held up a hand and he stopped, obviously shocked that she would dare do so. 'We're here to visit your sultan and mean no offence. We would be most grateful if some of your men would guard our... beast while we are gone.' The guard captain regarded Mahra uncertainly and then peered at *The Griffin*.

'What if I were just to kill this thing and then throw you children into the dungeons? You show no respect by arriving like this and...'

'As I said,' interrupted Mahra as she felt Quint bristling behind her. 'We mean no offence, we... children are ignorant of your ways and wouldn't wish to cause offence should our beast hurt any of you, or by us defending ourselves if you mistook us for enemies. It would be far better for all if we were to be allowed to explain ourselves to the sultan. As a man who has risen to your rank, I'm sure you are blessed with a superior intellect and can see the wisdom of this. I commend you on your prompt, professional arrival and shall be sure to advise the sultan that his captain of the guards has acted both professionally and wisely in dealing with what must be a very strange event.'

Loras exchanged a nervous look with Quint as Mahra finished.

'I don't need *you* to explain anything to our sultan, who is also my brother,' spat the guard captain as he puffed out his chest. 'However, I will graciously grant your wish to see the sultan, and he shall decide what is to be done with you. You may see your bird thing again, or maybe you will not, now come with us.' With that he marched off towards a large arched entrance.

'Can you put some sort of spell on *The Griffin* to stop anyone touching her?' whispered Mahra to Loras.

'I already have,' he hissed back as they followed. 'If anyone tries to get close, *The Griffin* will snap at them, but if she feels she is under any real threat she'll fly away, and only one of us can call her back.' He saw a soldier listening to them so lowered his voice still further. 'Remember how I said to break the spell on the Isle of Skulls? Well say the same thing in a normal voice and she'll come.'

'Okay, well let's just hope that the sultan is a little more welcoming than his brother,' muttered Quint as they entered the palace. He cast a look back and saw *The Griffin* snap at a soldier that had prodded her with his spear. 'I'm pretty sure she's going to be gone when we come back out.'

'If you get out,' growled a soldier. 'Our sultan hates to be disturbed, and this, I think, will be very disturbing for him. Maybe he'll give you to us guards to play with.' He leered at Mahra and held out his hand to touch her but flinched back in a hurry when she bared her teeth and emitted a deep animal growl.

'Just pray that he doesn't,' she purred. 'You might not like the games I play.'

* * *

'My dinner is looking at me,' Pardigan whispered to Tarent. He was staring down at his bowl and sure enough an eyeball, or something very much like one, was peering up at him through a mass of tubes, gristle and liquid.

Tarent held back a laugh and elbowed him in the ribs. 'Shhh, just eat around it or something, at least we're being fed.'

'I wish they hadn't bothered, I can't eat this muck. Pass me more bread, will you?' They were sitting cross-legged around the edge of a large tent in the company of about twenty Dhurbar horsemen. No women were present except for two dancing girls in the middle who were swaying to a strange wailing sound coming from an old man blowing on a large bulbous flute.

'It's a shame Loras missed this, at least he would have liked the music,' observed Pardigan with a grin, 'and I'm sure he could have made this eyeball disappear as well.' He scooped up the eye, popped it into a wedge of bread, and then pushed it to the side. 'There... gone, magic!' He glanced around to be sure he hadn't been seen.

The conversations around them were taking place in Dhurban, which of course neither of them spoke. Most of the attention was for Azif Benhoudin Sharif as everyone tried to gain his favour. Azif was happily gorging himself and carrying on several conversations at the same time. Finally he wiped his mouth with a cloth and clapped his hands. The two dancing girls rushed off and a tall Dhurbar walked in and bowed deeply to Azif. He started to speak in Dhurban but Azif scowled and clapped his hands again.

'Please, I have guests who have no knowledge of our tongue; you will speak Freyan, if you are able.' He smiled and waved across at Tarent and Pardigan.

They had been invited to the tent by luck after asking to speak with Azif. While one of his people was trying to hurry them away, Azif had actually called them over. They'd told him of their need to reach Dhurbar and had produced a gold coin as good faith. On seeing the coin Azif had told them to follow and the whole group had retired to his tent, where the feast had started to take place.

The tall Dhurban swung towards them and bowed deeply. 'May you please forgive me,' he said in perfect Freyan. 'I did not see you seated amongst this noble gathering.' He indicated the other guests in the room with a bow and a casual gesture of his hands, then turned back to Azif and, bowing once more, swept aside his cloak with a flourish to show two belts crossing his chest holding a selection of deadly knives. 'My great Lord Azif Benhoudin Sharif, noble guests. If it pleases you I shall display my humble talents, for I am Mustep the Knifeman, *greatest* blade thrower in the entire known world.'

'I bet he's not,' whispered Pardigan. 'What do *you* think bread?' He held up his bread with the eye wrapped in between looking out. It looked like the bread was a real eye in a furrowed brow. Pardigan made it blink a couple of times then turned it from side to side. 'The bread is watching him and isn't convinced.' He laughed but had the sense to hide his mirth behind his hands.

'Shhh,' cautioned Tarent with a glare.

Mustep clapped his hands and a scruffy looking boy ran into the tent and stood in front of a large board. The boy stood still as the knifeman arranged him with arms outstretched and had him hold burning candles in each hand, he then placed a small pomegranate on top of the boy's head. The boy stood trembling, his eyes tightly closed. Mustep marched back, close to where Azif was seated then spun around and threw his first knife. It flashed across the tent snuffing the candle in the boy's left hand. A second knife quickly followed the first, snuffing the second candle. The diners all clapped enthusiastically, although it seemed to both Tarent and Pardigan that they'd all seen the display before. The third knife was sent spinning and the pomegranate split in two, juice dribbled down the boy's frightened face and he blinked it away from his eyes.

'If he'd set the knife to land flat rather than straight, he could have done that without spilling any juice,' muttered Pardigan. 'He's definitely not the best... but I'm keeping my eye on him.'

'*Shhh, shut up you fool!*' hissed Tarent.

Next, a young girl ran in and stood opposite the boy in front of a different board. Servants came in and set candles in each of her hands, and fresh pomegranates were placed upon their heads.

'My Lord, today I have extended my performance and shall amaze you by doubling the danger. I shall prepare myself and throw fast but true, proving once again that I am the greatest knife thrower in all the kingdoms.'

Azif glanced up from the conversation he was having with a small round gentleman in a bright flowing robe and waved his hand. 'Yes,

yes I am sure it will be a most wondrous display, Mustep.' He quickly returned to his conversation.

'And dangerous,' pointed out Mustep, 'for this requires great practice and preparation.' He bowed low offering an oily smile before returning to the centre of the room.

'Not dangerous for him though, is it,' snorted Pardigan a little too loudly. 'If I was one of those two, I think I'd run for the door about now.'

Tarent dug him in the ribs. '*Shhh.* For the love of the Source, Pardigan, why can't you just keep quiet?'

By now several people had heard him even if they hadn't quite caught what he'd said. Mustep the knifeman turned a stony face to Pardigan before addressing Azif.

'My Lord, I do believe that your young guest is trying to show his courage by volunteering to stand at the board for the young lady.' Azif leaned forward to peer at Pardigan who had sat back in shock.

'Young man,' cried Azif. 'I am heartily impressed with your valour, indeed with anyone brave enough to stand in front of Mustep's knives; they are not always known to find their mark. If they do, they are often in the children he uses as targets.' This brought a roar of laughter from the seated Dhurbar causing Mustep to turn red with shame and anger.

'Come, boy, show your courage,' urged the knifeman gruffly. Pardigan glanced over at the girl. She was holding out the candles with a pleading look in her eyes, the pomegranate wobbling precariously on her head. He glanced over at Tarent who shrugged.

'I did try and warn you to keep your big mouth shut. Now get up there, close your eyes and say nothing if that's possible, then sit back down when it's over, all right?' Pardigan took a breath.

'At least I can stretch my legs and don't have to eat the muck in that bowl,' he whispered. He saw his Dhurbar neighbour prodding suspiciously at the piece of bread that had the eye peeking out. 'Oh, and keep an eye on my food will you, Tarent, it keeps winking at people?' With a sigh he stood up. 'Very well, I would be happy to stand for the lady. I have great faith in your ability, oh wondrous knife man.' He walked over and a servant helped him with the candles and pomegranate.

Mustep paced to the centre of the room and let fly his first knife. It flew towards Pardigan who screwed his eyes shut and stood completely still. He heard it thud into the board to his left and he opened his eyes to see that the candle in his hand was split in two, the knife only a hairsbreadth from his fingers. Hot wax dripped onto his hand, but he gritted his teeth and held firm. Mustep grinned at him showing black rotting teeth. Pardigan glanced across to Tarent who shook his head and frowned. The message was clear, just hold still and get it over with.

The next knife flew at the boy and the candle in his hand was snuffed out, another knife immediately followed towards Pardigan who again closed his eyes and prayed to the Source. It thudded home and his mind reached out to see if any pain had accompanied it before he opened his eyes, the candle was snuffed. Loud clapping came from the diners and even Azif was applauding happily. The next knives flew and the pomegranates on both Pardigan's and the boy's heads were split, dribbling juice onto their faces. Pardigan squinted open his eyes and saw everyone, including Tarent, laughing and pointing at him. Pardigan hated being laughed at; it had always been a problem and had gotten him into many a scrape. He felt his anger rise and the urge to spin the knives back at Mustep began to overwhelm him. He took a step forward and saw Tarent shaking his head urgently, but Pardigan just smiled and pretended not to notice.

Chapter 19

Walking the Knife's Edge

It had taken almost two days to get to Freya, which was where Matheus Hawk was sure the thieves had gone. He'd renegotiated his position with Bartholomew Bask and they'd agreed that Matheus would now receive any magical goods as well as a third of any captured cargo or coins. He was especially pleased with the deal, as magical goods would most certainly include a boat that transformed into a flying creature. The trail was somewhat cold but Matheus wasn't known as the best tracker in the entire kingdom for nothing. They'd questioned the nervous official from the Customs boat on leaving Minster, and been told that a small craft had been seen heading away from the island in much the same direction as the bird thing, towards Freya.

After arriving and much rooting around in the port, they had found the boat and Matheus had watched, amused as Bartholomew half destroyed it in his anger at finding neither the thieves, nor indeed any sign of his goods. Bartholomew had finally realised that the boat itself would possibly be worth something, and ordered two seamen to patch it up and sell it. Happy to be at least a little up on the deal, they were now supping Elder ale in front of Blake's while discussing where to go next. The heat was intense, more so here in Freya than in Minster, or of course the open sea, and Bartholomew was constantly mopping his brow with his now shabby lace handkerchief.

'By the life of me, I have no idea where the brats would be going. I've half a mind to call it quits and get on with me business now that damn demon has seen fit to depart.' He drank deeply from his tankard, then wiping his mouth on his sleeve glanced around for a serving girl to order more.

'Half a mind is about right, my fat friend. It was I that dismissed our demon tormentor; I've explained that to you. It would be bad business to abandon our search now when we're so close; besides, I think the prize is far richer than just the contents of your cabinet. There's too much interest in these young thieves. This is all about some bigger prize, you mark my words; your cabinet was just one small piece of this puzzle.' Matheus drained his tankard, a thoughtful expression on his face.

'Yes but it was my small piece of puzzle, wasn't it, and *I won't be robbed*,' snarled Bartholomew, his temper rising once more but then he sagged back down; it was too hot to get cross and he wanted more ale. They sat and continued to drink as the day went on, until finally the sun set and the shadows became night. When a girl came out to light the oil lamps in front of the inn, the two of them were laughing together like old friends, making jokes about demons and drinking far too much ale for their own good.

A short way to the left of Matheus Hawk a small tear appeared in the fabric of space and a finger forced itself through making a faint ripping noise. Muted sounds of panting and a struggle could be heard, but it wasn't until the hole finally forced itself closed again with a small pop, that Matheus finally noticed.

'What was that?' he glanced around, startled.

'What was what?' said Bartholomew dreamily, staring into the bottom of yet another empty ale pot.

'A sound,' said Matheus peering into the shadows. Seeing nothing, he returned to his drink. 'Come on, we should get back to the ship; we've still to plan what we'll do from here. We know those brats can't be too far ahead of us.' They stood up and leaning on each other, staggered back to the *Esmerelda* to plot their next move.

Walking the Knife's Edge

* * *

Belial sat back exhausted but happy. He had worked out how to follow the trail back to the right dimension and was satisfied that he could find it by concentrating his magic on the Hawk. Now he simply needed to gather his strength and some followers and he would be ready.

* * *

Loras was feeling two emotions as he studied the old man in the over-large turban. The first was complete and utter awe that he was facing a real live magician, one that had obviously spent a lifetime studying and perfecting his art. The second was a small amount of fear and uncertainty that he may be about to embark on his first magical duel with this strange opponent.

It had all started innocently enough; they'd been escorted into the throne room of the palace to find the sultan, seated on a large cushion raised upon a platform. He was deep in conversation with three advisors, one of whom was this funny little man. They had bowed deeply and Quint had started to speak.

'Your Majesty, we have come here...' Although Quint had got no further, a guard had struck him from behind and everyone had started screaming, it was as if the world had suddenly gone mad. As Quint lay prone on the floor the guard had lifted his spear as if to stab him, which had been enough for Loras. Before the guard had time to strike down, Loras had frozen him with a simple wave of his hand. He'd changed the heat in the guard's body for something opposite, cold, and the guard had literally frozen to the spot.

Mahra, by this time, was crouching on all fours, a Black Panther, teeth bared and growling, prepared to leap at the other guards who had at first rushed in but were now scrabbling to back out. The magician had stepped forward and thrown a ball of fire directly at Loras who had merely swatted it aside, which was why Loras was now prepared for a duel, his emotions already at war.

The magician lifted his robes around his skinny legs and leapt high into the air with a strange ululating cry, *'aaaaya-ha-ha-ha!'* He came down not three steps from Loras and pushed his hands out, and a thick wall of air knocked Loras to the ground.

'Wow!' said Loras instantly understanding what the magician had done. 'That was great, and so easy!' The magician shrieked, formed a flaming sword out of thin air and ran forward, his robes flapping wildly and yelling his strange shrill war cry. Loras simply formed a similar wall of air, which the magician bounced off, landing on his bottom; the sword disappeared. Loras grinned down at him and held out his hand.

'Can I help you up?' he offered. 'How did you make the sword? It was really good!' The magician started spluttering with rage and slapped Loras's hand aside. The other advisor jumped down; a regal looking Dhurbar with a forked beard and a huge curved sword. Quint, who had made it back to his feet, drew his own sword, ready to do battle.

'I'm with you, Loras,' he muttered, swaying a little as he sized up his opponent. Seeing things were starting to get out of hand, the sultan stood and bellowed in Freyan, *'Enough hold fast!'* and everybody stopped. The sultan scowled down from his platform. 'Who are you that brings madness to my court? Children shouldn't travel without an adult.'

Quint by now had recovered most of his wits but was still staggering slightly from the blow.

'May I speak, your highness?' he rubbed the back of his head, checking his hand for signs of blood.

'When I give you leave young man, then you may speak. Until I give leave, it is an insult. Yes...now you may speak, but do so quickly before my magician and my men are allowed to kill you.' He glanced uncertainly at his magician, whom he'd believed invincible, right up until he'd seen him foiled by a small boy.

He waved his guards back and sat down, Mahra resumed her human form and Loras grinned at the magician who stared at him shaking in anger, his eyes promising the exchange wasn't over.

'So who are you? Speak,' said the sultan with a scowl. Quint spoke. He spoke of their regret at causing any insult to the sultan or his court and then he spoke of their Quest and the skulls they sought in the name of the Source, and of the balance that was necessary to stop the world from tipping into Chaos. When he finished speaking some time later, the court was silent and the sultan was sitting stroking his beard thoughtfully.

'I must think on this story. My men will take you to rooms and you will be guests of my palace. Please do not attempt to leave without my permission, it would be most insulting.' He clapped his hands and the guards formed up and escorted them out of the room.

They were taken to a suite of rooms high up in the palace that gave a good view of the gardens where they'd landed earlier; *The Griffin* was no longer there but Loras wasn't concerned.

'She'll come back when we call,' he said dismissing Quint's concerns. 'This is an incredible place! How did the magician make that sword? That's what I want to know,' he continued excitedly. 'I wonder if I'll get the chance to speak to him?' Mahra and Quint exchanged glances.

'So where do we go from here?' asked Quint, addressing Mahra.

'Well, without the book we have no direction, so we just have to wait for Pardigan and Tarent to turn up.' She sighed. 'I just hope they're all right.'

* * *

Pardigan was all right, but Tarent's day was taking a bad turn as he watched his friend approach Mustep. *Why can he never sit back and keep quiet?* He fumed.

Every eye in the tent was on Pardigan as he walked towards Mustep, wiping juice from his face.

'Have you finished with your party tricks or are you going to do something really clever now?' Mustep frowned at Pardigan's words.

'My lords, our friend Mustep here is indeed a great knife thrower but then he is, I believe, using trick knives.'

A murmur of voices filled the tent. 'What are you doing, boy?' hissed the knife thrower.

'Are they trick knives? How do they work?' asked Azif, showing more interest now than at any other time in the spectacle.

Pardigan ignored Mustep and pulled one of the knives from the board behind him.

'Well I think they're trick knives, let's see.' He picked up a large melon from the closest table and hurled it over his head. A heartbeat later he sent the knife flashing over his shoulder, making it obvious to all that he hadn't taken aim. The knife caught the melon at the top of its flight and split it in two. One half fell to the floor, with the knife stuck in it, the other half fell and landed on Mustep's head. The room erupted in laughter and Pardigan turned to see Mustep shaking away melon pieces and wiping juice from his face, glaring at him. Pardigan gave him a big grin.

'I'm not sure what you did but make a joke of me boy and you make an enemy of me as well. You'll do well to watch your back, for one day I'll come back and I *will* have my revenge.' He stomped off out of the tent to derisive hoots and laughter.

'Come, sit, boy, bring your friend and talk with me.' Azif beckoned them over to where he sat and room was made for the two boys.

'You're going to get us into a lot of trouble one day, Pardigan,' hissed Tarent as he sat down. 'Now one of the greatest knifemen in the kingdom is going to be out to get you.'

'Us, Tarent, I'm sure he'll want to get both of us,' said Pardigan grinning. 'But at least we're going to get to Dhurban now, aren't we, and anyhow, he's not the greatest knifeman in the Kingdom, I am! The book saw to that.'

As they were welcomed into the caravan - Pardigan was delighted while Tarent felt a deep unease that he tried not to show.

Walking the Knife's Edge

We may be going to Dhurban, but at what cost? he thought as he watched his friend talking with Azif. Why couldn't I have gone with Mahra and the others? I'm sure they're having a far easier time.

* * *

It was two days before the caravan got underway amid a well-organised chaos of movement. The stabling grounds had been a hive of activity with tents being disassembled, people shouting, horses being saddled, camels being loaded and several covered platforms or palanquins as they were called, hastily constructed. Each palanquin was swung between two camels and then draped in a colourful mixture of silk and canvas to protect the occupants from the boiling sun and harsh conditions of the desert. Pardigan and Tarent had been persuaded to purchase the use of one of these and because of their newfound popularity with Azif; they rode second in line behind him. The other fare-paying passengers were towards the back of the long line; either in palanquins if they had sufficient coin, or on camels or horses exposed to the heat and dust if they didn't.

'This is horrible,' moaned Pardigan, lying back on the pile of many coloured cushions that filled the swaying platform. 'Oh Source, I feel sick.' He pulled a cushion over his head. They were only halfway through their first morning, barely started on the three-day journey across the wide expanse of the desert and both boys were already regretting the experience.

'If you hadn't found such favour with Azif then we could have just hired a couple of camels and ridden instead, *that* I could have dealt with, but this is ridiculous,' said Tarent falling back as the camels negotiated a hillock and the platform jolted up. Pardigan scrambled to the edge, nearly falling out in the process, and threw up noisily over the side.

'Three days, we're never going to last three days like this,' he gasped back over his shoulder.

Tarent stared at him. 'Serves you right for showing off; it's me I feel sorry for.'

The caravan moved along at a slow plodding pace across the dunes, negotiating a route between crumbling ancient mountains and across the seas of flat sandy expanse. The palanquins creaked, the harnesses with their bells jingled and sometimes the camels called to each other, their strange grunting cry passing up and down the line. The only other sound was the occasional call of the Dhurbar as they urged each other on but for the most part, the camel train was silent as man and beast did their best to deal with the ever-increasing heat as they went deeper and deeper into the desert.

* * *

After two days of waiting as prisoners in their rooms, a messenger arrived with an armed escort and bowed deeply.

'The great sultan regrets the inconvenience of your waiting here and begs you indulge him a little longer while he confers with his advisors on this and several other important matters. If there is anything that I can get for you, please tell me and it shall be yours.'

'We just wish to speak with the sultan again. We don't want more of these fruits or pastries.' Quint kicked a tray of delicacies into the air and Mahra moved forward, resting a hand on his arm.

'Calm yourself, Quint, this does us no good.' She turned to the messenger.

'I apologise for my friend's behaviour, he is a little…frustrated about our journey being delayed.' The messenger bowed again as he backed towards the door.

'It is quite understandable but regrettably unavoidable. I am sure you will be called for soon.' The door closed with a click and a turn of the lock.

'I'm sorry but this is driving me mad.' Quint stomped off to the balcony and gazed out over the grounds of the palace and into the city beyond. The sun was beating down without any mercy upon the city as it had done on every single day in its history; as if trying to prove that a city had no right to be here in its desert. It had never rained in Dhurban.

'Somewhere out there is the skull we're searching for, is there no other way for us to locate it?' asked Quint quietly as Mahra moved up beside him.

'The book said that the sultan's daughter would tell and then guide us down through hell. We have to wait and wait and then wait longer if that's what's necessary.' Mahra reminded him. Quint stared at her.

'You're right! We don't need to see the sultan again at all, it's his daughter we want, yet I haven't noticed more than two girls since we got here. There were none sitting with the sultan, so how is she meant to find us and guide us anywhere?' He glanced up. 'You have to go flying, Mahra. *We* can't get out of here and make contact, but *you* can.' Mahra edged away, shaking her head.

'We've been told to remain in our rooms; I don't think they'd take too kindly to finding me missing, do you?'

Quint stared at her, while Loras put down the large book he'd been reading.

'He's got a point, Mahra. I mean how is this daughter meant to know about us or know she has to tell us this vital bit of information? Why don't you go and look about, see what this palace is all about?'

After a moment she nodded. 'All right, I'll fly tonight. Owls don't fly during the day, but to be honest owls don't spend an awful lot of time in deserts either, at least not barn owls.' She walked over to a pile of cushions and leaping forward turned into the cat and curled up, falling instantly to sleep.

'It does make sense,' said Loras in a vain attempt at appeal, but the cat didn't stir. She'd be like this now until dark; the boys had witnessed several of her sulks and this was one of them. Loras went back to his book and Quint returned to watching the city, the shimmer of heat that covered it and the distant mountains beyond.

Chapter 20

What's a Mudlark?

Figures shuffled in the gloom, large dark silhouettes framed against the red glow that emanated from molten pools of lava. The walls of the cavern oozed a thick syrupy liquid while sulphurous fumes belched continuously from the pools, making the atmosphere thick and fetid. The only sounds as the gathering assembled, were the hiss and burps of the lava and the rasping breath of everything in attendance.

The meeting was being held for the elite of the brethren and Belial's nostrils flared with pride. Pride at the mighty that had gathered at his word and in delight at breathing the thick heavy gases of the demon realm, rather than the tasteless sweet nothing of the realm he had so recently departed. He gazed out into the gloom and saw the shadows gathering, eyes glowing red in the steamy atmosphere. Judging that the meeting was almost complete, he brought a large stone down upon the altar rock, sparks accompanying each crash that echoed around the cavern.

'My brothers, my people, I have returned from the realm of man and their flesh is as sweet as you all remember; soon I shall go back and you shall come with me. The time of the demons is at hand.' The demon horde roared its support and Belial smiled. A king must lead and this would be his greatest moment as he brought his people back to the realm of man.

'But how will you go, my King?' The question came from a hunched figure standing to the side of him; Curohl, one of many brother princes and a pretender to his throne. Word had reached him that Curohl had started to plot against him as soon as he'd left, and it could be that he would test him for the throne here and now if allowed.

'Were you not dismissed back to us?' Curohl started to walk towards him. 'Were you not... *Aauughh!*' He never finished his sentence as Belial's knife embedded itself into his brother's eye. Curohl fell to the floor whimpering and kicking out in his death throes. Such was justice dispensed in the realm of the demons. No other moved to give aid, no voice was raised in protest as Belial's gaze swept the cavern. If Curohl had friends and sympathisers, they wisely chose to do nothing. He continued as if the interruption had never occurred, delighting once again in the power that was his to control.

'I have the key to go back, I can return whenever I desire, bringing as many of you with me as I wish. Do you not crave to return with me and fill your bellies with the flesh of man, to feast upon their pain and their suffering? Am... I... not... your... King?' He held up his hands, inviting an answer and received it as the gathering roared his name over and over.

'Belial, Belial, Belial...' He smiled and drank in the attention. Now if he were only able to find the final piece of the puzzle he could indeed return with this army of demons and their minions. He could locate the Hawk and make the gateway, but how to hold it? The cavern continued to resound with the echoes of his name and for now he satisfied himself in the worship of his people. In front of him the body of Curohl twitched one last time and he observed it with interest as the final moments of his brother's life ebbed away.

* * *

After two days, both Pardigan and Tarent were becoming relatively used to the swinging momentum of the palanquin. Neither was enjoying it, both still felt ill, but so far today neither had been sick.

The evening before they'd been deliriously relieved when the caravan had eventually stopped and they were able to crawl out and feel solid ground. They hadn't noticed Azif watching them, a huge smile on his face as he stroked his immense stomach in anticipation of the evening meal.

'How you like our Palanquin, eh? Is this not true luxury to travel the desert in comfort and shade while those of a lesser class ride the camels?' He waved his hand derisively towards the back of the caravan, with riders still arriving amongst a huge cloud of dust. 'You are lucky Azif has decided to like you, yes? Come, eat with me at my tent.'

What the boys really wanted to do was crawl into their own tent and sleep. Riding in the unpleasant palanquin all day was far from restful and the only sleep they'd been able to manage was unsettled and filled with strange dreams, giving little rest between bouts of vomiting. They'd eventually relented and gone to Azif's tent, but only after he'd sent one of his retainers in search of them. Once seated, they had sat through and endured an evening of entertainment, while tray upon tray of food was left mostly untouched. Finally, they had slid off to find their own tent, to sleep an exhausted sleep filled with more strange dreams.

The current day had been one of torture. At midday, as the sun reached its highest point, the caravan came to a welcome stop at a watering hole. The camels had smelt the water some distance off and had been calling and grunting in anticipation for some time. They now gathered with heads hung low, sucking great mouthfuls deep into their huge stomachs. Pardigan and Tarent had crawled from their palanquin and were sitting with their backs propped against the side of a shallow cliff, observing the milling throng around them.

'I feel awful,' muttered Pardigan. Tarent did no more than glance at his friend. There was nothing left to say.

The Dhurbar organised the brief stop as efficiently as they did everything else. All the camels were seen to and watered before the Dhurbar themselves gathered in small groups, lighting fires and cook-

What's a Mudlark?

ing up small cups of the thick black beverage they favoured over the Freyan brew and baking flat gritty bread.

Tarent picked up a stone and tossed it towards the water; it bounced a few times but didn't quite make it to the edge. 'I'm so tired, I'm going to sleep for a week when we get to Dhurbar and find a proper bed and I don't ever want to be the one travelling alone with you again. You always manage to get us into trouble of some sort.'

'At least I make life interesting, eh? We are...' Pardigan stopped short as all around them the ground literally exploded. Earth and mud flew up wrapping around camels and Dhurbar alike.

'*Mudlarks*' came a cry as Pardigan and Tarent watched for a moment, trying to make sense of what was happening as the Dhurbar slashed at the mud forms with their swords.

'What's a mudlark?' asked Pardigan glancing wildly around him. Tarent felt something slide around his neck and jumped up, tearing himself free drawing the twin swords from his staff. A mudlark, if that's what it was, leapt out from the bank he'd been resting against, the swords flashed and what had looked and felt like a solid being a moment before, splattered to the ground into separate lumps of wet sticky clay.

'I think that's a mudlark,' said Tarent, but Pardigan was already engaged with two others. One had a brown sticky arm around his neck and was fast covering his face, trying to suffocate him. The other didn't last long as his knife found some source of its life and it dropped as a puddle of mud to the ground, coating him to the waist in thick brown goo, the second lasted only moments longer. Tarent spun around and watched as the Dhurbar fought the attackers, swords flashing. To their right a camel was being dragged into the pool and two Dhurbar had jumped to its rescue only to be attacked by more of the strange beings. Up and down the caravan similar scenes were unfolding accompanied by the scream of terrified beasts and the shouts and cries of the Dhurbar.

'Come on,' shouted Pardigan, any thought of sickness or fatigue forgotten as he threw his cape to the side, pulled his knives and tripped a mudlark, sending it flying as it lurched past. He finished it and ran on.

Azif was standing on a rock shouting orders and directing his personal guards as they fought savagely around him. A mudlark vaulted up and over its fellows, flying towards the stout caravan master and Pardigan let fly a knife that literally exploded the creature in mid air. Azif waved cheery thanks as they ran past; Pardigan retrieved his knife, and they went searching for where they were needed next.

For what seemed an age they travelled the length of the caravan helping out where they could. The mudlarks were interested in both humans and camels as they successfully dragged both into the pool and down into its depths. The boys quickly realised that once into the water, there was very little help they could give man or beast as hundreds of muddy arms grabbed and dragged their struggling burdens under. On land the mudlarks were easier prey and the boys became covered in sticky mud as they fought; swords and knives flashing alongside the Dhurbar. Towards the rear of the caravan the fighting was heaviest and the boys ran to help as a group of mudlarks began tearing and pulling at a palanquin and its camels, its helpless occupants squealing in terror. Tarent and Pardigan went in with blades flashing.

When fighting in a group, the mudlarks tended to attack from as many directions as possible, trapping legs and feet and attempting to bring an opponent to the ground where they could then drown them in mud. The boys fought bravely and were aided as at least one of the palanquin's occupants attacked from behind. As the mudlarks were beaten back, Pardigan glanced up to thank the man who had just knifed a mudlark that had got too close, only to realise he was face to face with Matheus Hawk. Both reacted at the same time; Matheus screamed an oath and reached out for Pardigan while Pardigan jumped over a slippery pile of former mudlarks, desperate to get some distance between him and the angry hunter. Tarent turned to see what was happening and taking in the situation, called to Matheus.

'For now we fight together, our differences can wait until we've beaten back the mudlarks, agreed?'

Matheus stopped and glared at him, then nodded an agreement. Tarent studied the palanquin but could see no sign of Bartholomew Bask under the pile of quivering cushions but knew he must be there. A new wave of attackers erupted from the ground and once again the caravan was a heaving mass as mud, men and screaming terrified camels fought for control. Tarent and Pardigan began to move away from where the Hawk stood fighting alongside a handful of Dhurbar, and made their way back towards the front of the caravan and their own palanquin.

'We may well need the good favour of Azif. The Hawk and Bartholomew Bask are going to come looking for us when all this is over,' Tarent muttered, and sure enough they did.

As the fighting subsided and the caravan attempted to pull itself back together, Matheus Hawk, accompanied by the indignant Bartholomew Bask, came marching up to where Pardigan and Tarent were standing alongside Azif.

'Hold them young thieves there,' shouted Bartholomew. Azif glanced up from a report an aide was trying to give him.

'You have thieves, hoodlums and pirates riding with you, man.' Bartholomew strode across and attempted to grab hold of Tarent, who ducked out of the way and drew his two swords with a flourish. Bartholomew retreated hurriedly, allowing Matheus Hawk to come up alongside him. Matheus bowed slightly to Azif and addressed him more politely.

'My companion is correct, I fear. We've been tracking a band of young thieves for some time now and these are indeed two of them. We ask you for justice. That you hand them over to us, unarmed, so that we may take them to stand trial.'

Pardigan bristled and fingered the sword at his hip; Tarent stood alone making no move to reform his swords into the staff. Azif smiled pleasantly.

'I am sure you good gentlemen are mistaken. These two fine fellows are under the protection of the caravan, and indeed are my personal guests...' a spluttering red-faced Bartholomew Bask interrupted him.

'Mistaken! Why I'm as sure as eggs is eggs that...' he never finished as Matheus clamped a hand across his mouth.

'As you see fit, my lord, but I take it that the protection of the caravan will only extend until we arrive in Dhurban City?'

'If it is protection as you call it, then yes, my obligation is over when we reach Dhurban but having seen these two young fellows in action, I feel it may be you two gentlemen that will need protecting if you seek to tangle with them.' He laughed and every Dhurbar within earshot joined him.

Matheus Hawk inclined his head in acknowledgment, but said nothing and dragged the still spluttering Bartholomew Bask back to their palanquin at the end of the line. Azif addressed Tarent and Pardigan.

'Pirates! And what was it he called you? Ah yes, thieves and hoodlums, what interesting lives you boys lead. We will have much to discuss around the fire tonight, I'll wager.' He returned to his aides, to deal with the ragged remains of the caravan.

'How did they find us here?' hissed Pardigan as Tarent slipped his swords together with a twist and stood leaning on his staff.

'I have no idea, but I think we'd better make plans to depart the caravan, before reaching Dhurban. While the caravan is underway I don't think they'd dare do anything to us, but when we get there...' he left the sentence unfinished and shrugged. They watched the departing figures of Matheus Hawk and Bartholomew Bask and were dismayed to see Mustep the knifeman running over and talking with them. 'Well at least our enemies are all getting to know each other. Old Mustep must have heard the whole exchange and recognises a friend when he sees one.' The three were all staring back at Pardigan and Tarent.

'I'll be glad to be back with the others,' said Pardigan, giving Bartholomew a little wave. Tarent slapped his hand down crossly.

'Oh, give it up, Pardigan! You just never know when to stop, do you?' Pardigan grinned.

'I just like to annoy the merchant; he asks for it, doesn't he?'

'Yeah, but he doesn't need it, he hates us enough already, honestly, look at him!' Tarent shook his head and walked off.

Pardigan stared at the red glowering face of Bartholomew, waved again, and then chased after Tarent.

The caravan rested at the pools only long enough for the camels to be reloaded and the palanquins to be hitched up, before it once again resumed its plodding pace back out into the desert towards a range of distant mountains and the far off city of Dhurban. Pardigan and Tarent lay back in their palanquin, quickly returning to their former sick and unhappy state. While at the back of the line, Bartholomew and Matheus Hawk lay in grim silence in the swaying murky heat; all awaited their arrival in Dhurban, still more than a day away.

* * *

It really was good to fly again, but Mahra hadn't needed Quint to tell her that. She soared out over the city riding the thermal waves of warm air rising up from the buildings below. Above her the stars shone brightly and she was experiencing one of those 'good to be alive' type moments that came rarely after a thousand years of life. Earlier she'd flown over the city and spent some time around the palace listening at windows and doors for any titbits of information. The palace was divided, as they'd thought, into one half for males and the other half for females, with common rooms in between. The royal wives and their children, of whom it seemed there were many, were in yet another separate section at the rear of the palace. For all of her listening and eavesdropping on conversations she'd yet to identify the princess they sought. She had finally decided to fly out over the city and the desert beyond, simply for the fun of it, before heading back for one last round of the royal apartments.

Gliding down on silent wings she spied the sultan himself with a group of people. She landed softly on the roof just above where the exchange was taking place.

'Why, my daughter, do you always seek to anger me with your foolishness?' The sultan's voice echoed around the chamber below. 'Thirty-eight sisters you have and forty-seven brothers, and who is it that I am always having this conversation with? Why, it is always you!'

'But, Father, I am not like my sisters, happy to be sitting all day in the palace, and my brothers have some freedom, able to leave when they wish. I just have to get away some time...'

'*Get away?*' the sultan's voice became angry. 'You are the daughter of the sultan, you cannot just get away like some common housemaid whenever you like. Three days you have been in those mountains and three days I have mourned the loss of you. You were in the mines again, I know it. I've told you before and now I must set a guard upon you, for you cannot and will not go there again. There are travellers here asking about the mines. They shall never be allowed to find them and you shall never visit them again either.'

'But the guardian is kind and the skull speaks such wisdom, Father.'

The sound of a hand slapping against skin echoed around the hall and Mahra heard the girl sob with the shock of the blow.

'You will never seek the mines again... and you will not leave this palace until you leave with a husband, as befits a daughter of the sultan. Now go to your chambers and think upon what I have said here this evening.'

Mahra heard the princess run out, a door slamming behind her. She took off and flew in the same direction, hoping to see where the princess had gone. She heard the voice of the sultan echo as she left.

'What can I do with her? I ask you, that girl...' His voice faded as she sought out the next window to see the princess and saw the flash of red silks, the same as she'd seen with the sultan. She followed the sound of running feet as they went down corridors and in and out of rooms. Finally the princess arrived at what must have been her chambers and Mahra heard sobbing coming from inside. Landing softly on the balcony, she saw the girl lying on a large bed, thumping her tiny fists on the mattress in frustration.

What's a Mudlark?

Well, I think I've found our princess, thought Mahra as she returned to human form and walked into the room.

Chapter 21

The Guardian and the Flail

A feeble ray of light found its way through the dirty windows past fading grey curtains. It fell upon a figure lying under a thin blanket, the cover gently rising and falling with each laboured breath. A hand, barely more than skeletal bone and parchment-thin skin, reached out for a tattered book. He was desperately fighting the need for rest, but unwilling to give in to the desire, after waiting so long to complete the task which had occupied him for so many years. Muttering incoherently, he fumbled with the knife, his old fingers finding it difficult after so long with little use. After several attempts, he finally fitted the thin blade into the spine transforming the book into another, so completely different from the first.

'One more, just one and then we can end it... end the waiting... end the torment.' He studied the words he'd so carefully written, guiding the heroes from one skull to the next, forcing stiff fingers to move the pen. Where were they now? What was happening? Until the next skull was located, he would know little more of the Quest. When would it all end, allowing him to sleep, to rest ... to finally die? He coughed and clutched the book to his chest

'Hurry, Mahra, hurry my daughter... hurry...'

* * *

Mahra's conversation with the princess had been an interesting one; the princess hadn't seemed at all surprised to see a stranger walk into her room and had been delighted to chat about the guardian and the skull he protected. It was there and apparently waiting for them.

'The skull is wise and has counselled me on many things,' the princess had explained. 'It told me that one day I would guide some strangers to it, helping fulfil its destiny, and now I am happy that this day has come.' She had appeared downcast for a moment. 'Except that my father has forbidden me to leave the palace again, especially to go to the mines, but I can escape, I've done it many times before.' Her face had once again, shone with hope.

Mahra looked at the princess. 'Isn't it an awful place? The mines were described to us as some kind of hell.'

'No,' said the princess seeming shocked. 'It is no hell, the mines are only tunnels, and the guardian is a sweet old man who loves to have company. He and the skull are like two old friends arguing back and forth - they're really very funny.'

Mahra thought back on their conversation as she soared above the city enjoying the night air. It was late now and below her, darkness surrounded the sleeping buildings. The mountains rose from the gloom to one side and the great expanse of the desert lay to the other. She gazed out over the endless void.

The Dhurbar had a saying, that should a man and his camel walk out into the great expanse, then it would be his grandchild that would eventually reach the other side. How he was meant to father a child out there was anyone's guess, but then it was merely a saying to show that the great expanse was a vast patch of sand, and they basically hadn't a clue what lay on the other side. She dipped a wing and turned towards the crumbling mountains, feeling the warm air rising from the rocky cliffs, sending her circling higher and higher towards the stars that crowded the sky above. On the far side she could see the twinkling lights of campfires, a caravan heading to or from Dhurbar. She gave a cry and headed down to take a closer look.

* * *

'Oh they make my blood boil and no mistake.' Bartholomew Bask paced beside the small campfire that Mustep had managed to light from dried camel's dung.

'You're burning what!' Bartholomew had exclaimed, wrinkling his nose.

'Turds, Mr Bask, turds to keeps us warm - this is the desert; there are no trees.'

Bartholomew had watched with a look of utter disgust as the knife-man had bent over the strange pile coaxing a flame.

He stepped away from the smoke, careful not to breathe in any fumes. 'We get close - they get away. We capture them - they give us the slip. We surround them - they *fly right over us!* Today we should have just snatched them and been done with it. The Dhurbar wouldn't have done anything once we'd overcome them.' He eased himself down onto a cushion and chewed on his handkerchief in frustration.

'Nobody was holding you back from capturing them, Mr Bask. I didn't see you making a huge effort to get close to those blades.' Matheus sneered at Bartholomew's discomfort. 'Those boys fight like devils, there's nothing natural about them.'

'Devils?' Bartholomew started and glanced nervously about him.

'Don't worry, Mr Bask - they're gone, there are no more devils or demons to disturb your night.' The hunter laughed but Bartholomew ignored him.

'Oh, but tomorrow, Mr Hawk, we arrive in Dhurban and we shall have them.' He clenched his fist around a handful of sand and with a look of frustration and anger squeezed his fist. Matheus watched as most of the sand slipped through the merchant's fingers and silently prayed it wasn't an omen. He felt a chill run through him and, try as he might, just couldn't shake it off.

* * *

Pardigan emerged from the palanquin stretching his arms as he gazed about. All around him the desert reflected the orange of the rising sun and he stood shielding his eyes from the glare as he took in the caravan waking around him. Most of the travellers were still asleep or in the process of waking, but a few Dhurbar were up tending their precious camels or cooking a leisurely breakfast. The smell of thick Dhurbar brew and baking bread filled the chill morning air making Pardigan's stomach rumble. He then noticed Tarent walking towards him, grinning.

'What's making you so happy this early in the morning?' asked Pardigan, accepting a steaming cup of brew.

'I had a good night that's all. We're getting close to Dhurban now; it's just the other side of these mountains.' They both glanced up towards the cliffs and the narrow canyon through which the caravan would be passing.

'Morning, boys,' came a friendly voice. They turned to see the beaming face of Bartholomew Bask standing with Mustep the knifeman.

'I'm told we'll be in Dhurban by sundown today and then we can all have a friendly chat about the property you stole and whatever illegal errand it is that you've been on, dragging us all around the world like this.' Both Bartholomew and Mustep were being careful to stand well back from the boys, with the rising sun behind them.

'Well, Merchant Bask,' said Pardigan. 'We're flattered that you've visited us with your new boyfriend. We've already been introduced to Mr Mishap the child tormentor.' Bartholomew glared at him and Mustep reached inside his robes.

Tarent stared unsmiling at the knifeman. 'Now that would be silly, Mishap, you really wouldn't want to take out that knife and be shamed by a twelve-year-old boy again, would you?'

Mustep's eyes flicked from one boy to the other, deciding if he should take a chance with his knife. Decision made he started to pull it out and Tarent's staff rang as the twin swords were pulled clear, one stopped at Mustep's throat the other rested upon the hand still in his robe, tapping it gently.

'Mr Bask, please explain to your monkey that he should be good, will you. How the Hawk let you two out of his sight, I have no idea. When we have all walked through the gates of Dhurban together later today, we'll gladly sit down, surrender our weapons to your superior force, and tell you everything.'

Tarent glanced from one surprised face to the next as both Pardigan and Bartholomew Bask echoed the same thing.

'*Really?*'

'Sure we will, now go find the Hawk and give him the good news.' Tarent waved them away, and caught off guard, they walked off.

'*I'm* not giving myself up to them, what are you up to?' said Pardigan scowling.

'We had a visitor last night. Mahra was here. We're meeting her at the other end of the pass with *The Griffin.*' Tarent took delight in his friend's relief. 'We won't be walking through the gates of Dhurban, so we won't have to give ourselves up.'

'Thank goodness for that,' exclaimed Pardigan, letting out a sigh. 'I thought you'd gone soft. How are they getting a boat into the mountains, is there a river?' Tarent put his arm around his friend's shoulders as they walked off in search of breakfast and explained his conversation with Mahra.

The final day in the desert wound on and was easier for the boys. They didn't have to ride in the palanquin, as the hills and rocks around the canyon that ran through the mountain prohibited their use. Walking was hard work but the canyon was out of the direct sunlight and it was cool. They were sure Bartholomew was having a worse time of it. He would be right at the back huffing, puffing and using any spare breath he may have to complain. When they spoke to Azif he was delighted to hear of the boys' escape plan, although a little sceptical of magical creatures.

'So this big bird thing will come down, pick you up, and fly off, whisking you away from those gentleman who believe they will be skinning you alive in only a few hours time?' His booming laughter echoed throughout the rocky corridor they were walking through, startling a flock of roosting birds far above their heads, their cries mingling with the sounds of the labouring caravan below. 'The nasty cool one, with the hooked nose paid me a visit earlier today,' Azif continued. 'He wanted my assurance that my men would not hinder your arrest when we arrive in the city. Of course I told him it would be the will of the Source if he were to arrest you, but that I could not and would not hamper his efforts. I think he must have more people waiting in Dhurban, because he seemed very sure of success. I'm glad you have a flying beast to come take you away.'

It was past noon when the last of the stragglers emerged from the rocky canyon and into the bright sunlight, squinting across the desert plain at the walled city of Dhurban. It seemed deceptively close in the shimmering haze, its towers and minarets appearing to float above the desert, the lakes in front of it a non-existent seductive silvery mirage.

Bartholomew emerged from the canyon supported by Mustep as one of the last in the line. He sank down to sit on a rock and wiped his brow with a lace handkerchief that was dirtier than he was. Drinking greedily from the water flask that Matheus Hawk offered him, he gazed across the plain at Dhurban.

'So we're nearly there, are we, about time as well. Just keep your eyes on those rascals and no letting them give us the slip when we walk through those gates.' He squinted upwards as the Hawk replied, a dark silhouette against the bright sky.

'If your Dhurban agent and his men meet us at the gates as arranged, we'll stop them with little trouble, let's hope your message made it through.' Matheus took back the water bottle and frowned when he discovered it nearly empty.

Bartholomew sighed. 'I'm tired chasing that scum around, not knowing where they're off to next or even what it's all about. There are riches involved here, I'm sure of that and I'm about due for some riches.'

It was then that he noticed a commotion, and guessing it was the caravan getting underway once more, he reluctantly stood up, dusted himself down and searched round for his palanquin. Then the shouting and waving coming from the far side of the bunched group increased.

'What's going on?' asked Matheus, his suspicions aroused.

A shadow crossed the sun and the three of them, along with everyone else, gazed up to see a large creature descending. Its huge wings flapping as it slowed its descent; two figures perched upon its back guiding and coaxing it down to land amid a cloud of dust and sand.

'It's that Source damned bird thing!' shouted Bartholomew, but Matheus had already started running, anticipating where it was landing.

'Stop them, a thousand sovereigns to the man that can bring the beast down,' screamed Bartholomew. He tried to run after Matheus Hawk, only to fall to the ground in his haste.

The crowd drew around *The Griffin* as Mahra and Quint helped pull their friends up onto its back. The great creature was breathing and snorting, its wings flexing in agitation as the people started to crowd it, calling and pointing at it in awe. The great eagle head eyed the crowd and snapped her beak, daring them to come too close. Quint had to make an effort to keep a firm control upon her.

'See you some other time, Azif, it's been fun to travel with you,' shouted Pardigan over the rising noise. Azif was beside himself with excitement.

'This is a wondrous beast, and to think that I disbelieved you boys.'

They heard shouting and guessed that Bartholomew and his friends were on their way.

'So long, Azif, thanks for your help,' shouted Pardigan as *The Griffin* flapped its wings forcing the crowd back. They began to lift from the desert and the crowd covered their eyes and mouths from the dust and sand that blew up around them. Matheus Hawk came bursting through.

'Stop, I command you to stop.' He held out his hands, his lips moving silently as he wove his spell and *The Griffin* stopped its slow ascent, held by some invisible force. Letting out a loud cry, it scrabbled at the air with razor-sharp claws and snapped angrily at whatever invisible

The Guardian and the Flail

force held it. All but Matheus Hawk stepped back from the struggling creature.

'Come down!' commanded Matheus. His eyes flashed red as he forced his hands lower. Behind him Bartholomew arrived, watching the problems the boys were having with a thin smile on his dusty face.

'I'll be having you yet, me young thieves, oh yes I will!' He was breathing through his dirty handkerchief but his voice reached out to the riders as they stared down at the crowd around them.

'Do something!' yelled Pardigan and Quint drew his bow.

'Where's Loras when we need him?' Tears came to Quint's eyes as he sighted down the arrow, ever reluctant to take a life. Seeing his dilemma, Mahra launched herself from *The Griffin* and the large Black Panther dropped upon Matheus with a roar. The crowd turned screaming in panic while *The Griffin* lurched away, no longer under the spell. Matheus was down, trying unsuccessfully to stand as Mahra changed into an owl and flew after her retreating friends. Azif, standing a distance away, was laughing and clapping his hands in delight while Matheus glared up at him.

'You make an enemy of the wrong people,' he spat. 'You allowed those criminals to escape and did nothing to stop them, you will be held responsible for their disappearance.'

'Oh yes *you're* responsible, you will pay and I'll...' Bartholomew didn't get a chance to continue as a sharp sword was pressed to his throat. Azif stood watching as his guards surrounded the bedraggled pair.

'You obviously do not like this caravan. We are in sight of the city, thus the law of the desert is satisfied; we shall allow you to leave here.'

Bartholomew's jaw dropped. 'Let us leave? You're going to strand us here and make us walk to the city from here?' He stared across the shimmering desert at the distant city and licked his lips nervously.

'Yes, you shall walk. You have offended me and my people and you shall walk like a camel into the city and no man shall respect you.' Azif waved to his men who pushed Bartholomew away.

'And you can have Mustep to keep you company. I believe he is your friend, is he not?'

Mustep fell to his knees with a cry of anguish and frustration, hands set in a prayer of appeal, but the caravan master simply turned his back on him and walked away. Mustep fell forward into the sand with a sob, beating his fists at the injustice of life.

The caravan continued its slow march to the city, while Bartholomew, Matheus and Mustep sought to keep a little dignity and silently walked after them in the ankle-deep sand.

'This is so unfair,' muttered Bartholomew, 'so unfair. All we seek is justice. I simply don't understand why the Source treats us so.'

* * *

After dropping Pardigan, Tarent and Mahra in a high, sheltered area of the mountains, Quint guided *The Griffin* back towards the palace to pick up Loras and the princess. Mahra had told the princess to prepare to leave and she'd been excited at the thought of a magician coming to rescue her. Mahra only hoped that Loras would live up to the princess's expectations.

Finding Loras proved to be no problem; he was perched high up on one of the palace roofs waving up at the approaching *Griffin* with the princess at his side. Below them a group of the sultan's guards were attempting to climb up but Loras was keeping them back with a whole array of different spells; the princess clutching his arm giggling and clapping in delight at each one. As *The Griffin* approached, Loras stood and started whirling his arms around his head and smoke began to fill the area below them confusing the guards even more. The sultan's magician had been trying unsuccessfully to counter every spell that Loras had used but his magic was nothing compared to that of Loras - the old magician could be heard screaming in frustration and rage. If he did something that Loras hadn't known before, then Loras learned how it was done almost instantly, and it became little or no threat to them or was sent straight back to confound the old magician further.

The Griffin landed, sending roof tiles crashing to the courtyard below as it scrabbled for purchase, and they came running over. Quint helped them both up and showed the princess where best to hold on.

'My daughter, I forbid your leaving! Listen to me, I am your father and your sultan.' The voice came floating up out of the smoke. Quint glanced at the princess but she tossed her head, wrapped her arms tighter around Loras then poked her tongue out in the sultan's direction.

'He may be my father and also my sultan, but he doesn't even know my name. Let us leave here.' She shook her head dismissively and motioned them on with a regal wave. *The Griffin* lurched up with huge beats of its wings and several arrows flew past them as the smoke was blown away. They could hear the sultan berating his guards.

'Don't shoot, you fools, that is my daughter! If you hit her I will make you die a thousand agonising deaths.'

Glancing back, they watched as all but the sultan started down from the roof, leaving him to stand alone to watch without moving until they were well out of sight.

The entrance to the mines was high in the mountain range at the base of a huge cliff, and had only a narrow path running up to it. If they hadn't had the princess to guide them, it could well have taken weeks to find amongst the rocks. *The Griffin* set them down and then flew off so as not to attract unwanted attention to the entrance should anyone be watching. Gathering round, Mahra introduced the sultan's daughter as Princess Fajera and she quickly took the lead.

'There's only one torch here. You'll all have to follow me closely as the tunnel is treacherous. It will take us some time to reach the guardian's cave.' The princess struck a flint and lit the torch, holding it out in front of her.

'I can give us light as well,' said Loras happily as two glowing blue globes appeared in his hands and floated into the entrance, instantly lighting the path. The princess smiled in approval then led them inside.

The tunnel was dark and narrow and appeared to be as treacherous as the princess had promised. It angled down, branching out in several places as other tunnels disappeared off into the darkness. Loras, who was at the back, made sure to mark the wall so they'd be able to find their way back if, for some reason, they didn't have the princess to guide them. From several of the branch tunnels they could hear strange sounds and moaning, water dripping or rushing, and at one part the crash and thump as, within another tunnel, something gave way.

'What is it that lives down here making all those sounds?' asked Quint, fingering the sword at his belt nervously.

'Nothing lives down here except the guardian.' The Princess giggled. 'Maybe a few mice or rats,' she poked Quint with her finger. 'You're not afraid of mice are you?'

Quint ignored her. 'So what's making all the noises?'

'It's the wind or water moving, or maybe the earth shifting,' answered Tarent. 'The earth is constantly moving and shifting beneath us, we just don't notice when we're happily walking around on the surface - down here it's different.'

They followed the princess down and down, twisting and turning until they all felt completely lost.

'How did you find these caves, princess?' asked Mahra when they stopped for a rest. 'I mean this is hardly the type of exploration trip that most princesses would make, is it?'

'I'm not like most other princesses. I should know, I have thirty-eight sisters, who are also princesses, all of whom are happy to sit and sew or sing and dance prettily, acting like perfect dummies as they wait for a husband to be found for them. I, on the other hand, want more than all that sitting around and I don't want a husband.' She gazed at Loras. 'Well, not any old husband any way.' She smiled. 'I want to choose my husband, not be found some smelly old merchant's son to spend the rest of my life with. So I escape as often as I can and come to these hills. On one of those trips the skull called to me and guided me down to its cave.'

At last, after what seemed like most of the day, they saw that the blue globes had halted their travel at the entrance to a large cave. The princess placed her torch into a holder to one side of the opening and bade them follow her in.

'Hello?' she called. 'Guardian? Are you here?'

'Child? Is that you?' a weak voice drifted from the dim confines at the back of the cave. Do you bring me visitors?'

'No, she brings *me* visitors and well you know it, you old fool,' said another voice.

'*Silence!*' hissed the guardian. 'Come forward, child, bring these visitors to me. I've waited so very long to meet them.'

'They will be more of a match than you think, old man,' came the second voice again.

'I said *silence!*' screamed the guardian. 'You have promised me for countless years of waiting that you would not interfere at this final time of reckoning.'

'I did, so I shall say no more and remain silent, my old friend. You have waited long and dutifully for this day and I shall now cease to interfere.'

The Griffin's crew followed the princess into the darkness, nervously fingering their weapons, unsure of the strange conversation they'd been hearing. Out of the gloom came a wizened old man with a long white beard. He supported himself upon a stick that was nearly as bent as he was and it was with obvious effort that he lifted his eyes to see them. The princess ran over to him.

'Let me help you, guardian, please...' but he shooed her away.

'Stay back, girl. Your task in these things has been completed and I thank you, but stay back while we talk.' He waved his old hand towards the side of the cave and the princess, crestfallen, backed away.

'Welcome, visitors. Allow me to introduce myself to you. I am the guardian of the skull.' He cast his watery old eyes over the group. 'So young,' he murmured. 'So very young.'

'I'm fed up with people telling me how young I am,' growled Pardigan in a low voice.

'*Shhh,*' muttered Quint.

The guardian shuffled a little closer. 'I am the guardian of the skull and I was set here...' He thought for a moment, obviously trying to work out how long he'd been sitting in the old cave, guarding the skull. 'I have been here too long. That's how long I have been here, far too long. I was placed here to guard this skull against the one thing that my masters feared most. The one thing that might turn time against them... *you!*'

What had been a little old man only a moment before exploded into action in a flash of red light. The staff was flung up turning into a flail, a short staff with five long strands running from it, each strand tipped with the head of a poisonous snake hissing and spitting venom. The guardian had grown to almost twice his previous size and with eyes glowing red and yelling a terrible cry, he pulled back his arm and sent the spitting heads at the group of heroes as they stood mesmerised in shock before him.

The flail snapped down and the snakes each struck for a different member of the crew. Finally jolted into action, they tried to defend themselves as best they could. At the front of the group, Quint drew his sword and cut the head from the first snake but his triumph was short-lived as the head fell to the floor, hot acidic blood sprayed over him and he fell down in agony, his hands covering his face. Tarent had drawn his twin swords but seeing what had happened to Quint, he replaced them into each other with a quick snap and struck out with the staff instead, instantly causing one of the snakes to fall limp. Mahra had turned into the Black Panther and had succeeded in shredding another of the heads with a swipe of her claw, but had suffered much the same fate as Quint. She was now whimpering at the back of the cave nursing a badly burnt paw that hissed and steamed as the venom burnt into her.

'Guardian, guardian, please stop!' wailed the princess, sobbing at the madness erupting around her.

Pardigan threw a knife at the guardian but it was turned aside as the flail came up to strike again, the snakes renewed and five fresh poisonous heads came flashing down towards them. Loras stepped forward and held out a hand forming a solid wall of air, momentarily stopping the forward motion of the snakes. The guardian shrieked in anger, the cry echoing back into the caves.

The flail was pulled back and then struck down once more sending Loras crashing to the floor with the force of it, yet somehow, he still managed to maintain the defensive wall.

Seeing that different measures were called for, Pardigan scanned the dim shadows behind the guardian and with a shimmer was gone, place-shifting to where the skull lay.

The skull pulsed a deep blue. 'About time, young man. I knew one of you would have this ability. Now shift us back and out of here before my old friend hurts somebody.' Pardigan picked up the softly glowing skull and shifted back to behind his friends.

'We have what we came for, let's get out of here,' he shouted and Mahra limped out whimpering, followed by the princess. Quint was edging back towards the door, his face a mask of agony while Loras held the guardian at bay, but the young magician was weakening. Each crackling strike of the flail was draining him as the red Chaos energy of the guardian met the blue Order energy of Loras's wall of air in a shower of light and sparks. Tarent stood at his side ready to defend his friend if he possibly could.

'The roof,' the skull muttered from the confines of Pardigan's cloak. 'The roof is weak.' Pardigan looked up to see that the roof was indeed fragile, a series of cracks running all over it. 'The largest crack,' came the muffled voice of the skull.

As Tarent and Loras made it to the entrance of the tunnel, Pardigan sent a knife flying underhand at the largest crack with all the force he could muster. A load groan echoed round the chamber and several large pieces of rock came crashing down - but the roof held. Seeing what his friend had done, Quint strung an arrow and sighting as best he could through burning eyes, let it fly at the same spot. Several more large pieces of rock came crashing down, smashing onto the cave's floor causing the guardian to spin round, fear and uncertainty now etched upon his monstrous face. Another knife from Pardigan and a large slab of rock fell crashing down, pinning the guardian to the floor. He writhed there unable to move, the snakes hissing and spitting, dragging themselves towards the group, eyes glowing red and poisonous venom dribbling from their mouths. Loras dropped the wall of air and sent a bolt of blue energy at the roof and a large section exploded with a crash. There was a heartbeat of hesitation, and then the whole roof, carrying the weight of the mountain above it groaned and then dropped with a *'whump!'* sending dust billowing out into the tunnel, ending the guardian for good.

Now in the total darkness of the tunnel, they were choking on dust until Loras lit two glowing blue globes and sent a crackle of energy into the air. The energy bolt caused the dust to drop to the floor, and they were at last able to breathe again, all of them noisily sucking air into aching burning lungs.

Bending over Quint, Tarent poured healing energy into his friend who lay, eyes closed with relief, as his burns were slowly healed. Loras moved over to Mahra and tried to do the same for her but the Black Panther bared her teeth at him and growled. He stepped back in shock.

'Don't be such a baby, Mahra! I'm going to heal you, it won't hurt.' The panther shimmered and Mahra the girl stared up at him, teeth gritted in agony, tears running paths down her dusty face.

'Just heal me, boy! And hurry, cats don't like pain.' She held out her hand and soon her face relaxed and her scorn turned to thanks.

It took them quite some time to get to the top of the tunnel. Slowly helping each other retrace their earlier steps, as they sought out the signs left by Loras. They smelt the fresh air before seeing any light and when they did finally emerge it was to a star-filled sky and chilly night air. They sat down to rest while Mahra shimmered into an owl and did a fast circuit of their surroundings to see if anybody else was up on the mountain. She was soon back, allowing herself to drop down exhausted besides the others.

'We're quite alone up here; we can rest safely until morning.'

The Guardian and the Flail

'I cannot believe I have been such a fool,' sobbed the princess. 'The guardian deceived me. I thought he was such a sweet old man, yet he turned into...into...a monster!'

'You were not deceived,' said the Skull, pulsing a deep blue from the rock where Pardigan had set it.

'It was written in the annals of history, that you would do exactly what you did. You fulfilled your task beautifully, my dear. The guardian was indeed a sweet old man and a great friend to me as well during all these years. We spoke many times of how the final events would play out, and towards the end, I believe he had no wish for victory at all. His mentors misguided him many years ago and set him on a path that he had no way of leaving, at least not before today. Now he is finally at peace. Be happy for him, child, remember him as the kind old man that he was, not the monster that his destiny forced him to become.'

'Wasn't so kind when he was flinging that whip thing about, was he!' muttered Pardigan.

'No he wasn't, but that wasn't the man, that was the guardian, and he fulfilled his role in things admirably, the same as did you all. And now we must go on to finally complete the great spell. Rest now, heroes, in the morning you may read your book and see the final pages.' The Skull became silent and the blue glow faded away.

They managed to start a fire and set an order of watch before turning in. Pardigan, who had drawn the first guard duty, sat contemplating the valley below and the silent city of Dhurban, with its twinkling lights still showing across the desert.

I wonder what Bartholomew is doing down there right now, he mused.

Chapter 22

Tipping the Balance

Loras and Quint took the princess back to the palace in the early hours of the morning. She was still upset at the death of the guardian, but the Skull had spoken kindly of him and the long years they had spent together.

'He was a good man given a bad duty. For hundreds of years I was his only company, the very object that he had been told to defend the world against. When you started to visit him it was the happiest he had been for centuries. You must try to understand that death was a blessing to him, a long-awaited release from the task in which he had lost all belief. You both played your parts in the events splendidly.'

As *The Griffin* landed on the roof of the palace, the princess wrapped her arms around Loras's neck and planted a huge kiss on his lips. Taken by surprise, Loras's hands went up and, with a *pop*, two blue bolts of energy shot off into the air. Smiling, the princess scampered away before turning back to wave.

'Don't forget me, Loras. I'll always remember you. Come back for me, won't you?' She blew him a kiss and with that she was gone, leaving Loras quite unable to move. Quint had to slide down off *The Griffin's* back and nudge him for Loras to respond in any way.

'Got a bit excited there eh, Loras,' said Quint with a grin. 'Come on; let's get out of here before the guards come.' He helped the still dazed Loras onto *The Griffin's* back and they soared aloft on silent wings, back into the star-filled night, a thoughtful Loras gazing back at the twinkling city already far below.

* * *

> *At last you have the skulls all three,*
> *Congratulations, now come to me.*
> *In Sterling temple you shall find.*
> *Three places for the crystal mind.*
> *Place them all, then slot the knife*
> *For only this will save all life.*
>
> *Beware now heroes Chaos burns*
> *To stop your Quest at this last turn.*
> *A final battle you will make*
> *The Source's priest a choice must take.*

'That sounds fairly simple,' said Pardigan, leaning over Tarent's shoulder.

'It tells us where to go, if that's what you mean,' replied Tarent, 'but I don't much like the sound of *the Source's Priest a choice will make*, that's me, and as for a final battle, that last one was nearly the end of us.'

'It was not,' snorted Pardigan. 'He wasn't so tough after we dropped half a mountain on his head, was he?' He glanced around at his friends.

'Pardigan, please don't make light of someone's death. Besides, if we hadn't been able to drop the roof on him, have you any idea how we could have beaten him?' said Tarent with a frown.

'I'm sure Loras would have thought of something,' said Pardigan, 'and whatever choice you have to make, I'm sure it will be the right one. I wonder what you're going to have to choose? Well whatever it is, there's no point in us all getting down about it is there?'

Mahra decided to step between the two friends when she saw Tarent was about to lose control. 'I think we'll have to go to Sterling to find out what Tarent's choice is and then end this thing at the same time. Maybe when all this is over we should take a break and go fishing back at that reef at Minster Island, what do you think?' The change of subject to something other than the Quest worked and they discussed what they would do when everything was complete. A fishing trip to Minster was firm favourite and they spent some time discussing the best way to trick the fish.

* * *

Belial stood high upon a rock observing the heaving mass before him, the gathered army of demons truly magnificent to behold. Rank upon rank of demon warriors of every cast stood ready, the red and gold of the demon dawn glinting dully off heavy black armour.

Clouds of yellow sulphurous gases wafted by spewed forth from bubbling pits of lava, offering their own special flavour and colour to the event. Belial drew a deep breath, savouring the pleasure of command.

'My people, my brothers, it gladdens my heart and pounds the blood throughout my body with pride, to see you, the greatest army ever assembled.' He gazed about and saw the rapt attention upon every face within sight.

'The time is now fast approaching when we shall cross into the realm of man once again and feed upon them as they feed upon their cattle, fattening themselves for our table.' The warriors pounded their feet and beat weapons against shields in salute to the words of their king.

'Sharpen your swords, find an edge for your hunger, for soon I shall breach the curtain that divides us and take you into the Promised Land.' The army responded with a mighty roar that would have deafened mortal ears.

'Belial, Belial, Belial, Belial...' Belial raised his arms and accepted their praise as his captains attempted in vain to hold some semblance of order among the writhing ranks of hungered beings.

*　*　*

The journey back to Sterling was broken by a visit to the Moorings; the flight was uneventful, if not a little cramped with five of them on *The Griffin's* back. Mahra who had transformed into the cat and curled up inside Quint's Cloak for the journey, was the only happy passenger. It took them all of two days and half of the next to get back and it was with great excitement that they finally sighted their home port far below, set amongst the twinkling waters of the river system. *The Griffin* spiralled downwards before gently gliding in and allowing her tired passengers to drop gratefully to the ground. She peered around at them and let out a soft cry. Large golden eyes regarded the group and she dropped her head for Loras to scratch her beak. They all stroked and petted the wonderful creature, thanking her and saying their good-byes before Loras changed her back into their beloved boat and home.

They spent the remainder of the day relaxing and recuperating from their ordeals. Quint especially needed to rest after the burns he'd received. Energy of Order could heal the physical wounds; the mental wounds and exhaustion they'd caused would take longer.

It was a full five days after leaving Dhurban that the little boat made the overnight trip from the Moorings, and crept into Sterling Port in as inconspicuous a way as it always had. The sea journey had done them all good, the wind and salt spray cleansing them of any remaining desert sand. The sailing had been fun and the night watch had been entertaining with porpoises and phosphorescent waters making it a special trip for all of them.

Quint had recovered enough to enjoy his own game of riding the bowsprit, and managed to rid himself of a lot of his frustrations by once more screaming, yelling and cursing at the sea.

In Sterling they tied up and took their time in putting the boat in order, then Loras and Tarent paid their harbour fees and went in search of cinnamon buns.

'I suppose there's not much delaying what we have to do,' said Tarent sipping a glass of freshly squeezed lemon water once they had returned. 'Let's go to the temple early tomorrow morning when there aren't so many people about, and place the skulls then. If we're to fight our last battle, we may as well get a good night's sleep and choose our own time when there's no one else to get hurt.' Everyone agreed and while Loras went into town to poke about the bookshops, the others sharpened weapons and made ready for the morning.

Tarent placed the three skulls upon the table and attempted to talk to them but they remained silent, perhaps gripped by the same nervous feelings as the rest of them, now so close to the end of their journey.

Loras returned with fish and vegetables and he and Quint prepared a stew that they later sat on deck eating as the sun set and the stars came out.

'That may well be the last day that the sun shines down on a world sliding towards Chaos,' ventured Pardigan as the final rays of sunlight disappeared.

Mahra set her finished plate aside. 'It had better be. I've not waited a thousand years and gone through this Quest, only to find that tomorrow doesn't change anything. We've done all that the book has asked and we're now ready to finish what was started so long ago.' She looked about her at the people she'd only recently met, yet already shared so much with, and raised her tankard to each of them in turn.

'After a thousand years of waiting, it's been a pleasure and a privilege to finally meet you and Quest with you my friends.' She smiled. 'Here's to us, to the heroes at the end of time.'

'*To us!*' echoed the crew, smiling and raising their tankards in turn.

* * *

Pushing back the thin blanket, the old man started the laborious task of standing up, something he hadn't done in such a very long time. Indeed today was the first time that he'd done it with such anticipation in many years. His bones cracked and he rubbed at his legs trying to get his circulation moving, willing himself to find the strength necessary for this day of days.

'Not long now,' he cackled, his voice dry and strange to his ears after so long with little use. 'The heroes return and the skulls are here in Sterling. I almost thought it would never happen, almost.'

This was the morning he'd looked forward to, for over a thousand years. It was possibly the greatest morning since man first walked the earth.

'Hmmm, well maybe there were one or two other mornings to compare since the dawn of man, but not many.' Giggling happily he began to wish he could jump up and *click* his heels together, but knew he couldn't, such foolishness was for people several centuries younger than he. He tried to gather his thoughts; he would need all his faculties together for the day's events and no mistakes.

He sat for a while before finally raising himself up to totter precariously upon stiff awkward feet. Magic was one thing and a good thing at that, but at some point reality had to take the strain and this was its moment with him. It took several attempts but finally he pulled on a robe, then brushing cobwebs and dust from the door-latch, let himself out into the street and the cool early morning air.

* * *

It was still dark and the stars were twinkling overhead when the crew emerged from *The Griffin*. The sky to the east was beginning to lighten and it was cold, the air smelt clean and fresh, but that wouldn't last long before the city once again started to heat up. The crew drew their cloaks around them and huddled together on the harbour walkway while Loras set the guard spell on *The Griffin*. Pardigan, Tarent and Mahra all carried bags over their shoulders, each of which held one of the crystal skulls and Loras had the knife with him. At this hour nobody was about. Even the chance of bumping into the watch was unlikely.

Pardigan blew onto his hands, his breath a white mist in the chill air.

Quint smiled. 'Don't worry it will warm up all too soon.' He was shielding his bow under his cloak to protect it from the damp and was shivering as much as Pardigan.

Empty streets echoed to the sound of their footsteps as they moved along bunched together, glancing up at shuttered windows, the occupants fast asleep, yet they still expected attack from the shadows at any moment. As they walked, the sunrise began to paint the streets with a warmer orange revealing a thin mist hanging low in the air. A baker came out and opened the shutters to his shop, the smell of freshly baked bread wafting out with him; he glanced over, startled, and quickly hurried back inside, slamming the door behind him.

They took a turn and started to walk a bit faster, the burning need to complete the Quest now overwhelming in each of them.

'Let's go back and visit that bakery when we've done the skull stuff, okay?' whispered Pardigan, his breath a plume of orange caught in the early light.

Loras's stomach gurgled as he replied. 'I'm with you on that.'

An old man dressed in brown robes came out of a door and stood back to let them pass. He kept his eyes low and backed into the shadows as they trudged past, they barely noticed him.

'How much further is it, Mahra?' asked Quint. 'Are we nearly there?'

'Look,' she pointed. 'The street starts to rise just up ahead. When we turn right at this next corner we'll be on Temple Street.' She shifted the weight of her bag from one shoulder to the other. 'It's not far.'

Temple Street turned out to be a street of orderly houses. One of the *better* parts of the city as the merchants would say, for it was they who lived here.

Two maids in crisp clean uniforms came out of a house and pushed past them, consumed by a whispered conversation that was making them giggle. Smells of cooking filled the air and lamps were now being turned out up and down the street by uniformed butlers. The crew hurried on, aware how out of place they were here amongst this world of servants and masters.

The houses were eventually left behind and the temple was sighted some distance ahead, standing alone amongst the trees, a path winding up towards where it perched on the small hill that bore its name.

The air was beginning to warm as they reached high ground, they turned and gazed back over the city seeing it bathed in the full glory of the sunrise. The sea was a huge sparkling golden band and from this vantage point they could even make out *The Griffin* far below in the little port.

A rooster crowed somewhere below and was answered by another, several dogs started barking; the city was starting to wake.

'Well, shall we?' asked Quint glancing round. They began climbing the temple steps, gazing in awe at the ancient building before walking inside.

The interior was cold and still, and echoed with their footsteps, the noise a rude intrusion upon the holy serenity of the temple. It was a beautiful building lined with tall stone columns, many of which were intricately carved as they reached up to support the ceiling high above them. Row upon row of stone benches stood awaiting the early morning worshippers, the cold hard surfaces ensuring the sinners remained repentant and that the Source blessed might remain awake. The temple was empty, but it wouldn't be that way for long, the Source priest would be holding Morning Prayer and the devout would be arriving soon now. Quint led them along the aisle, the tiles of which depicted the writhing tangle of branches of the tree of life, he held his bow drawn and an arrow cocked waiting for the first sign of the promised attack.

A shuffling sound to the side caused Quint to spin, drawing the bowstring back against his cheek. The others reacted behind him. Pardigan pulled out a knife and held it poised to throw as Loras cradled a ball of blue energy in his hands. Tarent held his staff, ready to pull the swords apart while Mahra stood tensed, waiting for whatever would emerge. For a moment all was silent save the distant barking of a dog.

The Source priest shuffled in, humming to himself. The moment he caught sight of the murderous looking group in the middle of his temple, he dropped the altar cloth and books he was carrying with a bang that echoed around the temple.

'*Whaooo!*' Spinning on his heels, he disappeared, the sound of his footsteps retreating hastily down the corridor. An unseen door slammed and the temple returned once more to silence.

'Of course this might mean that this morning's service is cancelled,' murmured Pardigan. Tarent frowned at him.

They approached the altar and removed the cloth that covered it along with an assortment of candles and incense holders. The altar itself was a large block of stone, carved on its four sides with scenes from the book of the Source. It sat on squat stone feet and appeared as if it had been there since time began and the temple had been built around it at a later date. The surface was flat except for three shallow depressions.

Wasting no time, Mahra took her skull from the bag and placed it in the first of the smooth hollows facing outwards. It pulsed blue once, then returned to being clear. Pardigan and Tarent did the same, both skulls pulsing blue when placed, then returning to their normal clear lifeless state. Loras handed the knife to Mahra who slid it into the slot in the centre of the table; nothing happened.

'There are *two* slots,' she hissed.

'What do you mean two slots?' Tarent rubbed his finger over the second slot in confusion. 'Nobody said anything about a second knife, what's meant to go in that slot? We can't have gone through all this for nothing, can we? Where on earth …'

'There they are!' The silence of the temple was broken. 'Thieves…Scoundrels…Scallywags…Stop right there!' Bartholomew Bask was waddling down the aisle waving his arms furiously with several people following him; sailors from his ship, Mustep the knifeman, and of course the tall gaunt figure of Matheus Hawk several steps behind. The temple echoed with footsteps as the group approached.

'*Ohhh*, they're going to spoil it all,' whined Mahra.

'How did they get here so fast?' asked Pardigan, pulling his sword free. The crew spread out to give each other room and the temple rang for a moment with the sounds of both groups noisily unsheathing swords and knives. Quint drew his bow and deliberately took aim at Bartholomew, who seeing it, stopped immediately, causing everyone behind to run into him with much clanging and cursing.

'Leave us be, you don't know what we've been through to get here today,' shouted Quint. 'I *will* fire, and it will be *you*, Merchant Bask, that gets my first arrow.'

'What *you've* been through!' Bartholomew stamped his foot and his face turned several shades redder. 'I've been dragged halfway round the world, consorted with demons and just recently chewed on sand for several days and all because of you riffraff robbing me!' Flecks of spittle flew from his outraged face, '...Villains, the lot of you!'

Three of the sailors started to edge along a line of stone benches in an attempt to get around them.

'Stand still.' Pardigan screamed the order, his voice echoing around the temple. The sailors didn't stop but continued edging along. Pardigan pulled back his arm and flung a knife; it struck the column next to the lead sailor and stuck fast between two stones. He place-shifted, slapped the startled sailor's face, retrieved his knife and place-shifted back to his friends all in the beat of a heart. The sailors abruptly reversed their direction, quickly shuffling back the way they'd come, pushing and shoving each other in their haste.

'It would appear that we're at somewhat of a stalemate,' called Matheus Hawk, moving past Bartholomew. 'You have some talents that most of us here don't posses, yet you don't wish to hurt anyone, that much is also obvious.' He took another step closer.

'Stay back, old man, or I *will* be forced to hurt you,' snarled Quint, changing his aim to the centre of the Hawk's forehead. The Hawk held up his hands.

'Let us not fight, my friend. Why not explain what you've been doing, robbing Merchant Bask here, traipsing around causing all kinds of mischief, and for what?' He suddenly saw the skulls behind them. 'And what, by the Source, are they?' He pointed to the skulls and Bartholomew shoved forward joining him, squinting to try and see what the Hawk was staring at.

'Whatever they are, I'll bet they're mine,' muttered Bartholomew. His nose wrinkled, trying to set a value on whatever it was. He suddenly straightened. 'What's that smell?' He cast about as if searching for something. Matheus did the same, saying nothing.

'What are they doing?' asked Pardigan in confusion. Now even the sailors were sniffing and murmuring. Mahra took a deep breath, her feline senses stronger than those of her friends.

'There's a bad smell, a really bad smell, it's...' She didn't get a chance to finish as, to the side of where Bartholomew and Matheus Hawk were standing, the air split in two with a tortured, ripping sound. A long black arm pushed through, followed by the head and shoulders of Belial clad in glistening black armour, his face contorted at the effort of breaching the dimensions.

'Well hello, one and all,' panted Belial. 'So glad to have you all gathered here to meet at this most auspicious of times.' He pushed the two sides further apart with all of his strength and it was obvious that he had others behind him also attempting to come through. He flopped to the floor and another face appeared. This one wasn't the same beautiful flawless human face as Belial's. It was hideous enough to chill the blood of the most seasoned of warriors, black as night with blood-red eyes, and a mouth filled with teeth that dripped saliva and gore. It gave a deep snarl as it fought with the dimensional rift. Large clawed hands took over enlarging the hole where Belial had left off and other hands started to help, grabbing eagerly at the growing doorway. Before anyone had a moment to react, three steaming demons were standing in the temple with more coming through.

Throwing its hands up to its face, one of the demons gave a high-pitched scream as Quint's arrow struck one of its eyes while Pardigan's knife quickly found its other.

'Remember,' shouted Quint, 'the only way to kill them is by striking deep through their eyes.'

The demon he had struck continued to squeal, clawing at its face, trying to pull both blade and arrow out at the same time. It fell to the floor, twitching, completely ignored by its comrades.

'Not so pleased to see us then?' said Belial with a smile. He bent down and pulled the knife from the demon's face and flung it at the closest sailor who fell to the ground with a gurgling cry, the knife protruding from his chest.

Quint confronted the Hawk.

'Are you with us or against us?' Matheus's answer was to slash his sword down at Belial who blocked it easily.

'We have to close that hole,' whispered Quint to Loras, who nodded. Two demons were fighting to get through, hindering each other's progress in their eagerness to get at the human feast. Belial began hitting at them, trying to force one back so the other could come through more easily and it growled and shrieked with anger.

The sailors launched themselves at Belial from behind with a flurry of blows, one lifting a large stone candleholder, striking it across the back of his head. The demon king turned in fury and struck out, hurling three sailors across the temple with a red burst of Chaos energy, to land in a heap against the wall. Two others spun and ran for the doorway. Belial's laughter was caught short as both *The Griffin's* crew and Matheus Hawk attacked, united against the common enemy.

Tarent and Mahra charged into a tall demon with long white hair that was walking hunched over, swinging a massive sword wildly about. The huge blade narrowly missed Mahra as she leapt, shimmering into the form of the panther and setting her teeth deep into its neck; unbalanced, it fell to the ground. Tarent ran to her aid and finished the demon by driving his blade through its head. Mahra hung on until the demon gasped its last breath and lay still. Then she rose looking for fresh prey.

Belial was defending the tear in the dimensional rift, trying to get more of his army through, which was proving difficult. His magic was almost useless, with Loras stopping anything he did and he'd already slapped down several arrows fired by Quint. The last he snatched from the air with lightning reflexes and hurled it back, striking Quint's shoulder. The armour held, but Quint was badly bruised and found he could no longer draw the bow.

As Belial became occupied with three seamen, Loras took the opportunity and ran over to apply healing energy of Order as the battle continued around them.

'I can't get close enough to that hole thing. If I could, I think I could close it without a problem, but I need to touch both sides at once.' Loras peered into his friend's face seeing the pain gradually subside.

'Follow me,' said Quint, rising stiffly. 'Let's see what we can do.'

Towards the back of the group, Mustep was with a panicking Bartholomew, desperately seeking some avenue of escape. Unfortunately, the front entrance to the temple was on the other side of the fighting and Quint and Loras were blocking access to the door through which the priest had escaped.

'Get me out of here and I'll make you a rich man,' gasped Bartholomew, clinging onto Mustep's robes. The knifeman glanced round and pulled Bartholomew from the floor.

'Come, come this way,' He dragged Bartholomew to the very edge of the fighting, intending to make a dash when the opportunity presented itself. However, a small demon saw them and charged from the group shrieking with glee. Newly arrived from the demon realm it was ravenously hungry and Bartholomew promised a tasty meal beyond anything it had thought possible. As it came, it raised a jagged sword, Bartholomew drew back in fear and Mustep threw a knife. The knifeman may not have been a match for Pardigan, but he was good. The knife glanced from the demon's nose and entered its eye, its only point of vulnerability, killing it instantly. Momentum drove it forwards towards Mustep and the sword came down delivering the unfortunate knifeman a deadly blow. He cried out in agony and his blood splashed across the cowering Bartholomew. The merchant jumped up screaming, driven beyond reason by panic and fear and dashed for the door.

Tossing aside the broken body of a sailor, Belial saw Bartholomew coming and held out an arm, grabbing the panicked merchant by the throat as he ran past. Bartholomew let out a squeal.

'*Eeeeekk!*'

'Are you going somewhere without me, my fat friend?' Belial threw back his head laughing, then with mouth wide and teeth bared he bit down onto Bartholomew's shoulder. Both screamed. Bartholomew screamed because of the madness and the pain and Belial because he now had sight in only one eye. Matheus Hawk, seeing his partner in trouble, had rushed forward and catching the demon king unaware for once, had driven his sword home. It didn't kill him, but Belial threw Bartholomew to the side and turned upon Matheus.

'*La-il-eb*,' shouted the Hawk in desperation as Belial's sword flashed forward in a series of lightning cuts, forcing the hunter to stagger back.

'That won't work again,' growled Belial through a mask of blood. He launched himself in another stinging combination, leaving the side of the dimensional rift for the first time.

Quint saw the opportunity and dodged past Tarent, who was keeping the only other two surviving demons occupied with the help of one of the last sailors still alive, then drawing an arrow, shot straight into the eye of the next demon attempting to come through the rift, it fell back with a hideous scream. Loras quickly dashed forward and cast a wall of air inside before running his fingers along the seam of the hole, searching for a means to close it. He turned and hissed to Quint excitedly.

'Help me hold them back; I can close this!' He added more strength to the wall of air that he had pushed through the hole, frustrating the attempts of most of the demons to get close. A horrific vision of snarling faces could be seen in the darkness beyond but now all that was emerging was an appalling smell. Quint's sword slashed down at a hand that managed to get past and hold the edge, it quickly withdrew. Without any force applied to it, the hole started closing of its own accord and frantic, desperate hands scrabbled to keep it open. Quint slashed and stabbed at the snarling demons, protecting Loras as he cast his magic on the hole to speed the process.

Behind them, Mahra had her jaws clamped around a demon's wrist, her weight stopping the huge creature from raising its sword. It was lifting its arm and swinging her around making it impossible for anyone to get in and attack it. The panther held on in grim determination and just as she was losing her grip, Pardigan place-shifted onto the demon's chest and stabbed a knife into its unprotected eye, blood spurted upwards over his hand and chest.

'Oh yuck!' he pulled out his knife and the demon let out a pitiful scream, falling to the floor with the two friends holding on as the final stage of its life twitched and bucked away.

At the back of the temple, oblivious to all else and unaware that his rift between dimensions was now far too small for any more of his army to join him, Belial was easily getting the better of Matheus Hawk. The tall hunter continued to fend his blows off and had cast a shimmering shield, which he held outstretched with growing desperation but the demon king was simply playing with him. Behind them, unseen by Belial, a lone arm thrashed about in mid-air from the shrinking rift, unable to go forward or return it was caught in an ever-tightening grip by the hole, which finally closed. The arm dropped to the floor with a soggy flop and twitched for a moment before going still.

One last remaining demon still fought but was losing to the blades of Tarent and Pardigan. At last it fell and the tired fighters confronted the demon king together.

'*Demon,*' yelled Quint.

Belial stopped the sword strike he was aiming at Matheus and, sensing the silence, slowly turned to see *The Griffin's* crew fanned out behind him. He pushed aside the shield of energy and grabbed Matheus by the throat.

'It would appear we are at an impasse. I have this human and you have... well nothing really, I think I'll simply kill him and be done.' His remaining good eye stared at Quint as he raised the sword and began to slowly push it into Matheus's throat, the skin broke and a trickle of blood dribbled down onto Matheus's chest. The hunter remained silent.

'*Wait!*' called Pardigan. 'Just leave him and...' an arrow sped past and imbedded itself in the bloody socket of Belial's former eye, the demon king screamed and was knocked back several paces. Somehow still alive and retaining his grip on Matheus, he raised his sword once more.

'Can't kill me, eh? I was once told you humans say that all beings are born equal, but unfortunately for you I was born a little more equal than anything else!' The gruesome face swung towards Matheus Hawk and the sword once again pushed at his throat. 'Your pretty skulls don't work, do they, the set is incomplete. You have failed.' His remaining eye scanned the crew as they stood around him, exhausted from the fighting. 'I shall kill this one ... then I shall kill all of you, one by one. I am Belial, King of demons, and you should have known you can never defeat me.' The blade slid deeper, drawing more blood from Matheus's throat.

Tarent stepped forward. It wasn't meant to be like this, he could sense it, feel it, and the priest in him knew it. He still didn't know what his choice must be but he was aware it was fast approaching. Walking slowly he closed on the demon, his twin swords drawn but held low at his sides.

'Demon, you are a lord of Chaos, and I am a priest of the Source. Let us end it, here and now, you and I. *This* is how it is meant to be, how it will always be, a battle between Order and Chaos, we both know that. Let the old man go.'

Gazing at Tarent through a mask of blood, Belial threw the hunter to the side. '*Source priest,*' he spat the words with contempt. 'So you choose to die before your friends do you? How...noble of you,' his voice dripped with scorn. 'So be it, if that is your wish; *then die!*'

His attack was one of blinding fury, a demonic whirlwind that drove Tarent stumbling back tripping over the temple's benches. But before the demon could hasten a finishing blow he cried out, as a knife struck a heavy blow to the side of his head. Belial snarled, his head jerking around, blood spraying through the air searching for the knife-thrower.

Tarent staggered back to his feet. 'No, Pardigan, this is my fight, I *will* find the balance. Please, believe in me and keep back, all of you.' Despite his words Tarent knew his friend's knife had just saved his life.

Now clear of the benches, it was Tarent's turn to attack and for several moments it appeared as if the fight may indeed go in his favour, then as one of his blades flashed forward, Belial managed to trap it under his arm. The demon tore it from Tarent's grasp and swiftly brought his own sword down, shattering Tarent's second blade, leaving the Source priest unarmed. The demon gave a great howl of triumph, his one good eye glaring around at the others in unspoken challenge as they moved restlessly about the two combatants, unsure of what to do.

Tarent felt the icy fingers of fear and uncertainty travel up his spine. Was it really all for nothing then? He saw Belial smile and make ready for his final strike. Had the Source deserted him in his final time of need? Had his understanding been so wrong, so misplaced? Would Chaos prevail? He began to wonder if his part in the Quest had been a waste; had the book chosen the wrong person? Had he ever really understood his role as a warrior priest? A priest who carried a deadly weapon? But then his moment of doubt ended and he knew the Source had chosen correctly, that the Book of Challenges had merely been its instrument. The Source was love, pure and simple. As a priest of the Source he could never strike from hatred or fear, but he *could* strike for a just cause, to restore the balance, he simply had to have the belief and conviction to carry it through.

Hearing his name shouted, he turned to see Quint throw a sword, the blade shimmering as it flew through the air. Leaping to catch it, his fingers curled around the grip and Tarent landed just in time to duck beneath the demon's slashing blade.

Tipping the Balance

Now armed, both with blade and conviction, he was once again ready for the fight. 'Killing you isn't the most important thing,' Tarent stared at the demon, 'it never really has been.'

'Then what are you doing here, boy?' The demon's tone was mocking.

'Sometimes it is more important to make a stand against evil, than to worry about beating it, that's all that matters to the Source. I'm *trying* to stop you, because you need to be stopped, and in doing so, I'm going to restore the balance.' He circled the demon, spinning the blade, his confidence returned. 'You would have us believe that the only way to beat you, is to become like you, but that isn't true. It only matters that I give my best, the Source sees to all else. It's not victory we seek but balance.'

'You speak in riddles, boy priest, am I meant to understand your babbling?' The demon wiped blood from his brow and for the first time Tarent recognised the first signs of doubt in his opponent.

'Your understanding isn't important, demon. You could never hope to come close to understanding.' He smiled, feeling the peace of the Source infuse him.

With a snarl, Belial launched himself at Tarent, confused and goaded into an angry attack. Their swords clashed and rang time and again as they circled, each seeking to break the other's defences.

Seeing an opening, Tarent feinted to his left and with a flick of his wrist at the last moment, pulled the blade back to his right; Belial blocked the move but the demon showed a new respect for his smaller opponent. Side-stepping, Belial pushed the sword clear and sent a vicious backhanded strike to Tarent's face. The Source priest jumped back, almost avoiding the strike, but the demon's blade drew a line of blood across his forehead and the Taint of Chaos burnt into the wound. Concentrating his power of healing as best he could, Tarent lifted his free hand and felt the blood sticky between his fingers. The demon smiled.

'You're too frail, little human, you all break too easily and have never really stood a chance against us, mankind never has and my demon army shall soon be feasting upon you all.'

Tarent returned the smile. 'The Source will always find a way to stop you demon, and someone like me will always be there to do its work.' As he spoke Tarent's blade snaked through the demon's guard and found Belial's one good eye. The demon screamed, dropped the sword, and brought both hands up to his face, a moan of pain and anguish echoing through the still temple air. Tarent swayed uncertainly.

'*Finish it!*' screamed Pardigan.

'I...He's unarmed, I...I can't...I...' Tarent dropped his sword and stepped back, a look of horror on his face. 'The Source doesn't seek victory, it seeks balance.'

Lunging forward the blind demon grabbed Tarent and drawing him into a fatal embrace, pulled out a knife and held it to Tarent's throat. His scream of triumph echoed around the temple.

Terror filled the Source priest, his emotions and beliefs at war as he struggled vainly in the demon's grip.

Then, from far away, a calm soft voice parted the curtains of his mind.

'This is the time of your choice, Priest of the Source. It is a choice for your Quest, but also a choice for your soul. You must now choose to believe in your path ... or not. Surrender to the Source and we shall find the balance, remember, it is not a victory that shall win the day. We seek...to find...the balance. Place courage in your convictions and...let...go...'

A wash of calm infused Tarent as he released his fear, lifted his head to expose his throat, and spread his arms to either side. A look of confusion then anger played across the blinded demon's ghastly face as with a cry, he lifted the blade then plunged it down.

'Nooooooooooo...' the cry echoed throughout the Temple as the rest of the crew dashed in.

The moment they did, unseen by any of them, an old man in brown robes walked up to the altar and slipped a second knife into the empty slot at the moment Belial's blade also sank home. There was a hideous smile of triumph on the demon's blood-soaked face, then he disappeared with a pop, the blade falling with a clatter to the temple floor alongside Tarent.

'What happened?' asked Pardigan, running forward to catch his friend. The others gathered around.

'We have another visitor,' whispered Loras and the whole group spun to see who he was staring at.

The frail figure in the brown robes stood still beside the circle of glowing blue skulls.

'The second knife!' exclaimed Loras.

'Who are you?' asked Mahra walking forward...then she slowed as recognition dawned upon her. 'Magician Pew...Father?'

Chapter 23

Fishing

The sun continued to beat down. *The Griffin* was lying at anchor just off the coast of Minster Island above a reef of teeming fish. They'd been here for two days now, fishing and lazing about, enjoying the fact that they had no place special to go and all the time in the world to fish in. Mahra was becoming the best and most dedicated fisherman of the group, squealing in constant delight as she watched the schools of fish swimming around her hook. Her fast reflexes often meant that she snagged a fish that was swimming past and hadn't even noticed her bait. The others were happy simply to lie back and wait for the bell on the end of the fishing rod to ring, announcing a moment of activity and another fat fish.

Magician Pew had joined them, explaining that Belial had disappeared as the balance was restored and that the heat would slowly pass, returning the lands to the normal succession of seasons. The great spell had been completed and the hold that Chaos had upon both the world, and on the minds of man, would slowly lessen. Chaos wasn't gone, it simply hadn't triumphed as it had expected to; that was what Tarent had accomplished with his act of selfless sacrifice. He had not sought to claim victory for Order, but found a way to gain the balance.

'And it didn't kill me,' said Tarent smiling.

Fishing

'No, it didn't kill you. That I think would have been asking a little too much.'

Nobody had seen Bartholomew Bask since the battle, but the *Esmerelda* his ship, was long gone by the time the crew, along with Matheus Hawk had returned. Matheus had slunk off disappearing into the streets of Sterling vowing that he would find them again and one day, claim what was rightfully his. He was in shock from his recent ordeals and with the power of Chaos gone, was feeling the change more than anyone.

'I've got another,' squealed Mahra, pulling a fat wriggling fish onto the deck. Loras was watching Magician Pew as he sat happily at her side, suspecting the magician of somehow getting the fish onto his daughter's hook but as yet unsure how. Loras followed the great magician around everywhere, and always had thousands of questions for the old man, but he also respected the new-found relationship between the magician and his daughter and allowed them time together as best he could.

Mahra had almost fainted at the sight of the magician back in the temple as her full memory came back with a mighty jolt that had rocked her. Memories were regained of what they had planned and accomplished together so many years before and the necessary decisions that had robbed them of much of their time together as father and daughter.

They spent several days fishing at Minster, their nights filled with stories, all of them true as they told each other of their parts in the adventure. They sat on the deck eating fish and sleeping under the stars, happy that they'd finally completed the Quest and discussing what would happen next.

On the last evening before leaving, as the crew slept, Mahra and her father sat on deck talking as they had done on several other evenings recently. This time when there was finally no more to say except goodbye, Magician Pew slowly disappeared, a smile on his face and a tear in his eye as he held his daughter's hand for the very last time. His final words as his body faded away were to wish her a long and happy life and of course many, many fish.